THE BEAST

BILLIONAIRE
BROTHERS
GRIMM

J. KENNER

"Many a man has a wild beast within him."
—The Brothers Grimm

CHAPTER
ONE

All around me, the party glitters. The ballroom is lit with tiny twinkle lights so that it looks as if the world has been drowned in magic. Outside the windows, Atlantic City gleams, and the froth from the ocean forty-seven floors below dances in the light of the moon.

Serving stations in each corner offer appetizers created by the world-renowned chef of the Monarch Grand Casino, and the soft music from the orchestra underscores the babble of conversation.

I take a glass of champagne from a waiter decked out in a perfectly fitted serving jacket, the silver MGC logo pin on his lapel gleaming in the soft lighting.

This is the world in which I was raised. Isabella Hart—the Hart Industries heiress with her jet set life split between Manhattan and Atlantic City, with side trips to our other casino/hotels in Tahoe, Monte Carlo, Vienna, Singapore, and London. A world of power and money and beauty. Because as far as my father is concerned, I'm more showpiece than daughter. Especially tonight. I twist the simple gold band on my right hand—my mother's ring, and the only piece of jewelry I'm wearing tonight that hasn't been borrowed from the Hart collection for tonight's performance.

And what a performance.

As I glance around the ballroom, it's the beauty that captures me. Unlike most of the elegant aristocrats mingling nearby, power isn't something I've ever craved, nor is money. Though I suppose I might feel different about the latter if I'd been born outside the trappings of wealth.

Still, I know myself well enough to know that it isn't what can be bought that entices me, but what can be seen. The red of a cardinal against the pale bark of a birch tree. The dappled sunlight thrown across a musty attic when the curtains are pulled aside. Even the mixture of colors without specific form, but with the power to create a feeling so deep and transcendent that it is almost religious.

That's how this ballroom seems tonight. Like a magical place you might stumble upon in a story from long ago.

I freeze, the thought hitting me hard, and I have to blink rapidly, forcing back the threatening tears as I twist my mom's ring.

Stories.

Fairy tales.

Grimm.

Gabe.

It's only with Gabriel Grimm that I ever truly felt that transcendence. Like I was part of something bigger than myself. Bigger even than the two of us.

My vision goes blurry, and I hurry toward the restroom to gather myself. I should have known better than to let my mind wander.

I should have known that—especially here—it's Gabe who would be hiding in the dark corners of this trap disguised as a party.

Gabe. The man I lost almost five years ago to fire and treachery and death.

The man I loved.

The only man I'll ever love.

I may be getting married in a month, but Gabriel Grimm will always live in my heart.

I'm still blinking back tears when I step out of the Ladies' Room, my mind lingering on the wedding I don't want in payment for a deal that I do.

A wave of sadness crashes over me as I watch bubbles rise in the champagne like tiny prayers that will never be answered. But melancholy is not allowed. Not tonight. So I force myself to plaster on a smile, then glance around, hoping no one has caught my mood.

This is supposed to be a joyous occasion, after all. A party to celebrate my engagement to the more-than-suitable David Mercer, a slice of blond-haired, green-eyed eye candy who is also, thankfully, one of my closest friends. Not that my father cares about that. No, he arranged this medieval pairing because David is the heir to a smaller, yet similar kingdom of hotels and casinos across three continents, and neither my father nor David's parents gives a flip about what he and I actually want.

I sigh, then take another sip of champagne. Then another.

And—just to take the edge off—I gulp down the last of it.

It's Cristal—one of the best my father's money can buy. And yet it tastes bitter. Like broken promises and stolen dreams.

Not that I let that show. As much as I miss Gabe, I know that he's lost to me. Even if I had access to all of my father's money, I couldn't buy him back from death. So I smile and sip and pretend that being engaged to David is something more than a convenience for both of us—a business transaction wrapped in Vera Wang and diamond solitaires.

A hand cups my waist, and I'm drawn back to the present as I realize that David's come over from where he'd been holding court on the north side of the room. Now, he leans in, those deliciously sexy green eyes wasted on me. "Do you have a kiss for your adoring fiancé? Or," he continues in a low whisper, "more accurately, do you have one for your father, my parents, and our more-than-tipsy guests?"

"Always," I say, then let him pull me in for a kiss that's long and deep and makes a very good show even if it doesn't make my toes tingle.

But at least I know it looks real. Back when David and I were both thirteen, we decided that we needed to know how to kiss, then practiced on each other until we got it down. We'd planned to be each other's firsts in bed, too, but Gabriel got that honor when I turned sixteen. He'd been eighteen, and we were desperately, wildly, in love.

"Don't you two make the most stunning couple?"

I look up to see Mina, my father's air-headed assistant and long-time sidepiece, smiling at me. The kind of smile that actually says *fuck you*.

Considering my trust fund was established by my mother before she died—so it's nothing Mina can get her hands on even if my father does deign to marry her—I assume her dislike for me today stems from the fact that my engagement/wedding present is this hotel/casino, whereas her last gift from Daddy Dearest was a simple necklace with only one rather small diamond on a pendant.

"There's the happy couple!" My father's voice cuts through my thoughts and the room like a blade, and a second later, he materializes at my side, smiling in a way that somehow manages to be both charming and full of warning. To anyone watching, it probably looks affectionate. It's not.

It's a reminder that even though this day is the first step in getting out from under my father's thumb, he still has the power to screw up my life. So I better keep the *Hart Industries Rules for Oppressed Daughters* firmly in mind.

Fortunately, this is a role I've been playing for all of my twenty-eight years, and so I flash a smile of delight and charm, then lean forward and kiss his cheek. "Daddy, the party is wonderful. David and I are humbled by how lovely it is."

I glance around, then fight a sigh of relief when I see that David hasn't wandered away. On the contrary, he's coming closer, and a moment later, his hand slides possessively around my waist. And why not? He knows the expected script as well as I do.

"It really is an exceptional party," David says. "Thank you, Sir."

"Only the best for my daughter and son-to-be." His smile is camera-ready, perfectly calibrated so that the society photographers positioned strategically around us can capture this warm and lovely family moment.

Yes, sarcasm is one of my many talents. Unfortunately, standing up to Father is not.

"David," Father says. "I believe your parents are looking for you."

David's eyes meet mine in a glance so fleeting I'm positive Father didn't even notice. And if he did, he certainly didn't read the unspoken message—*you okay if I leave?*

I give him a slight nod, and he leans close, then kisses me on the cheek. "Another for the Press," he whispers. "And for good luck with whatever your old man has up his sleeve."

I just smile and squeeze his hand, then watch as he heads to his parents, leaving me with my father. In other words, lost and alone, despite this ballroom filled with over four hundred people.

"You should be owning this room, Isabella," Father says, his voice pitched low to avoid prying ears. "The press is here, along with our peers. Not to mention those who would like to see a Hart slip so that they can rise by climbing over our broken backs. This is a good marriage—but as for the consideration to which we agreed..."

I stiffen. He's talking about the hotel. As of tomorrow morning, I'm the new manager. And upon our actual marriage, I'll become the fully-vested owner.

It's all on paper, documented and negotiated with at least as much fervor as the founders negotiated the Declaration of Independence.

Too bad my father is far less trustworthy than those men, and I fear that if I do anything to make my father look askance, he'll pull the Monarch Grand Casino right out from under me. All of it. Which would mean losing access to the hotel's tenants as well. Specifically, the high-end shops and restaurants on the mezzanine.

If that happens, I'll lose *La Galerie LaBete*—and that's something I don't think I could survive. Gabriel and I started that business. A dream we shared. And just the thought of losing it brings tears to my eyes. I mean, sure, I could find another location. But that space is where we started. Where we spent hours painting the walls and putting in the flooring. Where we made love on the lumpy couch in the storage room, and where I'd often snuggle under a blanket, getting cozy as I watched him stand shirtless at an easel as he lost himself in his art.

"— the crown jewel of the Hart empire."

I stiffen. "Pardon?"

Father's mouth curves into a frown. "I said that I expect you to make this hotel a shining jewel."

"Of course, I will, Father. You trained me well."

He didn't, of course. Not unless yelling and tearing down and criticizing without any constructive suggestions can be considered teaching.

But operating this hotel/casino has been my goal since Gabriel died. That's when I knew I had to grow up. When I understood that I both wanted and needed to succeed.

All of which is why I've spent the last four and a half years working in various capacities throughout my father's empire. But now school's over.

All that's left is to marry my best guy friend, locking us both into a life we don't actually want, but which wins us both some hefty benefits.

"The admin team will want to meet soon to go over your management plan," my father continues. "I expect you to be prepared. The transition needs to be seamless."

"Of course, Father. Anything else?"

I keep my eyes on his as I wait for his next volley. Probably some sort of pop quiz about the laws governing gambling venues.

It doesn't come. Instead, he asks, "And the gallery?"

My heart stutters, and I have to work to keep my expression flat. "What about it?"

His jaw tightens. "We've talked about this, Isabella. You'll need to scale back your involvement. Running a major casino property requires your full attention."

That's my problem now.

The words fly out of me—but sadly, only in my mind. What my mouth says is, "Of course, Father. That's a given." I keep my face bland and hope he can't see the lie. "The gallery practically runs itself at this point. Chris manages the day-to-day operations, and he does an excellent job. I only need to be involved for major exhibitions and acquisitions."

All true. The gallery may have become world famous over the last few years for the LaBete originals and the other abstract pieces we curate, but Chris—my assistant manager and one of the few people in this world I trust completely—could run the place blindfolded.

If I had to, I really could just walk away. But I never will. *La Galerie LaBete* is all I have left of Gabriel.

That, however, is a Fun Little Factoid that Father really doesn't need to know. So, I just look at my father, my expression bland, as if I'm finally, truly not giving a fuck about the gallery, and happy to let Chris step in.

Father studies me for a long moment, and I hold my breath, waiting for him to push. Waiting for him to demand that I choose between the casino and the gallery. Between the future he's planned for me and the past that I can't let go.

Finally, he nods. "Good. I'm glad you finally understand. The Monarch comes first, child. Always."

"Of course."

He releases my shoulder and moves away, but it's not until he disappears into the crowd of Manhattan's power players and Atlantic City's high rollers that I can finally breathe again.

———

HALF AN HOUR and two glasses of champagne later, I scan the ballroom, looking for Harper Lang, my bestie. I catch sight of her near the terrace doors, partially hidden behind a massive floral arrangement, watching me with those pale gray eyes that see far too much.

She tilts her head slightly— *you okay?*

I lift my champagne flute in a small salute—*I'm fine*—because that's the lie we both need right now.

Harper and I met back when Gabriel was still alive. Back when I was young enough to believe that love could conquer anything and naive enough to think that my father's approval was something I could eventually earn. She'd been best friends with Gabriel since childhood, with her, Gabriel, and his younger brother Elliott, making an unlikely trio that somehow worked. She'd loved Gabriel, too, in the same non-romantic way that I love David, and she'd been the one who held me when I got the news about the fire.

And she's the one who knows, without me ever having said it out loud, that I'm still in love with a dead man.

She makes her way through the crowd toward me with the kind of easy confidence that comes from knowing how to work a room. A PR professional, Harper can charm a journalist, schmooze a critic, and manage a crisis all before lunch. She's wearing red tonight, because why fall in line with *black tie only* if you can be Harper?

"Your father's in rare form tonight," she murmurs when she reaches my side, pushing a fall of unruly ebony curls out of her eyes. With her mix of black, German, and Asian heritage, she's got a style and beauty that rivals the models she often hires.

Now, she hands me a fresh champagne flute.

"He wants to make sure I don't embarrass him. Like I'm going to jump up on a table and announce that I can't possibly marry David."

"Probably true." Harper's tone is dry. She's known me long enough to understand the complex dance I do with my father as I try to make myself believe that I'm a competent exec and not a pawn on Father's chessboard.

Except I *am* a pawn on Father's chessboard. Reality, meet hope.

She reaches out to squeeze my hand. "I wish I could make it all better."

"It's as good as it can be, I guess." I lift a shoulder. "I mean, at least I really love David. Just not, you know, *that* way."

Her eyes narrow.

"What?"

"There's something else bothering you."

I grimace. "You really do know me too well."

"Let's just say you should never go into espionage. Your face is easier to read than *The Cat in the Hat*. Now, spill."

"I can't stop thinking about how much this sucks for David," I say. "I've never wanted to be with anyone but Gabriel, and since that's impossible, I'll be fine living my life as David's adoring little wifey. And I've got the gallery to fill the empty spaces, so I'll be okay."

"I see where this is going," she says.

"Right? David's way more screwed with this deal than I am. What if he meets someone? I mean, I'm fine with that, but if the tabloids think that Isabella Hart's husband is cheating on her…" I trail off with a shudder. "I know we're both getting something out of this deal from our parents, but I still think it sucks more for him than it does for me."

There's an odd expression on her face as she nods, then squeezes my hand. "He has his own reasons, just like you do. You'll both be fine."

"You will."

The words come from behind me, not from Harper, and I spin around, then find myself pulled into David's outstretched arms. I hug him tight, my eyes squeezed shut as I try to draw in all his support and love.

Then, with a sigh, I open my eyes to literally and metaphorically face reality.

That's when I see the man.

He's standing across the room in a shadow, so I can't discern any details. Only that he's tall and decked out in a suit that fits so perfectly that I'm guessing London bespoke. He has a full beard and mustache, and hair that's pulled back from his face into a tail. His shoulders are broad, and there's something about the way he holds himself that reminds me so much of Gabriel it makes my stomach do little flips.

I pull out of David's embrace. "Who is that?"

But the crowd has shifted, and Mr. Bespoke is nowhere to be found.

"Sorry, who?" Harper says, sharing a confused look with David.

"Nothing. I just thought I saw—never mind."

David holds out his hand, and I take it. "Come on, my beautiful bride.

Our orders are to mingle our way over to the photo set-up. Apparently, people in the future will want photographic proof that we leapt into the fire."

I squeeze his hand, part of me terrified that this arrangement will screw up our friendship, another part of me so thrilled that he's saving my ass that I can barely think straight.

And then, of course, there's the biggest part of all. The part that won't stop worrying about what Father will do when he realizes that David and I used each other, making lemonade out of the loveless lemon of a deal our parents foisted on us. David, so he could get early access to his trust fund, and me so I could get the gallery. Not to mention the hotel that houses it.

Most parents would lose their shit if they learned about such bold manipulation.

But this is Sterling Hart we're talking about. And maybe he'll be impressed that his daughter is a full-on, sneaky, manipulative chip off the old block.

CHAPTER
TWO

"We are just too pretty for our own good," David says, scrolling through Harper's phone to check out the snaps she took—and posted on social—while the official photographer did his thing. We make a damn fine couple."

I let out an exaggerated sigh. "If only either one of us had the slightest hint of lust mixed in with that love thing."

He's quiet for a moment, then gives my shoulders a squeeze. "Plus, there's that pesky problem of you not being attracted to nice guys."

I roll my eyes but don't argue. He pulls me close, comforting me while the party guests glance over, thinking it's just a warm moment between the happy couple.

"Shall we make the circuit again, then escape to your suite?"

And there it is—another life lesson about how things aren't always what they seem.

What I want is to escape right now, but if even one person misses that vision of happy, giddy Isabella Hart, I'll never hear the end of it from Daddy Dearest.

So we mingle for the next half hour. Thirty long minutes of accepting congratulations from people whose names I don't remember, making small talk about wedding venues and honeymoon destinations, and playing the role of the radiant bride-to-be.

When I can't take it any longer, I pull David away, kiss his cheek, and tell him I need some space. Then I make him promise to tell anyone who asks that I went to the powder room.

That, of course, isn't where I'm going.

The gallery is on the Monarch's mezzanine level. In the weeks before he died, Gabe and I had finalized the paperwork to create an LLC for our new business as gallery owners. Then, after his death, I became the sole shareholder of the company we'd so goofily referred to as our baby.

Now I pause in front of the glass door and soak in the familiar colors and lines. Since the gallery is closed, the only light comes from dim security spots that illuminate each piece.

With a sigh, I key in my code—the date Gabriel and I first met, because I'm that pathetic—and slip inside, letting the door close behind me with a soft click.

It's quiet here. Peaceful. The only place in this entire building that truly feels like home—and that includes my permanent, humongous suite on the penthouse level.

Originals hang on the walls, most with a price tag that would make even my father feel the pinch, but the art supports it, and we funnel most of the proceeds into the art community with scholarships and grants.

I run my fingertips over the sleek workstation near the entrance—one Gabe designed himself. I'd found his furniture sketches in a notebook after he died and hired the best carpenters I could find to bring them to life.

I can picture him watching those workmen, then hurling a measuring tape across the room if they didn't get the cut just right.

He could be so patient and sweet. So loving. So gentle.

But he also had a temper, my Gabriel. How could he not, with so many ideas battling for attention in his head? And though I know he'd spent years verbally sparring with his father and brothers, he and I rarely argued. And when his temper flared, he was never violent toward me. His rages were always directed at himself, and usually inspired by some failure in translating his imagination to canvas.

"I miss you," I whisper. Then, with a sigh, I make my way across the main gallery, past the vibrant abstracts and moody landscapes that showcase LaBete's range, past the smaller studies and experimental pieces from his early days. Still stunning, but only hinting at the genius everyone missed while he was alive.

Only Leo and I know that the recently deceased international art sensation LaBete was none other than Gabriel Grimm, the golden heir of the Grimm empire, who painted in secret because his father would have seen it as a weakness. To Gabriel, every brushstroke was an act of rebellion, every canvas a middle finger to Elias Grimm's expectations of what his eldest son should be.

I've kept his secret for years. Guarded it jealously, fiercely, like the last precious piece of him.

You're stronger than you think.

Gabe's words seem to curl around me.

Don't let your father shape you. Only you. You decide who you are, Izzy. No one else.

I smile at the memory. And at the nickname. No one in my life except Gabe has ever called me Izzy.

"You're an Izzy," he'd said after our first kiss. "You're soft like a Bella, but you have sharp edges, too. That's good," he'd added, tapping my lip with his fingertip when I scowled. "But it's only for me and for you, okay? For now, at least. Izzy needs to get a little stronger before she shows herself to her father."

I'd laughed, then bopped him on the head with the pillow beside me.

"I mean it," he'd said. "When you need help pulling out your power, just remember who you really are—you're Izzy." Then he'd kissed me, and all my thoughts about Izzy or Bella or Isabella vanished. But he'd given me one hell of a gift that night.

Thinking of that kiss makes me think of another gift he gave me, and I slip into the back showroom to stand in front of the piece that mixes both abstract design and brutal realism. "I needed both reality and non-reality," he'd said after I'd pulled down the sheet covering the image I'd posed for. "Truth and fiction. Hope and despair." And then, brushing a soft kiss over my temple, he'd added, "Love."

Now the painting hangs on the back wall, spot lit like the treasure it is, with the title etched on a bronze plaque: Caged.

It depicts a woman behind bars of her own making, reaching toward light she can't quite touch. The colors are gorgeous—deep blues and purples for the shadows, gold and amber for the unreachable light—but it's the expression on the woman's face that makes this painting extraordinary.

Longing. Resignation.

A kind of beautiful despair.

He'd painted it back when we were still planning this gallery. Back when I thought we had forever.

"Is that how you see me?" I'd asked. "Trapped?"

His expression hadn't changed as he met my eyes. "No, my love. It's how you see yourself."

I'd taken a step back, shaking my head. "No."

"Everyone starts in a cage, Izzy. The question is, can you get free?"

The question haunts me. *Can I?*

I didn't know then. I don't know now.

But as I look at my left hand and the engagement ring that marks the farce that is my life, I can't help but think that Gabe would be disappointed in me.

"I'm sorry," I whisper. "But it's so hard without you."

Once upon a time, I'd believed we'd be together forever. How could we not? I'd loved him desperately, with the kind of all-consuming passion that makes you believe you can survive anything as long as you're together.

Turns out you can't survive a fire that burns hot enough to melt gold.

Now, all I have left of him is his art. The two that hang in my bedroom at home, and the rest that live here, a tribute to the man who painted them. The man I once loved with all my heart and soul.

Whom I still love, even though he's gone forever.

CHAPTER
THREE

After quite a bit of mental urging, I draw in a shaky breath, then force myself to step back from Caged. I can't stay here all night, no matter how much I want to. There's a party upstairs full of people expecting to see the radiant bride-to-be. There's a father with a large stick up his ass who will notice my absence and make me pay for it. There's a semi-fake fiancé/best friend who deserves better than a woman who keeps sneaking away to commune with a dead man's paintings.

Time to put the mask back on.

I slip out of the gallery and make my way to the elevator, the click of my heels echoing in the silence. Then I gather myself as the car rises, and by the time the doors glide open and the hum of the party washes over me, my society armor is back in place.

The buzz of voices. The clink of glasses. It's the sound of celebration, and most of the guests are truly happy for me and David, with no clue that they're raising their glasses in honor of a marriage that will be nothing but a business transaction dressed up in white lace.

I've known that forever, of course, but it truly hits me now. I should run. But I can't leave the gallery—can't walk away from Gabe's memory. And my father would find me anyway.

I draw in a breath and step back through the doors of the ballroom like a mouse skittering into a maze.

Across the crowd, I can see my father holding court near the ice sculpture. He's laughing at something one of the investors said, his hand resting possessively on Mina's shoulder, the picture of charm and success—the benevolent patriarch celebrating his daughter's happiness—with his younger-than-me girlfriend on his arm.

I shudder.

Nope, this was a mistake. I can't do this. Not tonight. Not after standing in front of Caged, soaking in those brush strokes and colors, and feeling Gabe's absence like a physical wound.

I make one circle, being seen but avoiding conversation, then I slip back out the way I came in. I take a deep breath of freedom, then hurry to my penthouse suite. Just one little perk of being a Hart heiress. One of the few I truly enjoy.

It's quiet when I slip inside—blissfully, mercifully empty.

David is staying with me, of course. Just another hat tip to how very, very in love we are. And no, as we've told everyone, of course, we don't have separate rooms. That would be far too hard on our hearts.

Yeah, right.

I kick off my heels and leave them where they fall, then pad across the plush carpet to the balcony door. The Atlantic City skyline glitters below me. Somewhere out there, people are winning fortunes and losing everything. But in the end, of course, the house always wins. I press my forehead against the cool glass and close my eyes. That's when I hear the click of the door.

I whirl around, then immediately relax. *David.*

"Hey," he says as he tosses his jacket over the back of the sofa. "You okay?"

I should tell him I'm fine, that I just need some sleep, that I'll be back to performing tomorrow.

Instead, I say, "Not really."

He tilts his head, studying me. "You went down to the gallery."

I nod, and he comes to me, then pulls me into a hug. This is why I love David. He knows me. He gets me. We just don't love each other *that way*. Which is good. If I did, that would mean I'd let Gabriel go.

And I'm not ready for that goodbye.

"All this bullshit with our wedding," he says quietly. "I get it. It should have been him. A real wedding instead of this corporate merger our parents concocted."

"We agreed," I say with a shrug.

He grimaces. "We didn't really have a choice."

He holds me tighter, then releases me, stepping back and casting an assessing look over me. "You could use some wine."

I almost laugh. "Yeah. I really could."

David nods, flashing a grin that's almost devious. Then he moves to the kitchen and returns far too quickly with a tray holding two glasses of red wine and a bag of chocolate chip cookies.

"What on earth?" I look up at him, not sure if the pressure in my chest is delight or a knot of tears.

"So here are your options," he says. "You can cry, and I'll hold you and make sympathetic noises and pretend I know what to say. Or we can put on something funny and pretend the world doesn't suck for a couple hours."

Despite everything, I can't hold back my smile. "What are our movie options?"

"I may have bookmarked a few things." He grabs the remote. "Princess Bride, Buffy, or stand-up comedy?"

"I can't believe you planned this."

"I planned for the possibility that my fake fiancée might bail early from her own engagement party and need a distraction." He shrugs. "I know you, Bella."

He does. That's the thing. After twenty-plus years of friendship—summer camps and charity galas and school and all the glittering prison cells where children of dynasties are stored—David Mercer knows me better than almost anyone.

"*The Princess Bride*," I decide. "I need Westley telling me that death cannot stop true love."

Something flickers in David's expression, but he nods and queues up the movie.

I change out of my gown in my bedroom, trading silk and diamonds for yoga pants and an oversized sweater. When I emerge, David has transformed the living room into a proper movie-watching nest—lights dimmed, cookies on a platter within reach, a soft blanket draped over the back of the couch.

"This is perfect," I say.

He pats the cushion beside him. "Come on. Buttercup's about to make some questionable life choices, and I need someone to mock her with me."

I settle onto the couch, tucking my feet beneath me the way I've done a thousand times before. David spreads the small blanket over both of us, and I scoot closer to him so that I'm fully under the soft material. It's warm and comfy, even though I can't hide how many cookies I'm snarfing since our shoulders brush every time we reach for one.

Halfway through the movie, the cookies are gone. David sets the platter aside on the coffee table, and when he settles back, his arm comes around my shoulders, just as we've sat a million times before.

I lean into him, letting my head rest against his chest. His heartbeat is steady beneath my ear, slow and calm and comforting.

"Thank you," I murmur. "For this."

"That's what friends are for." His hand strokes my shoulder-length hair. "Whatever you need."

On screen, Westley and Buttercup are navigating the Lightning Sand. I'm only half watching. The other half of me is marveling at how nice it feels to just *be*.

The movie plays on. Miracle Max. The storming of the castle. True love's kiss.

"As you wish," Westley says, and something in my chest cracks.

Gabriel used to say that to me. It was our silly little nod to this movie that morphed into our thing. *As you wish, Izzy. However you need me. I'm yours.*

Except it was a lie. Because how I need him is here and alive. But he's not. And I'm in another man's arms, wearing another man's ring, preparing to spend the rest of my life with a friend I love. But it's the wrong kind of love, even if he's the right kind of friend.

David must sense the shift in my mood, because his hand stills in my hair. "You okay?"

"No." The word comes out before I can stop it. "I'm not okay. I haven't been okay in almost five years, and I don't know if I ever will be again. I'm sorry. I hate dumping this on you, but—I'm just sorry."

He doesn't say anything. Just holds me tighter, his chin resting on the top of my head.

"I keep waiting for it to fade." My voice is barely above a whisper. "Everyone says time heals everything. But it doesn't feel like healing. It feels like...learning to live with a piece of yourself missing. Like you just get better at ignoring the empty space where something vital used to be."

"Maybe that's what healing looks like. Not forgetting. Not moving on. Just learning that you can carry it and still have space for something new."

I shrug. I don't really want to be mollified. I want Gabriel. I always will. And right now, he doesn't just take up space in my heart, he fills the space, leaving only corners and crannies that maybe—*maybe*—someone else could someday fill.

"It hurts," I whisper. "But I don't want to spend my life alone with his ghost."

"He wouldn't want you to. He'd want you to move on. And you can, you know."

I want to believe him. God, I want to believe that there's more to my future than this endless ache.

But I don't.

I tilt my head back to look at him. The movie's credits are rolling now, casting shifting patterns of light across his face. He's handsome. Not in the sharp, dangerous way Gabriel was handsome—all edges and intensity, strength and power—but in a softer way. Warm. Safe.

He's the brother I never had—hell, he even looks the part with our similar pale skin and light brown hair that looks golden under the sun. Even our eyes support the illusion, with his emerald green eyes matching my left eye, and my right sky-blue eye left out of the party.

"You are earning so many friend points," I tell him. "I mean, you must have a zillion stacked up. And I know it must be a downer for me to keep moaning about Gabe every time you turn around."

"The man you loved died horribly, and now you're being trotted around as the glowing bride. I think some melancholy is allowed."

"Yeah, well, I still appreciate it."

"All part of the David Mercer Best Friend Kit. You need me, I'm there for you."

"Even if what I need is to marry you while I'm still in love with someone else?" I wince. Tears and wine are a bad combination. "Sorry. I didn't mean to toss our parents' bullshit arrangement back in both our faces. Honestly, if we have to play the medieval sell-the-bride thing, then I'm glad I'm being pawned off on you."

"*Pawned off*," he repeats. "I promise you, Bella, that's not how I feel. I mean, come on. You and Harper are my two best friends."

"That works out well, then, because you two are my besties."

He nods at the television, now scrolling credits. "Another movie?"

I shrug. "Honestly, right now I just want more cookies, but I'm going to force myself not to have any."

He laughs as I shift on the couch to face him more directly. "Remember Lori?" he asks.

"Sure. That's been a while. What's she up to?"

"No idea. It's just that was the last time I…you know."

I grimace. "Yeah, I have you beat by what? A year and a half?

"Fair enough. The thing is, I have a weird confession."

I shift to sit up straighter. "Yeah? What?"

He shifts away. "Actually, never mind."

"Oh, no, no, no. You started this."

"It's—well, okay. Do you ever miss *it?* Not Gabriel. Sex."

My cheeks heat. "Awkward, much?"

"Oh, come on. It's us," he says. Then he catches my eye, and we both start laughing. Not because it's funny, but because this conversation is just too weird.

"You, my friend, are drunk."

He nods. "I have definitely slid over into tipsy. But I'm serious. "Do you ever think about it? Us. Taking the edge off?"

"Not unless *ever* includes forty seconds ago."

He drags his fingers through his hair. "Why is the idea so verboten? I mean, Friends With Benefits, right?" Emphasis on the friends. I mean, it's a thing."

I laugh. We both do. Because—*O.M.G.*

But also weirdly tempting. Being held. Being touched. The release. Letting the crap of the day fall away under the force of pure pleasure.

Maybe it's not such a freakish idea…

I hug a throw pillow to my chest, then shake my head to clear it. "This is one of our more bizarre conversations."

"In other words, you're not into it."

I shrug. "Honestly?" I say to the flooring. "Yeah, sex would be nice." I hug myself, glance at him, then glance away again. "I cannot believe we are actually having this conversation."

"All part of the best friend package. You were about to say something else."

"Was I?" I guess, just I don't want to screw up our friendship." I knock back some wine from the glass he must have magically topped off.

"Impossible," he says. "You're like a sister."

I almost spit out my wine even as he barks out a laugh. "Right," he says. "That came out wrong." He cocks his head. "So bad idea?"

"Not bad," I say. "But maybe not the right idea."

He nods. "Fair enough. I don't want to risk messing up what we've got."

"Me neither," I say, meaning it with all my heart. "You going to crash? Or do you want to watch something else?"

"Stand-up?" he suggests, nodding at the wine bottle with maybe enough for one glass left in it. "Split it?"

I nod, then slide closer to him, purposefully leaning against him as we share the blanket to prove to both of us that the conversation wasn't the weirdest and most awkward in the history of time.

David empties the bottle into our glasses, and we drink as we scroll through some of the best—and worst—comedians of the last few decades. By the time we turn off the TV, I'm giggling at pretty much anything. "Bed," I say, wobbling my way to standing. "Time for sleep."

"Definitely, he agrees, taking my hand for balance as he stands, too, then stumbles back, landing with a plop on the couch —and pulling me down with him.

The next thing I know, his mouth is on mine, and he's kissing me. And I'm kissing him back. Then I realize what we're doing and pull away. He looks at me, his expression is more than a little broken. "I'm so sorry," he says. "I know we said—but then you— and I—and, wine, and oh, hell, Bella, I'm sorry."

I draw in a deep breath, every molecule in my body wishing that Gabe were alive. That I was in his arms. But he's not. And I need to move on. And David—just a friend—is a safe way to take that first step.

My voice shakes as I say, "Just friends with benefits, right? And if this destroys our friendship, I will hunt you down and kill you as painfully as possible in cold blood."

"Understood," he says. And then, when I whisper, "Okay," he pulls me close and kisses me. And damned if I don't learn something new about the guy I've known my whole life. For one thing, I wasn't imagining it before—he is a *really* good kisser.

For another, that's not all he's good at.

A few very lovely orgasms later, and I'm curled against him, thinking that this was a good idea. I mean, it would be sad for us to be married and never have sex or kids or any of that. And we're good enough friends that we'll be able to talk through any weirdness. So, who knew? Guess I'm a fan of the FWB arrangement after all.

I'm about to share that revelation with David when my phone chimes. And since my DND setting only has five people who can break through, and I'm in bed with one of them, I'm pretty sure it's my dad calling.

"Ignore it," David mumbles against my hair. "It's the middle of the night. Whatever it is can wait."

He's right. But twenty-plus years of conditioning are hard to override. When Sterling Hart summons, his daughter jumps.

With a groan of frustration, I slide out of David's arms and reach for the phone. Then my heart stops.

Because the text isn't from my father.

It's from Leo Grimm.

Five words. Just five words, and my entire world falls off its axis.

He called me. Gabriel's alive!!!

The phone slips from my fingers.

He's alive.

Gabriel. Is. Alive.

I'm out of bed before I've even made a conscious decision, my body shaking so hard I can barely stand.

"Bella?" David bolts up. "What's wrong?"

I can't answer. Can't form words. Can barely breathe.

I grab my clothes off the floor and pull them on with trembling fingers.

"Bella, talk to me. What happened between us, are you—?"

"We're good," I snap. "Really. We're fine. But I have to go." My voice sounds strange. Distant. "I'm sorry. I'm so sorry, David. I have to—"

I don't finish the sentence.

I just run.

CHAPTER
FOUR

Leo's text is burned like a brand into my mind.

He called me. Gabriel's alive!!!

Another text arrives.

He says he's coming! The GT penthouse.

It's all I can see, all I can think about. Just getting to Grimm Tower Atlantic City.

Getting to Gabriel.

I have never appreciated a VIP access elevator more in my life. I use my keycard, and even though it probably takes less than three minutes, I bounce on the balls of my feet until those doors slide open and I leap inside, then keep bouncing as I use my key to shift the elevator to express mode. I try to hold myself together as I text down my order for a Town Car to be pulled around. Then I try to will the damn elevator car to move even faster as it drops the forty-plus stories to the subterranean valet level.

When the doors finally open, I burst out, racing across the sub-3 lobby, my untied sneakers slapping against the marble tile. I probably look like a crazy person fleeing the scene of a crime. I don't care. I can't care about anything except the two words still burning on my phone screen.

Gabriel's alive.

The words keep looping through my head, a drumbeat drowning out everything else. Every step I take pounds out the rhythm. *Gabriel. Is. Alive. Gabriel. Is. Alive.*

And right now, all I want in the world is to get to Grimm Tower and throw my arms around my beloved.

Five years of grief. Five years of lighting candles on his birthday. Five years of visiting the gallery like it was his grave and my only solace. Five years pressing my hand against his paintings as if I could somehow reach through the canvas and touch him.

He's been alive this whole time.

And he's on his way to Grimm Tower!

Gabe and I used to crash regularly at the Grimm's residential penthouse. No one actually lives there. It's just available to the family as needed. Just like the ones in Houston, Los Angeles, Chicago, Paris, Rome, Sydney, and at least a dozen other places.

And how wonderful that he's here now when he could be at any other Grimm Tower around the globe. Or even back at their home in Connecticut.

Once I'm released from the elevator, I burst through the glass doors to the VIP car service area, startling a couple in evening wear who give me the kind of look you'd give a woman who just escaped from a psychiatric facility. I ignore them.

I don't ignore the on-duty valet. Him, I practically interrogate, and am assured that a car will be arriving for me at any moment.

As he scurries off to get the elderly couple's car, I rock from one foot to the other, twisting Mom's ring and realizing suddenly how much better I'm breathing. It's as if a ton of cement has been lifted off my chest.

He's alive...

Dammit. Where is the second valet? Do we really only have one working?

As I mentally add an audit of the valet service to my list of things to monitor and upgrade, it occurs to me that David has a car here. Maybe I could go get his keys and—

David.

All my breath leaves my lungs as I think of the man I left naked and confused in my bed. David, whose hands were on my body less than an hour ago.

A wave of nausea crashes through me. I slept with David while Gabriel was out there somewhere, alive, breathing, existing in a world I thought he'd left forever.

David must think I've completely freaked out, and the guilt is like a knife in my heart—toward him and toward Gabriel.

But I can't deal with that right now. I can't deal with anything except getting to Leo and actually seeing with my own eyes that my love is back from the dead.

A solid three minutes pass, and I'm about to fire the entire car department when—*finally*—a sleek Town Car pulls up. The driver's window is already down, and he steps out, then opens the back door for me. I tell him to take me to Grimm Tower, then slide in, noticing first that the overhead light didn't come on. Yet another thing to put in my report about this department.

Then, just as the attendant shuts my door, the door on the other side opens, and a man slides in beside me, though I can't see him properly in the dark. He shuts the door, and as the car pulls out, I hear the click of the locks.

I'm about to tell the driver to stop and let this apparently confused passenger out, but that's when we glide past one of the garage's interior lamps, and the light erases the shadows from the passenger's face.

For one disorienting moment, I don't process what I'm seeing. I can tell that he's tall, with a moustache and beard, along with broad shoulders and a familiar, commanding presence that I don't need to see because I can feel it.

That's when I recognize him—the man in the bespoke suit from the party. "Who—" I begin, and that's when he tilts his head, and I finally get a good look at his face.

His eyes.

My hand flies to my mouth in both delight and terror as I look into the eyes of a dead man.

A dangerous man.

Gabriel.

And yet not.

The Gabe I love was intense. Dangerous in a way that thrilled me instead of frightening me. His smile was rare, but when it came, it was like watching lightning crack across a dark sky—sudden and wild and impossible to look away from. And his eyes—those pale blue eyes that always reminded me of storms rolling in over the ocean. Those eyes always softened when they landed on me. Like I was something precious. Something worth protecting.

They're not soft now.

Nothing about him is soft. All that has been stripped away. He's leaner now, his face carved into sharp angles and cold planes. A scar I've never seen before runs along his cheek, partially hidden by the full beard. His hair is longer, and right now it's pulled back from a face that holds no warmth at all.

Instead, those beautiful eyes are looking at me like I'm the enemy.

"Gabe." His name comes out broken. A whisper. A prayer. "Oh my god. Gabe."

I reach for him without thinking, just as I have so many times in my dreams.

But unlike my dreams, he doesn't reach back. Instead, he catches my wrist before I can touch his face, his grip so tight it's almost painful.

"Don't."

One word, as cold as a blade. I yank my hand back, then cradle it against my chest like he's burned me.

I swallow, then whisper, "What happened to you?"

"Don't you dare play that game with me, you little bitch."

The word stings like a slap, and I recoil, trying to disappear into the leather seats. To get away from the accusation in his voice.

A wave of nausea crests over me, and I have to fight not to vomit. To not let him—whoever the hell he is now—win.

When I'm certain I can keep the bile down, I try again, as if I'm going to somehow find the magical combination of words that bring my Gabriel back to me. "Please," I say, hating that my voice is close to a whimper, but not able to manage any more force. "I've missed you so much. Please, please tell me why you're acting like this."

His eyes narrow. "Missed me? Next, you're going to say that you loved me."

"I did," I whisper. "I do," I add, then cry out and recoil when he cups my chin and yanks me to him.

"Don't you fucking lie." His voice is hard and rough and low, and I see hate in his eyes before he pushes me away. "I've had enough of your lies to last a lifetime."

I hear myself whimper, and tears are streaming freely now. I curl into a ball again and sob silently against my knees, my shoulders shaking. I don't know everything that's in his head—hell, I don't know anything. Nothing except that he truly believes I had something to do with leaving him for dead.

How?

How could he possibly think that?

For a moment, I consider jumping from the car at the next traffic light, but I can't convince myself that's a good idea, especially when we're heading into a dicey neighborhood and not toward Grimm Tower.

More importantly, I need answers. And to get them, I have to stay the course.

"Where are you taking me?"

I don't expect him to answer, so I'm unsurprised when he stays silent, watching me with eyes so cold, I'm terrified that the Gabe I loved doesn't exist anymore. That whatever horrors he's faced over these past years have broken him completely.

I tremble slightly, not sure if my heart can handle knowing that.

After a moment, I draw new breath, then try again. "Gabriel," please talk to me." I hate how desperate I sound. Hate that I'm already begging. But I can't help it. I've spent what feels like a lifetime dreaming about seeing him again, and now he's here—alive, real, close enough to touch—and he's looking at me like I'm nothing. Like I'm less than nothing.

Like I'm someone he hates.

"At least tell me what's happening." I try to keep my voice level, try to exorcise all hints of begging or pleading.

"I thought you were dead," I continue when he stays stubbornly silent. "I thought you died in the fire." Tears well, and my voice cracks. "I mourned you. I'm still mourning you. And now you're here, and you won't even look at me like...like…

"Like what?" Not words. A growl, low and harsh and dangerous.

"Like you even remember loving me." I blurt the words out, ahead of the rush of tears that follow. And maybe it's an illusion from those tears, but I think I see something flicker in his expression. There and gone, too fast to identify. Pain, maybe. Or anger. Or just contempt. I don't know. All I can tell is it's bad.

"We'll talk," he says. "But not here." His voice is still harsh, but at least we're moving toward answers, and I nod eagerly, clinging to his words like a dog with a bone. "Then where? And when? Can we go now? Please, Gabe. Can we just go now?"

I start to say more, but swallow my words because there's no way to express the chasm that looms between the reunion I imagined and this cold, hostile silence.

In my dreams, he was always so happy to see me. Always reaching for me the way I reached for him.

This Gabriel doesn't even answer me. Just turns to stare out the window at the passing lights of this illuminated city. The neon glow paints his profile in shifting colors—red, green, gold—and I study the new lines of his face like I'm trying to memorize a stranger.

The scar on his cheek. The beard and mustache. The hard set

of his mouth. The tension in his shoulders, like he's holding himself back from something. Violence, maybe?

Or perhaps he's holding out on telling me the truth.

All I know is that he doesn't say another word for the rest of the drive.

CHAPTER
FIVE

I don't recognize the hotel we arrive at.

It's not one of the big casinos that dominate the Atlantic City skyline. This hotel is smaller. More discreet and with an old money vibe. The facade is elegant but understated, with cream-colored stone, wrought-iron balconies, and the kind of architectural details that suggest it was built over a century ago.

It's called *The Obsidian*, according to the bronze letters lit by a backlight so that they seem to glow above the entrance. And looking at it, that name seems to fit.

A doorman in a crisp uniform stands at the main entrance, but the car goes right past him, pulling around instead to a side entrance. The driver gets out, circles the car, then opens Gabriel's door.

Gabriel climbs out without even a glance back at me.

I consider just staying in the car, but since that would just piss him off, I follow, sliding across the bench seat with my heart pounding.

Besides, despite Gabe's strange distance and horrible accusations, I'm curious.

Or maybe that distance and the hard look in his eyes are the reasons I'm curious.

Either way, I'm not losing him again.

The side door leads into a service corridor with poured concrete floors and fluorescent lights. I don't see even a hint of the elegance outside. Not surprising, though, since we're apparently in the bowels of the building.

But why? Why are we here at all?

Gabriel walks fast, and I have to practically jog to keep up with his long strides.

"Gabriel, wait—"

He doesn't slow down. Doesn't acknowledge me at all. Just keeps walking, leading me deeper into the building.

The corridor gets even less polished as we go. The industrial carpet gives way to bare concrete. The already unimpressive sconces replaced by harsh overhead bulbs. Even the air changes, taking on the slightly damp quality of a laundry room.

Despite a million questions, I stay quiet and follow him onto a service elevator. Gabriel punches the button for SB2, and the elevator descends with a mechanical groan as the voices in my head bombard me with questions—*What is this place? Where is he taking me? Why won't he just freaking talk to me?*

I don't know. And worst of all is the truly dark question that keeps repeating itself—*is he going to hurt me?*

I tell myself no. If that was his plan, he would have done it already. Would have had the driver pull over to the side of the road and then used his well-known temper to do more than a little damage.

The thought makes me shudder. *No.* He wouldn't do that. No matter what he thinks, he wouldn't do that to me.

I hope I'm right. I think I am. But at the same time, there are a lot of ways to hurt someone that don't inflict bruises or break bones. And I don't know this Gabriel anymore.

I realize my pulse is pattering along in double-time, and I try to breathe and calm myself. It's not easy. This is *Gabe*, and I'm teetering on terrified.

How is this even possible?

Another breath. Another reminder to myself to just stay calm.

So far, I've been more curious than scared. More in shock than in distress.

Now though…now I'm starting to think a healthy dose of terror might be called for.

I've never wanted to be wrong more in my life.

That's when the doors slide open onto Sub-basement 2, and I stare into a completely different world.

"Welcome to The Beast," Gabriel says. "Or one level of it. My club." His voice is flat, like he's daring me to be impressed. Or horrified. Or to comment on the club's name. Maybe all three.

Honestly, I don't know what I expected. I was already in Wonderland, after all. Maybe I assumed we were going down into a storage facility. Someplace where he could lock me in a box, then toss me away. Or even just something mundane like a parking garage.

This is none of those things, and I hurry to catch up to him while taking it all in.

The place is like something from a noir movie—all exposed brick and dramatic shadows cast by pools of amber light. The distant thump of a musical bass line vibrates through the concrete floor. And somewhere deeper in the building, people are talking. Even laughing.

A speakeasy, maybe?

I jump from a sudden roar—crowd noise, boisterous and drunk—followed by the dull thud of something heavy hitting the ground. So, apparently not a speakeasy.

I frown, wanting to ask Gabriel, but I've already figured out that he'll tell me only what he wants to tell me—and that only in his own sweet time.

I quicken my pace so I can get a bit ahead of him, then catch his eye. "All right. I give up. What is this place?"

He holds my gaze for exactly one beat, then looks away, very pointedly not answering me.

Seriously, what the fuck?

Is he trying to intimidate me? To freak me out?

Yes, dummy, my better angel whispers. *What reality have you been living in?*

I grimace because, well, yeah. Duh.

But screw it and screw him. I have absolutely no intention of giving him the pleasure of watching me gawk and gape. So I do my best to look bland. Not impressed or intrigued. Just hanging out. Just existing. As if this place isn't a walking question mark on the forehead of the man I love.

Or, rather, on the man I used to love.

Because, as much as I hate to admit it, I don't know this Gabriel. More, I'm starting to fear that the tidal wave of hope I'd felt upon getting Leo's text was premature. That my Gabriel really did die in that fire, and this man in Gabriel's clothing rose from the ashes, a new man whom I don't know, and who doesn't love me.

No.

I can't believe that. *I won't believe it.*

Somewhere in this Gabriel-clone is the man I love. He's traumatized, yes. But I'll fight for him.

I'll get him back.

I will. Because I don't think I can survive losing him all over again.

As we continue to move, we pass a doorway, and through it, I catch a glimpse of what looks like a high-stakes poker game—men in expensive suits gathered around a table covered in chips, the air hazy with cigar smoke, the tension palpable even from here.

Another doorway. Another glimpse. This time it's a bar—sleek and sophisticated, all dark wood and leather, with beautiful people draped over beautiful furniture while bartenders in black mix drinks with exotic colors and pour shots of whiskey for the hard-core patrons.

Then we pass a doorway that opens onto a sight that makes my breath catch.

A boxing ring.

Not the kind you'd find in a gym. This is something else entirely—a raised platform surrounded by well-dressed spectators, two men circling each other with bare fists, blood already speckling the canvas beneath their feet. I can barely see through the crowd that watches with the kind of avid attention usually reserved for high-stakes auctions.

They're betting on this, I realize. They're betting on men beating each other bloody.

"What is this place?" The question comes out barely above a whisper.

I glance at Gabriel, and something that might be amusement flickers across his face. "Home," he says, and keeps walking, until we finally arrive at a door at the end of a very long corridor.

He unlocks it with a keycard and holds the door open, waiting.

I draw a wary breath, then step inside.

The space is Spartan. Expensive, but cold. And small.

A leather sofa in charcoal gray. A bar cart stocked with top-shelf liquor. Floor-to-ceiling screens on one wall, currently dark. Everything sleek and modern and completely lacking in personality.

Home, he'd said? The hell with that. This isn't the home of the man I'd loved.

Gabriel's apartment in Manhattan had been a glorious disaster —canvases stacked against every wall, paint-splattered drop cloths covering the furniture only when he remembered, half-finished sketches papering every available surface. The smell of turpentine and linseed oil. The sound of classical music or brutal hard rock playing while he worked. The feeling that here was a space where creativity and passion came to party.

This place has no passion. No creativity. No life at all.

It's a bunker. Hell, it's a lair.

There's no art on the walls. No books, no plants. Not even a magazine or a grocery bag. Absolutely no evidence that anyone actually lives here.

Except—

There's one photograph, taped to the wall near the dark screens. The paper is crumpled—like someone balled it up, then changed their mind. From where I stand, I can't tell what it is because the image is hidden by the shadows cast by the crinkles. Still, there's something about it that feels familiar. I glance toward Gabe, and when he stays perfectly still and silent, I walk toward the wall, curiosity pushing me forward.

It only takes two steps before the shadows shift.

That's when I see it.

My body tightens, and I suck in a stuttering breath.

Me. David.

Our kiss for the cameras only hours ago.

My stomach twists— I know why the paper's creased. He crumpled it. Twisted it. Treated it like trash.

And then he taped it to the wall.

I turn toward him, part of me wanting to cry. Part of me wanting to race out of here.

All of me wanting answers.

I thrust a finger at him like an accusation. "You were there. And you just stood in a corner and watched."

"I wasn't in the mood to greet old friends."

A shiver cuts through me. He'd been there. Right there. But he'd never said a word to me.

I want to go to him. To shake him. To ask him to please, please tell me what is wrong with him. Why aren't I in his arms right now? Hell, why aren't I in his bed?

Why is he being this way?

But I ask nothing. I'm too scared of the answers.

Instead, I whisper, "You bastard."

He stays silent, but takes one single step toward me. As he moves, the overhead light catches that scar on his cheek like a warning.

"Now, sweetheart," he says, and his voice is so cold it makes me shiver. "I think it's time for you to explain—in excruciating detail—exactly why the fuck you tried to kill me."

CHAPTER
SIX

For a long moment, I can't speak.

Those horrible words hang in the air between us, incomprehensible. Impossible. I hear them—I understand what each word means individually—but strung together like that? Coming from his mouth in that cold, flat voice?

They just don't make sense.

"Kill you?" The words taste bitter, and I instinctively pull back as his expression darkens. "What are you talking about?"

"Don't play innocent." He pushes off the door and stalks toward me. I take an instinctive step back, then another, until the backs of my knees hit the leather sofa. "Don't pretend you don't know exactly what I'm talking about."

"But I *don't* know!" My voice is rising, edging toward hysteria. "Are you insane? I would never hurt you."

"Did you think I wouldn't find out?" His voice is low. Harsh. *Dangerous.* He takes another step closer.

I try to step back, but I'm trapped between him and the sofa. "Gabe," I whisper as tears spill from my eyes. "What the hell? How could you even think that?" My heart pounds against my chest, and my head is swimming. He isn't making sense. *Nothing* is making sense.

"I loved you," he says, his voice like ice that's near to breaking. "*Loved.* You were my everything. Hell, I would have given my life for you." He lifts his head. "I never once thought you'd just take it."

Something snaps in me. "Don't you *dare*." My voice shakes, but I hold my ground. "I spent five years mourning you. Five years of wishing I'd died in that fire instead of you."

His eyes are hard on mine, but I don't look away.

I can't stop shaking my head. *This is a nightmare.*

It has to be a nightmare.

I swallow, then force the words past the lump in my throat. "How can you think that about me?"

He says nothing, but he's close enough now that I can see the new lines on his face, the hard set of his jaw, and the harsh way he looks at me. Like he doesn't know me at all.

Like he hates me.

I taste tears, then only shake my head. *This is real.* He truly thinks I could kill him. That I *did* kill him. "You bastard," I whisper. "I've been dead without you. Your death was like a knife in my heart, and now you're fucking twisting it."

His lips curl into a sneer. "You tricky bitch."

I see the way his hands are clenched at his sides like he's physically restraining himself from pummeling me. "Did you think I'd just die quietly and never learn the truth?"

"What truth? Dammit, Gabe, you're not making sense!"

"Five years." He spits the words like venom, his eyes dipping to where I'm fidgeting with my ring. "Five years knowing the woman I loved—the woman I would have died for—tried to fucking kill me."

"Kill you!"

But he just talks right over me. "Five years watching from the shadows while you built your little empire on my bones."

I gape at him. "You think I wanted any of this? The gallery was *ours*, Gabriel. Everything I've done for five years has been about keeping your memory alive."

"And do you know what I found?" he asks as if I hadn't said a single word. "Evidence. Hard evidence." His head tilts as he looks at me, like a predator sizing up prey. "I found a shiny paper trail. Proof. As if I needed it. Your eyes, Bella. That's where guilt lives. That's what truly killed me."

I shake my head, my body going cold. *I'm literally in shock.* "Eyes? Proof? What the hell are you talking about?" My voice rises with each word, and more tumble out. "There isn't proof because I didn't do anything." My stomach roils, and I clamp my hand over my mouth, afraid I'm going to barf.

"I followed the money, sweetheart. And it led me straight back to an account with your name on it. Three hundred thousand dollars, gone two days before I took three bullets and got left in a burning cabin to die."

The room is spinning. I grab the arm of the sofa to steady myself.

"I didn't," I whisper. "I didn't do anything. I don't know what you think you found, but you are so, so wrong."

"Do you remember what they said?" He moves closer, so I have to tilt my head back to meet his eyes. "The men you were with. When they left me bleeding out in that cabin? Do you want to know the last thing I heard before I passed out?"

I shake my head, mute with horror.

"'*Say goodbye to your girlfriend, Grimm.*' And the last thing I saw was you raising a gun."

The world tilts. I grab the sofa harder, knuckles going white.

"No." It's barely a sound. "No, that's not—I didn't—I wouldn't. Gabe, you have to know that. I would never hurt you. And I wasn't there. I wasn't in Aspen until we realized you were missing. I didn't do this," I say again, my voice choked with tears.

"Didn't? Didn't what?" His voice is a snarl, lower and wilder than I've ever heard from him. "Didn't order the hit? Didn't know about it? Didn't fucking pull the trigger yourself? Or maybe you didn't think I'd be around to follow the money trail and identify you? Hell, I see the truth in your eyes right now."

"Dammit, Gabe, no."

"You wanted money? The gallery? I would have given you anything. And now I'm just ashamed I never saw the black inside you."

"You prick," I whisper, my body trembling with fear and fury. "You unimaginable bastard. How the hell can you believe that about me? I would never, *ever*, have believed you'd hurt me."

His smile is thin. "And that's why you thought you could get away with it."

I try to speak, but my mouth is bone dry. I want to pinch myself awake from this nightmare. Except it's really, truly happening. He believes it. I've never seen such fury on his face— and considering Gabriel's reputation, that is saying a lot.

I start to speak—though I have no idea what to say—but he cuts me off.

"Are you going to tell me that it was a setup? Because that's damn sure what I wanted to believe. Daddy trying to twist the knife as his people killed me. Trying to make me believe that the woman I loved was complicit."

He steps closer, and I shake, suddenly terrified.

"I wanted so badly to believe it wasn't you holding that gun. And that's what I would have believed, too. And I did. I talked myself into it. *She loves me. She would never…*"

His lip curls. *"What a fucking crock."*

"But I wouldn't," I say, barely restraining myself from shouting. "You were right. I truly wouldn't."

"If you'd wanted me to believe that, you should have paid more attention to the money trail. Because when I checked, sure enough—money gone. But that wasn't the kicker," he says before I can protest again. "The real proof? The rock-solid proof even tighter than that. Not just your eyes, sweetheart. No, it was that you were the only person on this planet who knew where my cabin was. I hadn't even told Leo."

He leans in, then traces his finger gently down the side of my face, then down my neck, then lower still until he's cupping my breast, and I'm trembling. Not with the desire that has always been my reaction to this man. But with fear. Pure, horrible fear.

"And now you have all those pretty paintings by a famous dead artist. Now you have a fortune in the gallery. And you're about to inherit one of the most profitable casino/hotels in the country. And I can draw a straight line back from all of those to my death."

I taste tears, but all I can do is shake my head.

"A bullet that barely missed my heart. Another that almost nicked my spine. Then another that got me in the gut. Fists and boots slamming against me until it wasn't even pain. Just nothing. *I* was nothing. And your fucking goons were right there, making it very clear that each and every blow was a present from you and Daddy Dearest."

He makes a scoffing noise. "The fire? They said that was from you alone. So congratulations, bitch. You worked the long con on me. But I promise," he adds, leaning so close I feel the whisper of his breath on my ear, "I will have vengeance."

He means it. He really means it. And fear courses through me, because I know what he's capable of. But it's not fear that drives me to speak. It's pain. It's fury. And it's bone-deep loss.

"You unimaginable bastard," I say, my voice low and flat. "I would never—never—have believed you would hurt me. And for *money*? In case it escaped your notice, you fucking prick, I have money. Not really starving on the street." I swallow, then lift my chin, hating that this is happening and not quite believing it's real. "If it had been me, I would never have believed that you'd hurt me. You could have put a gun to my temple, and I still wouldn't have believed you were the one holding it."

I wipe away the tears. "Five years. I've mourned you for five years, every day wishing you were beside me. And now…now all I can do is look back and think what a damn, stupid waste. Because I loved a man—I believed in a man—who didn't love me back."

His jaw tightens, but it's not belief I see in his eyes, but fury. As if he's pissed that I'm not playing my part.

Yeah, well, too fucking bad.

I take a step toward him, my rage having completely overtaken my fear. "Do you have any idea how many tears I shed for you? How many investigators I hired to find your body? I was there with the cops. I found your ring. Your teeth." I shudder. "The cops found blood and bits of burned skin in a shallow grave of leaves just a foot from the cabin's remains."

My voice shakes, but I hurry on, the words spilling out along with the tears. "They didn't know if you crawled away and ended up as bear food or if you got trapped back in the cabin and turned to ash."

Since my legs are suddenly too weak to support me, I sit on the sofa, then pull my feet up to hug my knees. "For years, I dreamed that you'd escaped somehow. That you were on your way back to me. And that fantasy was all that kept me going some days. The hope that I'd find you again. That we'd be together. We'd run the gallery and live happily ever after."

"By profiting off my work? That's why you did it, right? So you'd have the gallery? So all those LaBete paintings would skyrocket in value? How does it feel, sweetheart, rolling around in money wet with my blood?"

"Don't you dare say that." My voice is low, heavy with fury and hurt. "That gallery was our dream," I whisper. "And half of the funds we get from your originals go to fund art scholarships. The rest supports LaBete's legacy and keeps the gallery running. So don't you dare tell me that I dishonored our dream. I've been living it every day. Some days it's the only thing that keeps me going. The only thing I have left of you."

For a moment, I think his eyes soften, but I change my mind when he says—his voice cold and rough—"hard to hold onto something like that if you destroy the lynchpin."

I wrap my arms around myself, hating that I feel small. "You're talented—you are. I've always known that. "But I guess now's the first time I'm learning that you're an asshole, too. And a stupid, disloyal one at that."

His eyes narrow, and I look down. My temper's running the show at the moment, but the adrenaline's going to slow down, and I'm going to be a blubbering mess soon.

I really don't want him to see me that way.

I really don't want to see him at all. Not now.

Maybe never, I think as a hand seems to tighten around my heart.

"The truth is that you and your father tried to kill me."

I've scooted away, but he's at my side in two long strides. He grabs my chin, forcing me to look at him. His grip is hard, just short of painful. "The truth is that you knew about Aspen—my cabin, my private retreat, the place no one else knew about."

"The address was in my book," I tell him. "The address book you made me with the LaBete cover. My father could have found it. You know he used to snoop in my room."

"Convenient," he says. "Too convenient. The truth is that you and your father sent a team that ambushed me and left me for dead. The truth is, you're about to marry another man. And the biggest truth is that I will have my revenge."

"I *never* told anyone about the Aspen cabin. Only Leo, when I couldn't get in touch with you. You were late coming back, and I was scared something had happened, and he went, and he's the one who found the cabin burned. Who arranged a jet for me so I was there with him.

We searched before the police did. We found your teeth and your ring and your blood.

I just shake my head, then wipe away a tear and blink furiously to hold back more. "I died that day, too," I whisper.

"You should have," he says, his grip firm on my arm.

I try to pull away, but his hand tightens. "I swear on my life, Gabriel, I didn't hurt you. I would never hurt you. Every day, I prayed that the police were wrong. That you survived somehow.

But then I had to face that you didn't. I finally let myself believe it a year ago. I thought letting go of you would be a comfort." I look at him through tear-filled eyes. "It wasn't. But having you back?" I whisper as a tear trails down my cheek. "Well, I guess that won't be a comfort either."

He looks pointedly at my engagement ring. "Do not even try to play those games with me." His voice is low and smooth and as sharp as a knife.

I roll my shoulders back, anger winning over fear. "Don't you dare go there. You were dead, and I wanted a way out from under my father's thumb. I marry a friend, I get the casino."

"Just more proof that you're a manipulative bitch."

"You know what, Gabriel? Fuck you. You want to think the worst of me, fine. Do it. Hate me as much as you want, but you're the fool in this story. I am sorry—so damn sorry—about what happened to you. But it happened to me, too."

I wipe away the stupid tears that have decided to flow again. "I've dreamed about this day. Literally dreamed about you somehow coming back to me. And here you are. It should be the happiest day of both our lives. But now, all I can do is look back on all those nights I spent wishing you were alive and beside me, and all I can think is what a fucking waste of time."

I lift my chin and face him dead on. "I'm leaving now. I assume there's a valet outside who can call me a cab?"

He doesn't answer. Instead, he moves closer, slow and predatory. "You know what the cruelest part is?" He comes right up to me, so close I can feel his breath stir the hair at my temple. "I still want you. After everything you did. After everything you took from me. I still fucking want you."

My breath catches.

"Five years of hating you." His hand comes up, fingers brushing along the side of my neck. The touch is feather-light, almost tender, and it makes my whole body shiver. "Five years of dreaming about you. Remembering what you taste like. What you sound like when you come. How you feel beneath me."

"Gabriel—"

"I told myself it was over. That I'd burned it out of me along with everything else. But when I saw the engagement announcement in the paper, and then when I saw that ring on your finger tonight..." He trails off, his fingers tracing down my throat, over my collarbone, coming to rest just above my heart. "I wanted to destroy you. And I wanted to devour you, too. I still don't know which one I want more. But I do know this—you aren't his. You won't ever be his.

CHAPTER
SEVEN

I should pull away. I should run.

But I can't move. Can't breathe. Can't do anything except feel his hand on my skin, his breath on my neck, his presence surrounding me like a cage.

"You still want me, too." It's not a question. His other hand comes up, turning me to face him. "I can see it. Feel it. Your body remembers, even if you want to pretend it doesn't."

"I'm not pretending anything." My voice comes out barely above a whisper. "I never stopped wanting you. Not even tonight," I admit. "Not even with all the horrible things you've said."

"I think it's time to remind you," he says, his voice like a low growl in my ear.

"Of what?"

His mouth hovers over mine, close enough that I can feel the warmth of his breath. "Of what you threw away," he says, then yanks me to him, his mouth closing hard over mine.

It's nothing like the kisses we used to share—wild, yes, but full of hope and love. This kiss is punishment. Possession. Five years of fury distilled into the press of his lips against mine, hot and demanding.

I should push him away. Should run. He thinks I tried to murder him. He's spent years planning my destruction. This is manipulation, not desire. This is revenge, not love.

I know all of that. But god help me, I kiss him back.

Because underneath the rage and the scars and the coldness, it's still Gabe. Still the man who saw me when no one else did. The man who gave me a name that was just for us, who painted me like I was something precious, who made me believe I could be more than my father's little wind-up toy to torture and manipulate.

Who somehow—someway—will come to realize what he surely knows deep inside—that I would never, ever hurt him.

My hands fist in his shirt, pulling him closer. He responds by backing me into the sofa, then lifting me onto it, his body covering mine before I can draw breath.

"Tell me to stop." His voice is ragged against my throat, his mouth trailing fire along my skin. "Tell me you don't want this."

I can't. The words won't come. Because despite everything—despite the accusations and the hatred and the long years of grief—my body remembers his. Craves his. Comes alive under his touch in ways it never has for anyone else.

"I want it," I say, then look up to see a spark of something in his eyes. Surprise, yes. But also respect.

One hand slips up under my tank top to tease my nipple while he slides the other down, his fingers sliding into my yoga pants to find my clit. Electricity sizzles through me, and I arch up, gasping.

"That's it," he says, tugging my pants off, while I do the same with my top.

He's already shed his suit coat, and I fumble with the buttons of his shirt as his eyes travel over my bare chest with a hunger that makes my cunt throb.

"Still so beautiful," he murmurs. "I used to dream about this, you know. When I was recovering. When the pain was so bad, I thought I'd lose my mind. I'd close my eyes and imagine you. Imagine this. Imagine my cock inside you. My mouth on yours.

"Gabriel—" His name is a moan of pure need.

"And then I'd remember what you did." His hand closes hard over my breast, his fingers so tight on my nipple that I suck in air, wincing. "That's when the wanting would turn to hatred. And the hatred would turn back to wanting. Around and around, for five fucking years."

I stiffen, because for the first time ever, I'm truly afraid of this man.

His hand slips lower, his fingers teasing my core, and I have to fight to hang on to some semblance of rational thought.

I tell myself he won't hurt me—except I don't believe it. He thinks I tried to murder him. The man I have loved for years actually believes I had something to do with the horror in Aspen. I need to remember that.

Then all rational thought evaporates as he thrusts deep inside me.

"Already so wet," he murmurs. "Does this turn you on? Knowing I hate you. Knowing I want you? Does it make you feel powerful?"

I try not to, but I actually whimper. "Please."

"Please, what? Please stop? Or please make you come?"

I don't answer.

"Tell me you want this."

"I want this," I lie. Except—damn me—it's not a lie.

"Tell me not to stop."

I tilt my head so that I can meet his eyes. "Don't stop. Please, don't stop."

"There she is. The horny little bitch. And don't worry, sweetheart. I'm not going to stop."

His voice is dark velvet, promising things I can't name.

"I won't stop until you come apart. Not until you scream my name. Not until you remember who you belong to. And not until you truly understand how deeply I know you now. What you are. What you're capable of. You destroyed me, Isabella. You and your father. And I'm going to return the favor."

The words are horrible, but my body doesn't seem to care, and when he thrusts in another finger, I cry out, wanting both to escape and to stay like this forever, hating myself for wanting. For craving. For making up stories in my head that if I just surrender, he'll finally see the truth. That he'll be Gabe again.

But those are just sweet lies. I know the truth. I know that I'm surrendering to a man who hates me.

But I've craved his touch for far too long to care that this is a mistake, that I'm giving him an advantage. It doesn't matter. Right now, all I want is him. The rest is white noise.

He thrusts deeper, and I cry out, the rhythm of his thrusts designed to drive me insane—building me higher and higher, pushing me toward the edge with devastating precision.

"That's it." His mouth finds my breast, tongue, and teeth making me writhe. "You're close, aren't you? So damn close."

I whimper, barely managing to murmur a soft *yes*.

He whispers, "I know." And then he stops.

Just stops.

His fingers withdraw. His mouth leaves my skin. His body lifts off mine, leaving me cold and aching and so desperate I could scream.

"What—" I begin, but I don't finish the sentence. I know what he's doing.

He stands beside the sofa, tucking in his shirt and looking down at me with an expression of cold, triumphant cruelty.

"Get dressed."

I stare at him, gathering the throw over my half-naked body, still throbbing with unfulfilled need.

"I said get dressed." He walks to a bar cart and pours himself a whiskey, then takes a long sip without looking at me. "Get dressed. And get out. The valet can call you a taxi."

"Are you—*wait*. No. We need to talk." Panic rises in me. "We need to talk. You have to believe me."

"I don't have to do anything. Now get dressed, or you'll be

walking out of here wrapped in that blanket. You can thank me later for letting you have even that.

For a moment, I just stare at him. Then I nod. "You know what? Fine. And fuck you. You're being an ass because you're believing what you want to. And now I guess I know how little you cared about me if you truly think I would ever—*ever*—intentionally hurt you."

I spit the words out, but they miss their mark. He doesn't react at all. All he says is, "Tomorrow." Then he reaches into his pocket, pulls out something that glints gold in the low light. A token, like a casino chip. He tosses it to me, and I catch it reflexively, my hands shaking so badly I nearly drop it. "Give that to the man at the valet stand outside. He'll get you a ride back to the Monarch."

"Gabriel."

"We're done." He looks straight at me. "For tonight, anyway."

I stare at him. This stranger wearing the face of the man I love.

Then, slowly, I reach for my clothes.

"I didn't do it." My voice comes out steadier than I expected as I pull on my tee and my yoga pants. "Whatever you think you know—whoever told you I was involved—they lied. I love you, Gabe. I always have. Even now. Even after this. And you're a fucking idiot if you truly think I could ever, *ever* hurt you. And somehow, I'm going to make you see the truth.

Something that might be hope flickers in his expression. There and gone.

He inclines his head. "In that case, I look forward to our next conversation."

My legs are shaking, my body still humming with frustrated desire, and my mind reeling from everything that just happened. I cross warily to the door, half-afraid he's going to yank me to him. Half wanting him to.

I almost turn when I reach the door. To see him one more time. To give him one more chance to be the Gabriel I knew.

But he's already shown me how that Gabriel is gone. And I

don't want to look again into eyes that believe I could hurt him. So I close my hand around the token, open the door, and leave, letting the door close behind me with a click that sounds like a verdict.

CHAPTER
EIGHT

After the driver drops me back at the Monarch, I stand outside the entrance for a long moment, staring up at the building as if I've never seen it before. Somewhere up there, David is waiting. Wondering where I went and why I ran out on him like the building was on fire.

What the hell am I supposed to tell him?

Hey, sorry I bolted after we had sex for the first time. Turns out my dead boyfriend is alive, and he thinks I tried to murder him. Also, he finger-fucked me in his underground lair and then kicked me out before I could come. How was the rest of your night?

A hysterical laugh bubbles up in my throat. I swallow it down as the valet shoots me a questioning look. My cue to go inside.

It's a quarter past three, and the lobby is quiet—just a few die-hard gamblers stumbling toward the elevators and a bored-looking clerk at the front desk. No one pays attention to me as I make my way to the VIP elevator, swipe my keycard, and ride up to the penthouse level.

The suite is dark when I slip inside. David's bedroom door is closed, a thin line of light visible underneath. He's awake, of course. I left him naked and confused after the most intimate thing we've ever done together. Not exactly a recipe for a good night's slumber. He's probably been lying there since I bolted, replaying everything, trying to figure out what he did wrong.

The answer is nothing. He did nothing wrong. I'm the one who's wrong. I'm the one who's broken.

I ease to the other side of the suite, then slip into my own bedroom. As soon as the door snicks shut, I lean against it in the dark, pressing my palms flat against the cool wood and wondering for the twenty-seven millionth time what the hell happened tonight—and hating myself because whatever happened, it ended far too early.

I didn't get answers. Hell, I didn't even get an orgasm. But my body is still humming, and even now I can feel his hands on me. His mouth. The way he played me like an instrument, building me up to the edge of release and then—

Nothing.

I squeeze my eyes shut, but that just makes the memories more vivid. His face above mine, cold and triumphant. The contempt in his voice. The way he looked at me like I was nothing. Like I was less than nothing.

Like I was the enemy.

A sob catches in my throat. I press my fist against my mouth to muffle it.

Gabriel is alive.

The thought keeps circling back, no matter how many times I try to push it away. Gabriel is alive. After five years of grief, five years of mourning, five years of wishing on every birthday candle and shooting star that I could have him back—he's alive.

And he hates me.

I slide down the door until I'm sitting on the floor, my knees pulled up to my chest. The tears come then, hot and silent, streaming down my face in the darkness.

How can he believe it? How can he possibly think I would ever hurt him?

But I know the answer. I heard it in his voice, saw it in his eyes.

Your fucking goons were right there, making it very clear that each and every blow was a present from you and Daddy Dearest.

That's what they told him. That's the last thing he heard before he lost consciousness, bleeding out in a shallow grave.

Me. My family. Used as a weapon to destroy him.

And I was the only one who knew about his place in Aspen.

From his perspective, it all makes a horrible kind of sense. The woman he loved, the only one who knew his secret location, the daughter of a man who never approved of their relationship. Of course she was involved. Of course she betrayed him. Why wouldn't she?

Except I didn't. And it hurts my heart to know that he could believe that even for a second.

He needs to know the truth. Somehow, someway, I need him to know the truth.

But how?

I grab my phone, my hands shaking so badly I can barely type.

You awake?

It's after three, so I know it's a long shot. Even so, I stare at the screen, waiting for Harper to answer. "Come on, come on." She's my person. She's been my person since we were twelve years old, bonding over our mutual hatred of the ridiculous etiquette classes our parents made us attend. She's seen me through every crisis, every heartbreak, every moment when I thought I couldn't go on, and I've done the same for her.

She'll know what to do. She always knows what to do.

If she'd ever freaking answer.

Dammit.

Hello? You there? I hesitate, then send it again, but this time I don't really expect a response. Her phone must be on silent.

But then the three little dots appear, and if I wasn't already sitting, I'd have dropped to my knees in relief.

Unfortunately, yes. Weird night. What's up?

Can you come to my suite? Please. I need you.

On my way. 10 min.

I let out a breath I didn't know I was holding. Then I pull myself off the floor, splash some water on my face, and try to make myself look like something other than a complete disaster.

It doesn't work. The mirror shows me a woman with red-rimmed eyes, mascara smudges, and a look of shell-shocked devastation that no amount of cold water is going to fix.

Whatever. Harper's seen me worse.

The soft knock comes exactly ten minutes later. I ease open the suite door and usher her in, a finger pressed to my lips as I gesture toward David's room.

She raises her eyebrows but follows me silently into my bedroom.

The moment the door closes behind us, she takes one look at my face and opens her arms. I fall into them like a drowning woman grabbing a life raft.

"Jesus, Bella." Her voice is soft against my hair. "What happened?"

I don't even know where to start. The words tangle in my throat, too big and too impossible to get out.

"Gabriel," I finally manage. "He's alive."

Harper goes completely still. And then her face crumples.

Not the way I expected—not confusion or disbelief. No, Harper's pale gray eyes fill with tears, and her hand flies to her mouth, and for a moment she looks exactly like I must have looked in the back of that Town Car when Gabriel's face emerged from the shadows.

"He's—" Her voice breaks. "Bella, are you sure? How is that possible? The fire. His teeth. His cabin. And the ring—the one you gave him."

"I know. But it's true. Somehow, he survived."

I'd forgotten, somehow, in the chaos of my own grief and shock and confusion, that Harper loved him, too. Not the way I did—but she'd grown up with him, spent summers at the Grimm estate, been part of that strange little trio with him and Elliott. She'd lost her friend. One of her oldest, closest friends.

"Oh my god." She pulls me back into her arms, and this time she's shaking too. "Oh my god, oh my god. Gabriel."

"Leo texted me around midnight," I say when we finally pull apart. "I was here, and I got a text that just said *Gabriel's alive*. So I ran downstairs to get a car to go to Leo's place—"

"And?"

I hesitate, but tell her everything. The drive there. The Beast and the fights that take place deep in its belly.

"He has an apartment there" I tell her. "And he kissed me. Because that's what you do to people you think might have killed you."

Her brows rise. "Wait. What?"

I grimace, then nod, blinking to force back fresh tears. "It's true. He thinks I was involved. He thinks I killed him. They must have—I don't know—drugged him or something. He said I shot him."

Her hand flies to her mouth. "But—but he knows better."

I shake my head. "He's different," I say, my voice so low she has to lean in. "He believes it, Harp. He really believes I was right there. That I killed him. But I could never—" The tears are flowing again, and she pulls me back into her arms.

"He wants revenge," I whisper. "He means it, too. I know his face. He wants to hurt me. Probably to kill me."

"That's insane," Harper says, holding me tight. "Gabriel knows you. He knows you would never do that."

"I was the only one who knew about the cabin. He gave me the address once because I was going to Colorado for a ski trip. So from his perspective it all adds up. It all makes this horrible, twisted kind of sense."

"Except it doesn't because it's not true."

"Of course it's not true!" The words come out louder than I intended. I force myself to lower my voice. "I loved him. I still love him. I would have died for him. But he looked at me tonight like I was a monster. Like everything we had was a lie."

Harper's quiet for a moment, then she tilts her head and

furrows her brow. "You said he kissed you. But he thinks you tried to kill him?"

"The bastard was punishing me.

She hugs herself. "That's harsh."

"Yeah," I say. "But I'd wanted it to taste like hope. Especially when he…" I trail off, certain my cheeks are going to burst into flame.

It takes her a second, then she whispers, "That prick."

"I'm so fucked up," I whisper, after I break down and tell her the full-on NC-17 version of what happened." My tears are falling freely now, and I'm not bothering to wipe them away. "I wanted it, Harper. Even knowing what he believed about me, I wanted it."

For a moment, she just looks at me, then she holds out her arms, and I slide into them, losing myself in her hug.

"I should hate him," I tell her. "I should want nothing to do with him." My voice cracks. "He's been alive this whole time, suffering, believing I betrayed him. And even with everything he said, everything he believed about me—I still love him. What does that say about me?"

"It says you're human," she murmurs. "It says you loved someone with your whole heart, and you don't know how to stop just because he's become someone different. Probably because now he's wearing armor to protect himself. And god knows he was already hard enough. But underneath, your Gabriel is still there."

"Maybe. I don't know. It feels like he hates me."

"Maybe he does," she says gently. "Based on what he believes, he would. But you can't hate someone that intensely unless you loved them first."

I want to believe her. God, I want to believe that somewhere underneath all that ice, my Gabriel still exists. That he's just hidden, not gone.

But I keep seeing his face as he told me to get out. Cold. Triumphant. Cruel.

"There's something else," I say, pulling back from the hug.

"More? Oh, you poor thing. How can there be more?"

"David." I watch her face as the name lands. "Earlier tonight. Before the text came. We...you know."

Understanding dawns in her eyes. "You and David?"

"It just happened. We were watching a movie, and we'd been drinking wine, and we started talking about how neither of us had been with anyone in a while. And we might as well be friends with benefits, especially since, oh, we're going to be married."

"Wow."

"Yeah," I say. "I know. And then I got the text and bolted. So add another man who hates me to my karmic scorecard.

I scrub my hands over my face. "I didn't even tell David anything. I just saw Leo's text, and I bolted. He probably thinks I freaked out about the sex. About crossing the line with him."

"Did you? Freak out, I mean."

"No. I actually think it's a good plan. Or I did before Gabriel came back. From the moment I got that text, I didn't think about David at all." I look at her miserably. "What kind of person does that make me?"

"A person in shock. And let's be real. You weren't starting something with David—it was sex and solace. He'll understand."

"Maybe," I say. But the truth is, I know that David's feelings for me have always skewed toward romance. And that if I hadn't been so selfish, I should never have jumped on the FWB idea.

"You can talk to him tomorrow," Harper says, reading my mind in her Harper kind of way. "Right now, sleep."

"Will you stay with me?" I sound like a seven-year-old, but I don't care.

"Of course." She kicks off her shoes and climbs into bed. "We'll figure everything out tomorrow. Tonight, you just need to breathe."

I lie down beside her, letting her put her arm around me the way she used to when we were kids having sleepovers. Back when our biggest problems were mean girls and strict parents and whether the boy we liked would ask us to dance.

What I wouldn't give to have those be my problems now…

"He scares me," I whisper into the darkness. "Not physically—I don't think he'd actually hurt me. But the way he looks at me now... It's like he's already decided I'm the enemy and nothing I say will change his mind."

"Then we'll find proof. Evidence. Something that shows him the truth."

"How? If my father was involved, there probably is no proof."

"We'll figure it out." Harper's voice is firm. "We're smart. We have resources. And we're not going to let Gabriel Grimm spend the rest of his life believing a lie."

"And if we can't prove it? If he never believes me?"

She's quiet for a long moment. "Then at least you'll know you tried. And maybe that will be enough to let you move on. Besides, could you really stay with a man who doesn't trust you?"

"No," I whisper, my heart already starting to break. "I love him," I whisper. "Even now. Even after everything. Is that pathetic?"

"No." Harper pulls me closer. "It's love."

I don't remember falling asleep, but I must have, because suddenly I'm dreaming.

Gabriel is there, standing in a field of golden light. He looks like he used to—before the scars, before the coldness, before whatever forged him into the man who accused me of murder. His eyes are soft. His hand is reaching toward me.

Izzy, he says. *Come back to me.*

I reach for him. Our fingertips almost touch—

And then I wake up, gasping, as morning sunlight streams through the windows. And as Harper, already dressed, with a cup of coffee leans against the door frame. "Rise and shine," she says. "We've got a beast to tame."

CHAPTER
NINE

The Obsidian looks different in the daylight. Still stately, but the magical beauty of the old building is less in sunlight. As if it needs stars and moonbeams to come into its own.

And not a single thing about it suggests underground fight clubs tucked in near the city's bustling boardwalk.

Then again, it doesn't have a Billionaire Back From The Dead vibe either.

"You're sure that's it?" Harper asks, eyeing the doorman in his crisp uniform from our vantage point across the street.

"Yeah, but yesterday we entered through a service door. Gabe used a key card."

Harper nods. "Okay, so we go in through the front and chat up the desk clerk."

"And hope they'll give us directions to the secret underground lair of my presumed-dead ex-boyfriend, who thinks I tried to kill him. Perfect plan. Easy-peasy."

Harper snorts. "When you put it that way..."

We glance at each other, then cross the street and walk through the front doors like we own the place. It's a trick Harper taught me years ago—confidence gets you past more security than any keycard.

The lobby is all marble and crystal chandeliers, hushed and refined like the businesspeople dotting the leather chairs. A concierge looks up as we pass, but we're dressed well enough that she just nods as we head to the front desk. "Hi there," Harper says to the clerk. "I'm hoping you can help me. I'm looking for Gabriel Grimm."

The woman's expression flickers—just for a second, but I catch it.

"I'm sorry, I don't believe I know that name."

Harper leans on the desk, her *I'm serious now* expression pasted on her face. "You need to tell him that Harper Lang is here. He'll be irritated if you don't."

A long pause, then the clerk picks up her phone, turns away, and murmurs something too quiet to hear.

I've counted to thirteen when she turns back to us with a carefully neutral expression.

"Someone will be with you shortly. If you'd like to wait in the lounge?"

Thankfully, we don't have to wait long.

The woman who comes for us is about my age, with dark hair pulled back in a sleek ponytail and the kind of effortless beauty that makes you want to hate her on principle. She wears a necklace with a stunning crystal pendant, and I notice her slip a pack of Tarot cards into her jacket pocket.

She moves through the lobby like she owns it—which, given the way the staff defers to her, she might.

"Harper Lang?" Her voice is warm but guarded. "I'm Anissa Graves. I manage the hotel."

"And you know Gabriel," Harper says. Not a question.

Something shifts in Anissa's expression. "I'm terribly sorry to break sad news, but Gabriel Grimm died five years ago."

Harper's been running this show, but now she looks at me, as if she's curious what I'm going to say.

I shoot a quick glance at Harper, then shrug. "They're friends," I say. "And we know Gabe's alive."

I watch Anissa's face, but her expression reveals nothing.

"I want to see him," Harper says. "I spent five years thinking he was dead. And because—" Harper's voice wavers, just slightly. "Because he's family. And I need to see him."

Anissa studies her for a long moment. Then her gaze shifts to me.

"You're Isabella Hart."

It's not a question. And from the cool assessment in her eyes, I can tell she knows exactly what Gabriel believes about me.

"I am."

"He's not going to want to see you."

"He seemed fine with it last night."

Her brows rise, and I take a tiny bit of satisfaction in surprising her. And in wondering if she and Gabe are a thing. *Back off, bitch. He's mine.*

Harper glances my way and raises a brow—a silent order to behave. She really does know me too well.

"Bottom line," Harper says, "we want to see him. Both of us."

Her mouth twists, but she says nothing, just turns her attention toward the man who's now striding across the lobby toward us. He's mid-fifties, broad-shouldered, with a kind of weathered handsomeness. His eyes are fixed on me with an intensity that makes me want to take a step back.

"Anissa." His voice is low. Gravelly. "What's going on?"

"Hey, Dad. Visitors for Gabriel." She stresses the name. "Old friends."

It's subtle, but I catch the way his jaw tightens. "He's training. Doesn't want to be disturbed."

"I know." Anissa meets his gaze. "But I think he'll want to see Harper."

Travis looks at Harper—really looks at her. Something in his expression shifts. "You're the one from the pictures. The trio."

Harper nods, her throat working, probably in an effort to hold back tears. I'm not surprised. I've heard approximately eight billion stories about the fun and mischief Gabe, Elliott, and Harper got into back in the day.

Travis turns his attention to me, his eyes as flat as his expression. There's a long pause, then he sighs. "He's going to ream my ass."

Anissa shrugs. "Won't be the first time."

Travis almost smiles. Almost. Then he jerks his head toward the back hallway. "Come on. But I'm warning you—he's in a mood."

"He's been in a mood for five years," Anissa murmurs as we follow. "At this point, I think we can just call it his personality."

———

THE BEAST IS everything I remember from last night—the exposed brick, the amber lighting, the distant thump of music, and the muffled roar of a crowd. But in the daylight hours, it feels different. Less like a noir film, more like a gym. Men wrap their hands with tape. Heavy bags swing from chains. The smell of sweat and leather fills the air.

And there, in a roped-off ring at the center of the room, is Gabriel.

He's shirtless, his back to us, but I see his reflection in a wide mirror. Three puckered marks on his chest and torso set against a canvas of hard, scarred skin. I stifle a shiver and blink back tears. *Bullet wounds.*

And that's not all. A web of faded lines stretches across his back at his shoulders. More scars, and they're like a map of pain.

I blink even more fiercely, determined to hold my tears at bay.

"Oh, god," Harper says, taking my hand as we gape at the show. Except it's not a show. It's real—every punch hitting flesh, sometimes drawing blood. He's sparring with a man twice his size, but he's winning. Gabe moves with a brutal grace that steals my breath. Every punch is controlled. Precise. Devastating.

This is a man who'll never be a victim again. A man who doesn't need a gun because he's the fucking weapon.

Harper makes a small sound beside me, and I squeeze her hand.

To my right, Travis clears his throat. "Hey, Savage?"

Behind us, Anissa whispers, "He uses the name Lyon Savage here. Well, that or The Beast. And he is going to be so pissed."

Gabriel lands one more punch—sending his opponent reeling—then he turns. His eyes find Harper first, and for one breathless second, his whole face changes. The ice cracks. Something raw and unguarded breaks through.

"Harper?" His voice is hoarse. "What the hell are you doing here?"

She's already moving, ducking under the ropes, throwing herself at him. He catches her automatically, his arms wrapping around her, and for a moment, he simply holds on. Eyes closed. Jaw tight. Like he's afraid she'll disappear if he lets go.

"You asshole," Harper sobs into his chest, her fists useless against the muscles in his back. "You absolute asshole. Five years, *Lyon*. For five fucking years I thought you were dead."

"I was." His voice cracks. "I'm sorry."

"Sorry? Sorry doesn't cover it. I'm going to kill you. I'm going to bring you back from the dead just so I can kill you myself."

He laughs—an actual laugh, broken and rusty like he's forgotten how—and holds her tighter.

And I stand there, watching, as the hollow ache of misery and longing spreads through my chest.

This is exactly what I've been wanting. Gabe, alive and reunited with the people who love him. His frozen armor finally cracking.

But it's not cracking for me.

His eyes open, finding me over Harper's shoulder. And just like that, the ice is back. The warmth disappears like it was never there. His expression goes flat. Closed tight.

He doesn't say a word. He doesn't have to.

Harper pulls back from him, her gaze sweeping over me. Her face falls. "Oh, Bella."

"Stay," I say, forcing a smile that feels like broken glass. "Catch up. You two have five years to cover."

She shakes her head. "I'm not going to just leave you out here."

"It's okay. I'm fine." We both know I'm not, but Harper hasn't seen Gabriel in five years, either, and she deserves this moment. "I'll wait in the lobby. Take your time."

She hesitates, clearly torn. Gabriel's hand is still on her shoulder, but his eyes are on me—flat and unreadable.

"Go," I tell her. "Really. Shoo." Then I turn and walk away before she can argue.

I make it to the hallway before I hear footsteps behind me. "Isabella. Wait."

It's Anissa, her heels clicking against the tile as she catches up.

Something snaps inside me. I whirl around, tears streaming down my face, five years of grief and one night of accusations boiling over.

"What? You want to tell me he hates me, too? That I'm a murderer? That I don't deserve to breathe the same air as him?"

My voice cracks, but I don't care. "I didn't do it. I didn't try to kill him. I love him. I've loved him forever, and I spent five years thinking he was dead. Five years with my heart ripped out. Five years of lighting candles on his birthday, unable to let anyone touch me because I was still in love with a ghost."

Anissa stands frozen, her expression shifting from guarded to something else. Surprise, maybe.

"You want to talk about pain?" I'm shaking now. "He got to be angry. He got to plan his revenge and build his little empire down here.

"What did I get? I got to grieve. I got to fall apart. I got to watch everyone move on while I stayed frozen in the moment without a single goddamn answer." I wipe my cheeks and sniffle.

"So don't follow me out here to defend him. Because, I swear, I can't take any more."

There's a long silence as she studies me, her head tilted slightly. She stays like that for so long that I finally scoff and start walking again.

"Bella."

I stop, then turn back to her, my shoulders dropping with exhaustion. "What now?"

"You're not what I expected."

"Sorry." I cross my arms. "I left my horns and pitchfork back at the Monarch."

She starts to say something, bites her lip, then starts again. "I don't know what happened at the cabin," she says, her voice so soft I have to step closer. "But he recovered at my dad's place."

"Oh." For some reason, that hits me hard. "I didn't know that."

"Why would you? The point is, I've watched him for five years. Watched him train, and plan, and sketch."

She takes another step toward me. "He doesn't paint anymore, but I've seen him sketch. He doesn't show anyone what's in that sketchbook, but one day—"

She cuts herself off with a shake of her head. "I shouldn't."

"Hey, you started it."

She glances over her shoulder, then edges around a corner, urging me to follow. I consider bailing, but I'm just too curious.

"One day, he didn't lock the drawer. I was looking for a legal pad and, well, I found the book."

"And?" I catch myself leaning in.

"It's the same woman. He sketches her. Over and over. I found one once, crumpled in the trash. He'd tossed it, but I could see how much love there was in those lines. I thought maybe he was remembering his mother. Like from when he was little. But it wasn't." She looks me up and down slowly. "It's you, isn't it?"

I can't speak. Can barely breathe.

"Hatred doesn't look like that," she says quietly as she stands in soft focus beyond my tears.

From somewhere behind me, I hear Travis's voice. "Anissa?"

I turn as she takes a step toward him. He's standing at the end of the hallway, arms crossed, his expression a clear warning. *Don't get involved.*

She pauses before passing me. "I'm not saying I trust you. I don't know you. But I thought you should know."

Then she falls in step with her father and heads toward the elevator and the hotel above us.

I stand still for a moment, not sure how I feel. Confused? Hopeful? Angry? All of it, actually. But it's not just about what I feel, but what I see. And after talking with Anissa—after the night before, seeing my wadded-up picture pinned on the wall of his Spartan little cell—well, maybe I'm starting to see something really important. Like a crack in the wall Gabriel's built around himself.

And that, at least, is something.

CHAPTER
TEN

It's three minutes to eleven when I hurry back into the Monarch. Which means I'm due to meet with my father in eighteen minutes. And that means the warm and fuzzy buds of hope that Anissa planted inside me are about to get shattered—because no way am I meeting with my dad before explaining myself to David.

In the elevator, I silently will the car to go faster. It doesn't, and I make a mental note to speak to the elevator gods about forcing these devices to do my bidding.

I am manager, hear me roar.

I grin. Yeah, that talk with Anissa definitely kicked my mood up a few notches. Gabriel may be throwing darts at that picture of David and me, but at least I know he hasn't stopped loving me. No matter what horrible things he might think I did. More importantly, deep down, he must know I didn't—and wouldn't—ever hurt him.

Then the doors open at my suite, and suddenly I'm remembering the way I bolted from David last night. So much for not hurting people.

I dump my purse on the table by the door, kick off my shoes, then hurry to David's room. I hesitate for a moment, then tap softly.

Nothing.

I tap again, this time a little louder. "David? You up?"

Silence.

I try the handle, and the door swings open, revealing his rumpled bed. *Damn.*

Not that I'm all that eager for the awkward, *I bolted after sex because my ex is alive talk,* but at the same time, that's a conversation I much prefer to chatting with Daddy Dearest.

Mostly, I want to do this now while I still have the nerve. So even though it will make me even more late to my meeting with Father, I shoot David a quick text asking if we can grab a coffee. When his answer doesn't come right away, I sigh, then hurry to my bedroom to change into my corporate armor. Then I head out for the task I want to put off. Not just for the day, but for all eternity.

But I can't ditch my dad. I need answers. And not about gaming licenses and vendor contracts and slot machine repair. Father may think that's the extent of our agenda, but he'd be wrong. I want answers that matter.

And I'm getting them today.

I want to storm into his office, metaphorical guns blazing, accusations— *Did you do it? Did you try to kill the man I love? Did you use my name while your thugs beat him and shot him, and left him for dead?*

He'll deny everything, of course. He'll look at me with those cold eyes and tell me I'm being hysterical, emotional, foolish. He'll remind me of everything he's done for me, everything he's given me, everything I stand to lose if I push too hard.

And then he'll find a way to punish me for asking.

All true. But I don't slow down. I grab my bag, and I'm out the door. Maybe it's stupid. Maybe I should wait, plan, think this through. But I need to look him in the eye. I need to see his face when I tell him I know what he did.

The elevator ride down to the executive level feels endless. I use the time to rehearse what I'm going to say, but the words keep tangling in my head. How do you accuse your own father of attempted murder? Even a father as vile as mine. How do you have that conversation?

By the time I step out, my heart is pounding so hard I can feel it in my throat.

My father's office takes up an entire corner of the floor—a sprawling space with floor-to-ceiling windows overlooking the boardwalk and the ocean beyond. I can even see The Obsidian, and that gives me strength.

Mina sits at the reception desk outside his door, examining her manicure like it's the most important task she'll accomplish all day. It probably is. She looks up when I approach and gives me that smile. The one that says *fuck you* while pretending to be friendly.

"Isabella." She draws out my name like we're old friends. "Your father is in a meeting."

"I'll wait."

"It may be some time." She's enjoying this. "Perhaps you could schedule an appointment for later this afternoon."

"I said I'll wait."

She waves a hand toward the sitting area, her nails catching the light. "Suit yourself."

I don't sit. Instead, I pace the length of the waiting area, too wired to stay still. The clock on the wall ticks off the seconds with excruciating slowness. This, I know, is my punishment for being four minutes late.

I think. I pace. And I think some more.

What exactly am I hoping to accomplish here?

My father isn't going to confess. Even if I walked in with a recording of him ordering the hit, he'd find a way to spin it, deny it, turn it around on me. That's what he does. That's what he's always done.

And confronting him now, before I have any proof, before I have any protection—what does that get me?

Nothing. Worse than nothing.

He'll know I'm onto him. He'll know Gabriel told me about the attack. And he'll start covering his tracks even more carefully than he already has. Any evidence that might still exist will disappear. Any witnesses will be silenced or bought off.

And me? I'll be exactly where he wants me—under his thumb, dependent on his goodwill.

Most importantly, I'll lose the casino. My chance at freedom. The gallery.

My father could take all of that away with a phone call. He could tie me up in legal battles for years, drain my resources, and destroy everything I hope to build. He's done it to business rivals. He'd do it to his own daughter without blinking.

I stop pacing.

I've been thinking about this all wrong.

Going to war with Sterling Hart without ammunition is suicide. I know he tried to kill Gabe. I know it in my bones. But knowing isn't proving. And proving is what I need if I'm ever going to bring him down.

I need evidence. Documentation. Witnesses willing to talk.

I need to get my ducks in a row—protect myself, protect Gabe, protect everything I care about.

And then—only then—can I watch my father burn.

The door to his office opens, and a man in an expensive suit emerges. A moment later, Mina rises from her desk, smoothing her skirt with that practiced grace.

"Your father will see you now," she says, and there's a hint of triumph in her voice. Like she's won something by making me wait.

I look at her. Look at the open door to my father's office, where I can see him sitting behind his massive desk, backlit by the morning sun like some kind of dark god surveying his kingdom.

I flash Mina my best smile. "Tell him I had to run."

Mina blinks. "Excuse me?"

"But remind him, please, just in case he's forgotten, I'm engaged now. And I'll be taking over his duties come Wednesday, as we agreed. If you haven't already, it's time to pack up his personal items. As for anything related to the business...well, he can leave me a memo." I'm already turning, already walking toward the elevator. "Have a lovely day, Mina."

I don't look back. Don't let myself hesitate or second-guess. I just walk, my heels clicking against the marble floor, my heart racing with something that feels almost like triumph.

For once in my life, I'm not playing his game.

I'm playing my own.

The elevator doors slide open, and I step inside, jabbing the button for the lobby. As the doors close, I catch a glimpse of Mina's confused, simpering little face.

And even though I have no idea where I'm going, the moment feels like a victory.

Now I just need to decide what to do next.

David? Maybe it's time to track him down. Or I could grab breakfast—I haven't eaten a thing today.

But two seconds later, I've ditched both those ideas. I know where I want to be. Where I need to be.

La Galerie LaBete.

My gallery. My sanctuary. The place where Chris always has pastries and Gabriel's art lives. Where I've kept his memory alive for five years.

That's where I need to be right now. Surrounded by the work of the man I love, even if that man currently hates me. Maybe being there will help me think. Help me figure out my next move.

Or maybe I just need to feel close to him, even if it's only through paint and canvas. I don't know. All I know is that I need to go, because it's the one place that's ever truly felt like mine.

I draw a breath, then push the button for the mezzanine, and look forward to the rest of this day.

CHAPTER
ELEVEN

La Galerie LaBete is quiet this early, the way I like it best. Soft light filters through the windows, illuminating the bold strokes of works I know as well as my own heartbeat. Every canvas. Every brushstroke. Every piece of Gabriel that has been with me for almost five years.

It's Sunday, and the gallery doesn't officially open for a few hours, but my mind is buzzing—the victory of walking out on my dad just now. The confusion of seeing Gabriel in that ring last night.

And, yes, the jealousy that came from watching him draw Harper into that tight, loving hug. Not to mention the way my heart cracked when he didn't even acknowledge me.

Jealousy, thy name is Bella.

And yet I still have a few strands of hope to cling to. *"He draws you,"* Anissa had said. *"The same woman, over and over. So much love in those lines."*

The words haunt me, and once more, I shove them aside and try to focus on what's in front of me. The gallery. The art. The one facet of Gabriel that is still really and truly mine.

The bell chimes, and Chris strides in holding a stack of bakery boxes. I force a smile, half-wishing I'd thought to call and tell him I could handle the gallery alone today.

He's tall and tan with a mop of dark hair and a surprisingly lean build for a man with his weakness for croissants. Especially ones from the patisserie two blocks over. A bakery that happens to be owned by his husband.

At first, he'd arrive daily with a box. Now, he arrives with three, the gallery picks up the tab, and we share with customers, too.

"Morning, boss." He pushes a box toward me. "Chocolate or almond?"

"Almond." I take a bite of the offered pastry, then glance over to make sure the *Closed* sign is in the window before plopping into the chair across from him. "Tell Xander his team outdid themselves this morning. This may be the best croissant ever."

He grins. "I'll relay your glowing praise. And before you ask, we did great yesterday. Sold two prints from the Fractured Light series. And a woman from Manhattan asked about buying an original for her penthouse. I gave her the catalog, explained about the charitable donations we make in conjunction with sales, and she's going to get back in touch. She kept talking about what a hit the art world took when LaBete died, but how much value the pieces have now."

"She's not wrong." I take another bite, letting the buttery layers melt on my tongue. "If he were—"

I stop myself. *If he were alive.* That's what I almost said. But he *is* alive. And that changes everything. Maybe not for the art world. Not yet. But for me.

"If he were what?" Chris asks.

I flash him a casual smile. "Nothing. Just thinking out loud."

I'm saved from further explanation by the gallery door banging open hard enough to rattle the paintings on the nearest wall.

My father strides in like he owns the place—which he absolutely does not, though that's never stopped him from acting like the entire world is his personal property.

"Isabella." His voice is ice. "We need to talk. Now."

Chris suddenly finds something fascinating on his computer screen. I set down my croissant and stand, brushing crumbs from my fingers.

"Father. What a surprise."

"Don't play games with me. We had a meeting scheduled this morning. He stops in front of me, close enough that I can see the vein pulsing at his temple. "Do you have any idea what's happening right now? While you're sitting here eating pastries?"

"Since you're here, I'm going to say no. So, please, Father. Tell me what's going on."

He "ignores me, then glances around the gallery's lobby area. "*You*. To think that you expect to actually manage the Monarch when *this* is all you've done." He practically spits the words, the scorn clear in his voice. "You think you're ready for this? Well, sweetheart, you're about to be tossed into the deep end. I've got Gaming Commission investigations hitting three Hart properties. *Three*. Complaints filed through shell companies, anonymous tips backed with documentation that shouldn't exist outside our own servers."

My stomach tightens. We do not want to be on the Gaming Commission's bad side. At the same time, there shouldn't be anything on our servers that would interest the commission. Apparently, Daddy has been a bad boy.

"I'll handle it," I say, even though this is so very clearly his mess.

"You'd better. This is your problem now."

Technically, it's not my problem until Wednesday. But since I work for him and he's delegating, that little distinction is moot, and he knows it. "Of course, Father."

His smile is a razor. "Welcome to management, sweetheart."

"Is there more you need me to take point on? Some other

trouble you can't sort out and need my help with?" I balance that zinger on my most innocent smile. Out of the corner of my eye, I swear I see Chris gulp.

Father's eyes narrow. For a moment, I think he's going to hit me—right here, in front of Chris, in the middle of the gallery.

But he doesn't. He just leans in, his voice dropping to something cold and dangerous.

"Those investigations didn't just spring up out of the ether. Someone is coming after us, Isabella. I don't know who yet, but I will find out. And when I do..."

He doesn't finish the threat. He doesn't need to.

"Get your house in order," he says. "And answer your damn phone when I call."

He turns and strides toward the door, nearly colliding with someone as he steps out. I hear a muttered curse, a sharp "Watch it"—and then David appears in the doorway, rubbing his shoulder.

"Your father almost knocked me over."

"That's his favorite pastime. I was looking for you earlier," I add. "I'd hoped we could talk over coffee." Our eyes meet, and he nods. Yeah. He knows what I want to discuss. "Chris, can you give us a few minutes?"

Chris is already grabbing a bakery box. "I'll be in the back. Yell if you need me," he says, then *whoosh*, he's gone. Smart guy, Chris.

David sighs, then shoves his hands into his pockets.

I have no idea where to start, so I just dive in. "Listen, about last night. I—"

He holds up a hand, interrupting me. "No. Not that. Not now. There's something going down."

I shake my head, as if I'm resetting the system. "Um, okay. What's going on?"

He drags his fingers through his hair. "I've been hearing things all morning. Rumors about employees getting poached. Big offers, way above market rate. Offers started going out early Friday and just kept flying over the weekend. Some folks were buzzing about it during our party, but I guess they all agreed to keep you behind a firewall. Me, too, because of our impending nuptials. Why throw shade at the happy couple?"

"Well, hell." The words are barely out of my mouth when my phone buzzes. I pull it out and see a text from Maria Chen, our Front Desk Manager.

Hey, boss-to-be. Thought you should know—five of us got crazy job offers over the weekend. Nobody on the desk's taking them—so far. Figured you'd want an FYI.

"It's not just rumors," I say, showing David the screen.

"Jesus." He takes a breath. "There's more."

I rub my temples. "Of course there is. What else?"

David sucks in a deep breath. "My dad. He got a call last night. From Gabriel Grimm."

I go still. "He—what?"

"I know, right?" He swallows, then takes my hand. "Bella, it's crazy. But I think Gabe's alive."

"I know," I whisper, tugging my hand free.

David jolts like he's been hit. "You do?"

"Harper's with him right now, I think." I can't keep the edge out of my voice. Somewhere across town, my best friend is probably curled up on Gabriel's couch, catching up over coffee, laughing about old times. And here I am, wondering if the man I love will ever look at me with anything other than hatred. "It's been a hell of a weekend," I add.

David rocks on his heels, his eyes wide. "Yeah. I guess so." He studies my face. "You want to tell me what's going on?"

"I do," I say. "I really do." And so I start talking, telling him all of it. Leo's text. Racing to find Gabe. The accusations. The woman with mismatched eyes like mine. The money trail that leads back to my father. By the time I finish, David's face has gone pale.

"Christ, Bella." David stands, paces to the window, then back. "The Grimms are dangerous. Ruthless. Cold. And Gabe had a rep as the kind of man who obliterates his enemies." He looks at me hard. "He's a powder keg, Bella. And I'm fucking terrified you're going to get caught in the blast."

"I know," I whisper. "Me, too."

I close my eyes, hating this new reality. Never in a million years would I have believed back then that Gabe could hurt me. Now, it just is. It doesn't even need a leap of faith. He's not the Gabriel I knew. Which leaves one huge question—who the hell is he now?

I open my eyes as David takes my hands, his grip tight. "You need to stay away. Far away. Let lawyers handle it. And get Security to put a man on you."

I just shake my head. "I can't stay away from him." The words come out quiet but certain. Even with all the question marks and fear, I can't—no, I *won't*— stay away.

"Have you lost your mind?" His expression is a cross between fury and confusion.

I shrug. "Does it matter?"

David is quiet for a long moment. When he speaks, his voice is careful. Controlled. "I need to say something. And I need you to actually hear it."

I frown, not sure where he's going with that, but I nod.

He draws a deep breath, as if gathering courage, then shakes his head. "Forget it."

"What?"

He grimaces. "I just worry. That's all. I already told you, he's a powder keg. I don't want you getting burned."

I squeeze his hand. "I love that you look out for me. Truly. But I'm a big girl now. You don't have to be scared for me."

"I'll always worry. And I will always be here for you."

I grin, forcing myself not to think of Gabe. "In that case, can you be here for some manual labor?"

He laughs. "I walked into that one." He follows as I head to the back showroom, step through the arched entrance, and freeze.

The wall where Caged hung—where it's hung for five years, where I've stood crying more times than I can count—is empty.

Now, there's just a bare white wall, and four small holes where the mounting hardware used to be. Even the bronze plaque identifying the artist and the piece is gone.

Caged is gone.

CHAPTER
TWELVE

For a moment, I can't breathe. Can't think. Can't do anything but stare at the empty wall where my heart used to live.

Then I see what's hanging on the side wall.

It's smaller than Caged, maybe two feet by three, but it dominates the room with the force of a scream. The style is unmistakably Gabriel's—I'd know his brushwork anywhere, the way he layers color, the fierce energy that pulses beneath every stroke.

But this...

This is nothing like anything he's ever created.

A butterfly. Wings spread wide, caught mid-flight. The colors are gorgeous—deep purples and blues, veins of gold running through like rivers of light.

It would be beautiful, if not for the hands.

Human hands grip the butterfly from either side. And the wings—those stunning, luminous wings—are being torn away from the body. I can almost hear the sound. The delicate membrane ripping. The creature's silent scream.

Monarch.

The word surfaces through my horror. *Monarch butterfly. Monarch Casino.*

He's telling me he's going to tear me apart.

"Jesus Christ." David's voice is hoarse as he steps up behind me. "What the hell is that?"

"A message." My voice sounds strange. Distant. "From Gabriel."

"Do you like it?"

I spin around so fast I nearly lose my balance.

Gabriel is in the arched entryway, leaning against the frame. His arms are crossed, and he's watching me with those ice blue eyes. He's dressed in black again—black jeans paired with a black Henley, the sleeves pushed up to his elbows, revealing forearms roped with muscle and lined with scars.

David steps in front of me, his body tense. "How long have you been here?"

"Long enough." Gabriel pushes off the doorframe, easing into the room with that predatory grace I used to find thrilling. Now it just makes my pulse spike with something between fear and fury. "Came in early. I still have my codes." His smile is cold. "You never changed them, Izzy. Sentimental of you."

The old nickname hits like a slap. He's tarnishing it now—turning something tender into a taunt.

"Where is it?" I demand. "Where's Caged?"

He looks at David. "If you want to have a chat, ask your bodyguard to leave."

I tilt my head, indicating that David can go."

"Fuck, no," he says.

"Language." Gabe *tsks*.

"Please," I say. "David, please. Just to the front. He won't hurt me. Not here."

David starts to speak, but Gabriel speaks first. "She's right. Let's call this a detente. Now go."

"Please," I say, when it's clear David's not moving. This time, he agrees, and with one curt nod, he moves past Gabe, his footsteps disappearing down the hall.

"Where?" I snap. "Where is Caged?"

"Safe."

"That painting wasn't yours to take."

"Isn't it?" He moves closer, and I know I should step back, should maintain distance, but my feet won't cooperate. "I created it. I poured my soul into it. I painted you in it—every line, every shadow, every desperate reach toward a light you'd never touch." His voice drops. "And then you took everything else from me. So yes, Isabella. I'd say it's mine."

"I didn't take anything from you!" The words tear out of me. "And I'm done defending myself."

"And you built a shrine." He gestures at the walls around us. "Yes, I can see that. Very touching. The grieving girlfriend, keeping the flame alive." His lip curls. "Tell me, did you cry real tears when you hung these pieces? Or were you just calculating how much they'd be worth?"

"I loved you, you son-of-a-bitch. I still do. So dammit, don't make me hate you."

He lifts a brow. "Touchy."

I fight the urge to knee him in the balls, then say, very calmly, "I gave your work an audience. I found good homes for it— people who actually appreciate what you created. And the money?" I step closer, driven by a rage I can barely contain. "I already told you about the scholarships and grants, and unless you're a total idiot, you checked up on that. So you know that hundreds of young artists are getting chances they never would have had otherwise. All in LaBete's name. I did that, you arrogant prick. I did it because I wanted your legacy to mean something."

Something flickers in his expression. There and gone, too fast to read.

"I hate that you believe I could hurt you," I say. "That you could look at me and see a murderer."

Something shifts behind his eyes. Pain, maybe. Or doubt. Then it's gone, locked away behind that frozen mask.

But it was there. I know it. And that little thing called hope flutters in my belly.

"You decided for me. You and the men who left me bleeding at that cabin. Your eyes watching me die."

"Goddammit. Did that fire kill your brain cells? I didn't hurt you. I would *never* hurt you. I didn't know what happened to you. I spent months trying to find answers, and every door I opened slammed shut in my face."

My voice breaks, and I struggle to find it again.

"I gave up," I finally whisper. "Eventually, I just gave up. I brush away hot tears. "Maybe if I'd kept it up another day, another week, I would have found you. But I stopped. I stopped because I let myself believe you were dead. And I was wrong." The tears flow freely now.

"Months," he says. "You investigated for months."

"Yes. Of course. I thought someone had murdered the man I was going to spend my life with, and I was supposed to just accept the official story and move on?"

I shake my head. "I did everything I could think of. I hired private investigators. I bribed police contacts. I dug through my father's files when he wasn't looking."

He's watching me with an intensity that makes my skin prickle. "Your father's files."

"He hated you—we both know that. And I know he used to go through my room. So maybe he knew about the cabin." I shrug. "But I didn't find anything. Not surprising. We both know my father's the kind of prick who knows how to hold his secrets close."

"You hate him."

It's a statement, not a question, but I answer anyway. "That should hardly be news to you. The only reason I'm still in his orbit is to get the Monarch. Get it, cut it loose from the Hart Properties portfolio, and build it into something of my own."

"The Monarch," he says, with a tinge of menace in his voice. "You mean the property I'm going to dismantle piece by piece? The gaming commission investigations are just the beginning. By the time I'm done, it'll be worth pennies on the dollar. And then

I'll buy what's left of your father's empire and burn it to the ground. Sorry, sweetheart. Your inheritance is my prey."

It takes a moment for the full, horrible truth to sink in.

The Monarch is my escape. My future.

And he's going to destroy it.

I force myself to hold his gaze. "What am I in all this?"

Something flickers in his eyes—there and gone. "Sweetheart, you're the whole point."

"Then look at me." I step closer, refusing to flinch. "Really look at me. And tell me you see a killer."

He doesn't answer.

"You can't," I whisper. "Because you know. Somewhere underneath all that rage, you know I didn't do this."

He's so close now. Close enough that I can feel the heat radiating off his body, smell the familiar scent of him underneath something darker, something new.

I lift my chin, defiant even as my heart pounds. "Someday you're going to realize how wrong you are. And when you do, I hope it destroys you. I hope the guilt eats you alive."

He moves so fast I don't see it coming. One second, I'm spitting fury at him, and the next, his hand is fisted in my hair, and his mouth is on mine.

The kiss is brutal. Punishing. Meant to prove that he still has power over me, that my body will betray me even when my mind knows better.

And god help me, it does.

I should push him away. I should bite and scratch and fight. But instead, my hands are fisting in his shirt, pulling him closer, and a noise escapes my throat that sounds too much like a moan.

He breaks the kiss as suddenly as he started it, then steps back, leaving me swaying, breathless, my lips bruised and tingling from the feel of his beard. Without thinking, I reach up, my fingers brushing his face, no longer smooth and familiar, but rough and dangerous.

"You still want me," he says. It's not a question. "Even now. Even knowing what I came here to do."

I can't deny it. The evidence is all over me. My face. My ragged breathing. The way my body is still leaning toward his like a flower toward the sun.

"I hate you," I whisper.

"But you want me anyway. And that," he says, "is going to be your downfall."

"You're wrong about me. You're going to hate yourself when you finally realize the truth."

"Sweetheart, I already see the truth in your eyes."

He starts to walk away, then turns back. He nods toward the butterfly, still screaming silently on the wall. "Consider it a reminder. Of what happens to beautiful things that get too close to hands that want to destroy them."

As soon as he's left the back room, I slide to the floor, my hands shaking. A moment later, David rushes back in. "Bella? Are you okay?"

"I'm fine." But I'm not, and we both know it.

"Did he hurt you?"

I touch my lips. "Not the way you mean."

David looks at me for a long moment, then holds out his hand. "Come on," he says quietly. "Let's get you upstairs."

———

WHEN I'M BACK in my suite, I call Harper and tell her everything as my tears flow. She lets me cry and says all the right things, but it's not enough. Nothing will be enough until Gabriel trusts me again.

If he ever trusts me again.

Mostly, I'm afraid that the longer he pushes me away, the smaller our chance becomes. Because as much as I love him, I'm not going to wait for a man who hates me, no matter how certain I am that he's hating for all the wrong reasons.

"It's going to work out," Harper says when I tell her all that. Except I don't believe her. Not anymore. I'm not even sure she believes it herself.

Still, I haven't given up yet. "Can you talk to Leo for me? He sent the text about Gabriel being alive. He might know something about what happened to him."

I hear a light tapping, then her perky, "Done. Anything else?"

Some of the tension drains from my body simply from knowing that she's got my back. "Yeah. A list of everyone who knew about the Aspen cabin. Gabriel thinks I was the only one, but I can't possibly have been. At the very least, my father must have found out somehow. How can I dig into my father's movements around the time of Gabriel's death? Where he was, who he met with, unusual activity. That kind of thing."

She sucks in air. "That's going to require some creative sneakiness. Your dad's no idiot. He's going to keep his dirty laundry well-hidden."

"I know. But there has to be something. No one covers their tracks perfectly. I just don't know how to find it."

"Me neither," she says. For that kind of digging, you need deep connections and a lot of pull. The Grimm name might do it. I can ask Leo, and —Oh! Hold the phone. Remember when I handled the mess with that actress? The stalker thing?"

"Vaguely."

"Doesn't matter. Point is, I ended up working with a PI, and he happens to owe me a favor of the humongous kind. Any doors he can't open on his own, we'll get Leo on it."

I actually laugh, and it feels really good. "So, you'll call in that favor, and then I'll be the one owing you."

"Way of the world, my friend. Want me to set it up?"

"Yes, please. And if I haven't mentioned it, you are the best."

"Well, duh." I can actually hear her grin. But the humor fades as she continues. "What if he does find proof? What if your father really did try to kill Gabe?"

I stop pacing, then gaze out the window at the Atlantic City skyline. "Then I'll do whatever I can to help him take my father down."

The words are the absolute truth, but what I don't tell her is that my father could swear on every Bible in the world that I wasn't involved, and Gabriel still wouldn't believe him or me.

He's no longer the man who used to call me Izzy. Who painted me reaching for light I couldn't touch. Who promised me forever.

Now, he doesn't trust me. Not yet. And even if he comes fully around, for years, he truly believed that I tried to kill him, and that lack of trust is like a knife in my gut.

He thinks I hurt him. But he's hurting me right now.

And I'm not sure we can ever come back from that.

<h1 style="text-align:center">CHAPTER
THIRTEEN</h1>

G abriel stood in the dark, staring at the empty wall where Caged used to hang as the focal point of this room in their gallery. The painting was in his apartment now, locked with him beneath the ground where he could look at it whenever he wanted, torturing himself in private as he longed for a past he could never reclaim.

That's where he should be now, too. In that utilitarian room, his laptop open as he planned and strategized, and waged his private war. After all, he had an empire to dismantle. A woman to destroy. He should be sharpening the knife he'd spent five years forging.

Instead, he was standing in the dark, trying to call up the scent of her perfume, and losing his goddamn mind.

She'd touched his face.

Soft and gentle, her eyes both sad and hopeful.

He'd meant to punish her with that kiss. Meant to prove she was weak, that her body would always betray her. But then her fingers had brushed his jaw, and something in her expression had flickered. Grief, maybe. Or loss.

Like she was looking for someone who wasn't there anymore.

With a sigh, he crossed the gallery space and pressed his palm against the empty wall. The plaster was cold. *Caged.*

He'd painted it in three days, almost seven years ago, barely sleeping, barely eating. Just him and the canvas and the desperate need to get her out of his head and on to something he could touch.

That was what painting had always been for him—an outlet. A way to bleed without making anyone else bleed.

His father had seen the darkness in him early. Had cultivated it, even. Gabe was the oldest son, the heir, the one who would carry the Grimm name into the next generation. Elias had taught him to be hard. To be feared. To walk into a room and know that every person in it would bend to his will or break against it.

And Gabriel had liked it. God help him, he'd actually liked it. The power. The control. The knowledge that he would always come out on top.

But the darkness had a cost. It built up inside him, and if he didn't find a way to release it carefully, it found its own release. He'd learned that lesson early on—learned it in bloody knuckles and broken furniture and the fear of everyone around him.

Then he'd found art, and it was an epiphany. A way to pour all that rage and hunger and desperate wanting into something that couldn't bleed back.

He'd never told his family, but Izzy had understood. How could she not, when it was only Izzy and his art that kept the beast at bay?

Now, though, she was gone, and art was his only way of caging the beast.

He drew in a breath, shoving the thoughts aside as he recalled the hours spent painting *Caged.* The way he'd rendered the woman he loved in pigment and longing.

In the painting, she was reaching. Always reaching. Fingers stretched toward light that was just out of grasp, her face caught between hope and despair.

He'd painted her eyes last. Had spent six hours on them alone, mixing colors until he got the exact shade of her mismatched irises. That celestial blue. That verdant green. The colors that still haunted his dreams.

The eyes he'd seen behind the muzzle of a gun.

With a shudder, he forced the vile memory away. This was about the magic times. The fake times.

The times when she had fooled him. Like the way she'd cried when she first saw the painting.

"Is that how you see me?" she'd whispered. "Trapped?"

"Reaching," he'd said. "I see you reaching."

She'd kissed him then. Soft and slow and full of something that felt like promise. *That was it,* he'd thought. *That was the life I was supposed to have.*

He'd taken it from her, and now he didn't know why he'd come here except that he'd lost the battle to stay away. Now the wall was empty, and his heart was emptier.

He walked through the rest of the gallery slowly. The lighting was dim, but he didn't need light. He knew every piece by heart. Knew the nights he'd painted them, the music he'd been listening to as he focused only on canvas and color, the coffee growing cold on his worktable.

He knew the story behind each canvas. Which came from joy, which from pain, which from fury.

Most of all, he knew which came from the desperate, aching need to be seen by someone who understood.

Izzy had understood.

That was the worst part. The part he couldn't forgive—not her, not himself. She'd seen him. Really seen him. Not just the artist, but the monster underneath. The darkness he'd learned to leash but had never managed to kill. She'd looked at all of it—the rage, the hunger, the thing inside him that wanted to own and possess and destroy—and she hadn't run.

She'd loved him anyway.

Or so he'd thought.

He stopped in front of Fractured Light.

Three in the morning. Paint on his fingers. His throat clogged with emotion. Izzy asleep in his bed, her body curled against his pillow.

He'd felt something crack open that night. Something he'd kept locked down his whole life. And instead of terrifying him, it had felt like relief. Like maybe he didn't have to be the hard, cold thing his father had made him. Like maybe there was another way.

What a fucking fool he'd been.

He wanted to rip the canvas off the wall. Wanted to put his fist through it, just like the brutal creature his brothers had always seen.

He wanted to destroy the evidence that he'd ever let himself be that vulnerable, that naive, that soft.

He didn't touch it.

Instead, he stood there like a man visiting his own grave, and he let himself *feel*.

The longing. The loss. The terrible, treacherous wanting that years of hatred couldn't burn out of him.

He still loved her.

That reality landed hard and cut deep. He just couldn't fucking shake her off. He'd tried everything. Fought in underground rings until his knuckles were raw and his ribs were cracked—channeling the darkness the old way, the way he'd learned before the canvas.

He'd fucked women who meant nothing, hoping to burn her out of his system. Built an empire of underground clubs that spread across the whole damn country just to prove he didn't need her.

None of it worked.

How could it when every time he closed his eyes, she was there? Laughing at something he'd said. Tracing the lines of his paintings with reverent fingers. Looking up at him with those eyes that made him believe he could be more than his father's son.

And now she was here again. Real and breathing and close enough to touch.

And she swore she didn't do it.

He both wanted and didn't want to believe her. Hell, he couldn't believe her. Belief was weakness. Trust, too. And both could get you killed. He'd learned that lesson from Elias Grimm, and it had been proved right in blood and fire. Never would he forget it.

And yet...

I loved you, you son-of-a-bitch. I still do.

The words echoed in his skull, burrowing under his skin like shrapnel he couldn't dig out.

I mourned you. For five years, I mourned you.

He pressed his forehead against the wall, the cold, hard surface reminding him of what he'd become.

That was the joke, wasn't it? He hadn't *become* anything. He'd just gone back to what he'd always been. The hard, dangerous man his father had raised him to be. The one who took what he wanted and crushed anything that stood in his way.

Once upon a time, Izzy had made him believe he could be something else.

And yet there was Aspen. Where Isabella had reminded him, in the most brutal way, why softness was a luxury he couldn't afford.

With a sigh, he let his gaze skim across the walls of the gallery.

This place remembered the lie. Remembered the artist who'd painted a piece like Caged. Who'd actually picked out flooring. Who'd argued about lighting angles. Who'd spent hours debating which pieces should go where.

He wanted to hate her for showing him that other self. For making him believe he could be gentle. Different.

Kind.

So, yes. He wanted to hate her.

But goddamn him all to hell—he couldn't.

Because when he'd kissed her today—when he'd fisted his hand in her hair and crushed his mouth against hers—she'd kissed him back. Had pulled him closer instead of pushing away. Had made that sound in her throat, that soft, desperate moan that used to undo him.

And for one moment, one single, devastating moment, he'd forgotten why she was vile. Why she was the enemy.

Why he'd sought her out with vengeance on his mind.

That's the reason he'd come to the gallery tonight. Not to remind himself of the vengeance he'd meant to wield. Not to stoke the flames of revenge.

No, he'd made this pilgrimage because he was losing the certainty that had kept him alive. Because now, when he looked at her, he no longer saw the monster. Now—again—he saw the woman.

And damn him all to hell—he still fucking loved her.

But he'd spent years becoming something cold and hard and merciless. The kind of man his father admired.

The man she'd once loved didn't exist anymore, and maybe that was a good thing because that man had let down his guard and almost died from that mistake.

But *this* man—the Beast, the weapon, the thing his father had always meant him to be— this man had survived.

He needed to remember that.

At the door, Gabriel paused, then looked around. He should burn this place down. Should destroy every piece of evidence that he'd ever tried to be something other than what he was.

He wouldn't, though.

Because even now, even after everything, some small and stubborn part of him couldn't let go.

So instead, he locked the door behind him and walked away.

Tomorrow would be different. Tomorrow, the hatred would come back. Tomorrow, he'd remember why she deserved to suffer.

But tonight…

Tonight, he let himself miss her.

Just for a moment.

Just until the sun came up and he had to be the beast again.

CHAPTER
FOURTEEN

I'm still wrapped in the fog of restless sleep and fragmented dreams when my phone buzzes on the nightstand. I grumble and glance at the display. *David.*

"*Wtisit?*" Which, translated from sleep-speak, is *What time is it?*

"Tell me you're not still in bed."

"I'm not still in bed," I say dutifully. Then I sit up and push the hair out of my face. "I'm sitting on the bed. There's a difference."

"Get dressed. We have a problem."

The urgency in his voice cuts through the last of my drowsiness. "What's going on?"

"Only your psychotic ex-boyfriend trying to blow up the merger.

"Oh. Well, shit." Not exactly a hard-edged corporate response. But it's heartfelt. I rub my temples, fighting a headache. *Gabe, seriously. Why?*

"Okay," I say. "Tell me."

I hear him blow out a frustrated breath. "My parents got another call last night. Whoever's feeding them information about your father just upped the ante. They're talking about pulling out entirely."

105

I'm on my feet before he finishes the sentence, already moving toward my closet. "What did they say? What information?"

"Financial irregularities. Hints about unreported liabilities. Suggestions that Sterling Hart might be leveraging assets that don't technically belong to him. No specifics and no documentation. But their informant swears it exists, and that they'll reveal it unless the merger goes gracefully into the night." David's voice is tight. Worried.

"But that's ridiculous. I mean, my dad's an ass—no argument there. But we have an army of accountants and administrators looking over all that stuff. I can't believe there's that kind of monkey-business going on."

"And yet."

I sigh. "If this merger falls apart, you and I both get screwed."

"You think I don't know that?"

"This is really fucked up. Do you really think your parents will pull out?" I ask. "I mean, anybody off the street could allege that. Without proof it's just hearsay."

"You know my father. He may own a casino, but the man is risk-averse. And he's very, very nervous now."

I rub my temples, fighting a very pushy headache. "It's Gabriel. He's behind it.

"Got there all on my own," David says. "I talked my parents down last night, but they want a meeting. Today. All of us—you, me, my parents, your father."

My father. And just like that, my day went straight to apocalyptic. I close my eyes, picturing Sterling Hart in a room with the Mercers, spinning his web of charm and lies, convincing them that everything is fine while Gabriel circles like a shark smelling blood.

"When?"

"Noon. At the Monarch. I already booked conference room three."

"I'll be there," I say, albeit grudgingly. "But you can have the pleasure of inviting my dad."

"Fair enough. Listen, Bella," he continues, his voice softening.

"We can fix this. But we have to present a united front. You and me, committed to this marriage, committed to making this work. That's what they need to see."

The words land like boulders.

It feels like only seconds ago that David and I were on the way to cutting free of our parents and moving on with our dreams in our little bubble of an arranged marriage.

Yes, I'd still have had my broken heart, but at least I'd have the means to build something out of the rubble without my father's overbearing guiding hand.

But now everything is different. Complicated. And somehow I'm supposed to stand in front of David's parents and pretend I'm not in love with another man.

A man who's actively trying to destroy the Father-free life I've been trying to build.

I stay in bed even after we finish the call, my phone still tight in my hand as the fragments of my life swirl around me like crazed swallows. A merger to save. A psychotic ex-boyfriend to manage. A father who may or may not have tried to commit murder.

And there I am, right in the middle of the melee. A woman who used to know exactly who she was and what she wanted, now drowning in chaos she can't control.

And to top it off, this is the day I'm taking over management of the Monarch. Apparently, my day is going to be even more jam-packed than I'd planned.

Just another Wednesday in the Hart-land.

With a sigh, I start for the bathroom to shower and dress in my trustworthy-daughter-in-law mask. Then I stop, realizing I have one more call to make.

Leo answers on the second ring. "Bella?"

"Gabe's losing it, I say without preamble. "He showed up at the gallery a few days ago. He took Caged and replaced it with this horrible painting of a butterfly with its wings being ripped off, and he was waiting for me." My voice cracks, and I force the threatening tears back. "Just waiting there in the dark for me."

"He was at the gallery?" Leo's voice is like sharpened steel. "Did he hurt you?"

"No, no. But he—" I press my hand to my mouth, fighting back the sob building in my chest. "Oh, god, Leo. He's going off the rails. And he's fucking with the merger. It's like he's trying to keep me trapped under Father's thumb."

I draw a long breath, practically drowning in fear and fury and longing and loss.

"That stubborn son of a bitch." Leo's voice is tight with frustration. "Do you know where he is?"

"He's got an apartment under a hotel called the Obsidian. He's got a fight club down there, too. With a bar and a cigar lounge and who knows what else. I haven't seen all of it. That part's called The Beast."

Leo chuckles.

"Yeah," I say. "Apropos, right?" I draw in a breath. "Will you come? Can you try to talk him down? Because honestly, Leo, if he screws up this path to freedom, I just might have to kill the bastard myself."

"Somehow, I don't see that happening." I can hear the smile in his voice, and it erases a bit of my overwhelming fear and longing and hatred and angst. "Just, please? Will you?"

"Yeah," he says, and as far as I'm concerned, that's the most beautiful word in the universe. "I don't know if it'll help, but I can try.

"Thank you." I can barely push the words out against the flood of relief that surges through me so intensely that I have to sit down on the edge of the bed. "He'll listen to you."

"Well, I guess we'll find out. Ruby and I are in New York. We can be there in a few hours." For a moment, only silence fills the line. "Sasha and Liam are at their Santa Barbara house, enjoying some time with the kiddo, but I'll keep them updated."

"Thanks. Have you seen him?"

"No. That night when I texted you—he never showed."

I nod. Of course, he didn't. He hadn't come back for his family, not yet. He came back to torment me.

I draw a breath, then apologize for dragging Leo into the mess. "I didn't know who else to call."

"Are you kidding? This is about Gabe."

Is it still? I ask, but the question is only in my head.

CHAPTER
FIFTEEN

I come out of the meeting feeling like a prize-fighter who's taken a zillion punches while playing darts and landing them all dead-center.

In other words, bashed and battered, but triumphant. Not because my dad stepped up, but because I personally assured the Mercers that nothing fishy is going on, and then confidentially told them about Gabe and his plan to become a human tornado to level all of Hart Industries.

That didn't exactly give them a warm fuzzy feeling, but we're almost family. Even without the engagement, David and I essentially grew up in each other's houses. They remember Gabe, and they were shocked by what happened to him—and what he believes about me.

I can't say they trust my father, but they do trust me. And once Mr. Mercer firmly kicked Daddy Dearest out of the meeting, they agreed that the deal could stay in place, with the caveat that if my father—or Gabe—pushed too hard, they might still have to push back. "We don't want to," Mr. Mercer said. "We love you like a daughter, and you know that. But I do not—*not*—love your father like a brother."

And that was it. Somehow, I'd bought us more time. And

despite the icky feeling that came from the whole situation, I walked out of that room feeling proud. I went in to do battle, and my corporate armor didn't fail me.

So, yay me!

And yes, I realize negotiating with almost-family is different than deals I'll be making in the future with foreign hotel magnates, but especially these days, I'm taking my victories where I can find them.

"You were amazing," David says once we're back in my suite and I've changed out of my suit and am now comfy in leggings and an oversized shirt.

"Yeah, well, you were a great—I don't even know the word. Wingman? Can you be my wingman when you were technically on your parents' side?"

"I will always be your wingman," he says. He comes to sit on the sofa, then pats the space beside him. I settle there, then shift and turn my back to him. Since this is David, he knows exactly what I want, and he puts his hands on my shoulders and starts to rub. Within seconds, I'm moaning and melting in relief and pleasure at the way his strong fingers are working out my kinks.

"Oh, yes," I whisper. "That is exactly what I needed."

"Then close your eyes," he says, his magic fingers working a miracle on my shoulders and my neck. I'm about to slip to the floor and beg a full-on back massage when I feel his breath at my ear, then the soft press of his lips.

I close my eyes—not to melt into this moment, but to draw a bit of courage. "David," I say. "We can't."

"I'm pretty sure our FWB pact says we can. And nobody's going to come looking for us until after lunch. Besides, we both need some stress relief."

His voice is soft and teasing and damnably tempting. I close my eyes for a moment, because yes, I do want what he's offering.

The trouble is, I don't want it from him.

Well, hell.

I shift around to face him, then take his hands. "I'm sorry," I say. "I just can't."

For a moment, he says nothing, and there's nothing I can say to fill the gap. I'm about to repeat that I'm sorry when he looks at me hard. "He wants to destroy you." His voice is flat. Resigned.

"I know." I lift my chin, finally meeting his eyes directly. "I know he does. And I know this doesn't make sense. But I just...I can't." I swallow. "I can't believe he really wants to hurt me. And even if he does, I can't stop loving him."

I take David's hands. "I do love you. I always have. But it's a different kind of love. And I know you feel more, and I know that it hurts, especially now when I'm saying no because of a man who might be the worst thing in the world for me."

"But the heart wants what it wants." His voice is dry and a little harsh, but there's understanding, too.

"Yeah," I say. "It does."

For the length of two heartbeats, he just sits there. "Okay," he says. "I get that."

We share a sad little smile. "Yeah," I say, leaning forward to brush a kiss over his cheek. "I know you do."

I'm afraid this uncomfortable conversation is going to segue into an uncomfortable silence, but I'm literally saved by the bell. Or, rather, the chime of my phone. I grab it up, feeling lighter when I see that it's from Leo. If anyone can transform Gabe back into the man I used to know, it's him.

Come to the penthouse.

He doesn't bother with an address.

"Leo," I tell David, pointing to the text. "I need to go." I wait, expecting him to say he's coming, too. That we've been friends our entire lives, and if I'm trying to rescue the love of my life from a barrage of horrible lies about me, then he's going to be at my side whacking away at the bullshit, too.

But he doesn't say that. Instead, he picks up the remote and goes straight to a streamer airing Disney's *Beauty and the Beast*. Figures.

I sigh, then head to the door. I pause once to look back, but he's absorbed by Belle. Or pretending to be.

Fine. Whatever. I've gotten used to things not being easy.

I text Harper on my way to the elevator. *Grimm penthouse. The gang's assembling. I need you.*

Her response comes before I hit the lobby. *Already on my way. Elliott called me. He's stuck in London, so I'll be him.*

No surprise there. She'd been one-third of The Trio growing up—her, Gabe, and Elliott. And even though they've all sworn they were just friends, I always suspected Harper had been a little in love with Gabriel back then. We all were, weren't we? Before I became the one he chose.

Twenty minutes later, I've walked off my David pissiness and am stepping into the Grimm penthouse. It's exactly as I remember—sleek, floor-to-ceiling windows overlooking the Atlantic. Dark hardwood floors, furniture that costs more than the gross national product of a small nation, and art on the walls that—

Whoa.

I stop. Stare.

There's a LaBete original hanging above the fireplace. One of Gabriel's earlier pieces. I've never seen it before, but I recognize his style. The bold strokes that aren't yet as confident as they'd become. The dark palette with hints of light, as if the artist was staring into a bright future hidden behind a wall of gloom. I swallow, wondering if when he'd painted that, Gabe had been thinking of a future with me.

Leo catches my eye, his mouth curving into a slow grin. "I saw Gabe painting once—never bothered to tell him, but after that day, I paid attention. Even bought a few from local dealers, but Gabe never knew." He points to the canvas. "I hung that one here the week after Gabe died. That's when I told the rest of these clowns and our dad about his secret identity," he adds, pointing to his brothers.

"Pretended to die," I say, with an edge in my voice.

"*Touche,*" Leo says with a nod. "Anyway, I wanted it to be a fuck-you to my father, but the bastard went and landed in a coma, so he still hasn't seen it." Leo shrugs. "But no way am I taking it down. Gabe belongs here."

"Yeah," I say. "He does." What I don't add—though of course Leo knows it—is that I appreciate the quiet fuck-you to Elias Grimm and the secret tribute to the brother Leo thought he'd lost.

I don't realize that I've moved across the room until I reach out, and my fingers lightly brush the canvas.

"You look like hell."

I turn to find Ruby Ryder beside me. Well, Ruby Ryder-Grimm now that she and Leo are married.

I've known Ruby since elementary school. I was one of the girls who "belonged," and she was a scholarship kid. She may not have grown up with money, but she was surrounded by it. Raised by her grandmother, who was a housekeeper for Reed Cosmetics, she ended up being besties with Sasha Reed—now Liam Grimm's wife.

Ruby and Leo met in school, then fell in love and fell apart. Not in the usual way of young love, but in that horrible, brutal way that seems to follow the Grimm name.

They're blissful now, though, and that gives me hope. What also gives me hope is that Leo and Ruby now run some sort of security-related, secret, badass, Liam Neeson in the *Taken* oeuvre, kind of business.

I don't know the details, but considering someone who was not me tried to kill the eldest Grimm brother, I figure we're chasing some badass people. And that means I want all the badasses I can muster on my side. Not just to keep Gabriel safe in case his would-be killers try to finish the job, but to keep me safe, too.

Because Gabriel thinks I'm one of that ilk. And that's something I never, ever could have imagined before.

"Earth to Bella."

My chin jerks up, and I refocus on Ruby. "Sorry. I keep zoning out. All of this is just surreal."

"I know. I'm so sorry. Except I'm not. I mean, sweetie, he's alive." Before I can respond, she pulls me into a fierce hug, then pushes me back, her assessing gaze raking over me.

"You need coffee."

"And that's why I love you."

The door opens behind me, and Harper slips in, slightly out of breath. She crosses straight to me and pulls me into a hug without a word. When she releases me, her eyes are bright.

"I still can't believe it," she says. "I keep thinking I'm going to wake up."

"I know. Me too."

"Elliott's losing his mind that he can't be here," she adds. "He's stuck in London—some deal that's been in the works for months. He can't get out of it without tanking the whole thing. But he told me to tell Gabriel—and I quote—'to get the fuck over it.'" She almost smiles. "He said he'd tell him personally, but transatlantic travel takes longer than Gabriel's stubbornness deserves."

"That sounds like Elliott."

"He'll come if we need him," she says. "He made that very clear."

As I settle into a corner of the massive sectional, Ruby disappears into the kitchen for coffee, and I sink into the cushions, letting myself feel, just for a moment, how exhausted I really am.

The penthouse is filling up now. Leo by the windows, still on his phone. Harper beside me, her hand on my arm. And in the corner, quiet and watchful, stands a man I've only met once before.

Alexander Grimm.

He's the most polished of all the brothers—impeccably dressed in a charcoal suit that probably cost more than the annual budget of a small nation. His dark hair is swept back, his face composed into an expression of perfect neutrality. He has the kind of stillness that makes you nervous without knowing why. I've heard rumors that he gives Gabriel a run for his money as to who's the most dangerous Grimm brother. Looking at him now, I believe every whisper.

He catches me staring and offers a slight nod. No smile. No warmth. Just acknowledgment. Then his gaze slides away, and he goes back to watching. Taking it all in. Filing it away for later.

I suppress a shiver and turn back to Harper.

Ruby returns with a tray of steaming mugs and settles beside me, tucking her feet underneath her. Leo finishes his call and joins us, dropping into a chair across from the sectional.

"Liam wanted to be here," he says, reading the question on my face before I can ask it. "But Sasha's exhausted—the baby's been fussy all week—and he didn't want to leave her alone. Apparently, the army of baby-related staff isn't sufficient," he adds with a grin. "Guess my big brother's a softie for his little girl. But he's on standby," Leo adds. "If this goes sideways, he'll be on a plane or chopper in a heartbeat."

I look around the room, and something loosens in my chest. I'm not alone. Gabe's friends and family are here, and not one of them believes that I tried to kill him. They're on my side. They're rooting for Gabe and me.

More than that, they're actively helping me get him back. Not the Gabriel who exists now—cold and vengeful and consumed by rage—but the man he used to be. Hell, yes, he had an ego and a temper. But this fury that now drives him—that isn't him. I want to excavate his cutting wit. His sharp mind. His way of looking at the world as if he could see straight through to the truth of things.

My father broke him. I'm certain Father was behind it. I want proof. I want to hand Gabriel proof and then stand back and watch the shit storm. And then I'll be the one smiling the widest as my father rots in jail.

Because I'll have my Gabriel back.

Please, please let me have him back.

Ruby settles closer to me on the sectional, her voice dropping. "How are you really doing? And don't say fine. I've known you too long for that."

"I'm..." I stare into my coffee. "I'm a mess. And a goddamn fool."

I take a long sip of coffee, wishing it were more of a whiskey kind of blend. Or, hell, just straight whiskey. "He hates me," I whisper. "And instead of being sane and getting the fuck away from the entire Grimm family, I'm here, still loving him, and desperately hoping that I'll stumble across a magic wand that will put his goddamn head back on straight." I bang the heel of my hand against my temple. "Clearly, I'm pathetic. And a fool."

Ruby's smile is gentle. "Love makes fools of us all. Trust me, I know."

I think about Leo. About everything they went through before they found their way back to each other. "When did you get so wise?"

"Three days ago. A sale on wisdom at Amazon. I grabbed a few pints."

That does it. I actually laugh.

She grins. "I'm not saying this is going to work out the way Leo and I did. But if there's even a chance that the man you love is still in there under all that pain and rage..."

"I have to try."

"You have to try." She squeezes my hand. "And if it doesn't work—if he's really too far gone—at least you'll know. At least you won't spend the rest of your life wondering."

Across the room, Leo lets out a sharp whistle, making us all jump. He's been making calls, pacing by the windows, and now he settles into a chair, his jaw tight, his whole body radiating barely contained frustration.

"I've been piecing together what Gabe's been doing for the past five years," he says. "For one thing, he owns the Obsidian under about a hundred layers of corporate rigamarole. As for the operation in the basement, well, The Beast is just the tip of the iceberg. He's built an entire network—fight clubs, underground gambling, information brokerage, bars, and cigar lounges. Pretty much anything potentially shady you can dream up, he's got a finger in it under that name you told me," he says to me. "Lyon Savage. He's not into any sort of prostitution, but he's into pretty much everything else. It's all there, along with hefty payoffs to the authorities, so it doesn't get shut down. Bottom line—the Beast is just one slice of Gabe's very big pie."

Harper's eyes widen. "Well, shit. He's not just sliding into a new lifestyle, is he? I mean, he's not thinking, "Hey, an underground empire sounds like the catalyst for a jolly good income stream, right?"

Leo chuckles. "Actually, from what my people have dug up, it's pretty damn lucrative. But no. The information he pays the most for is very focused."

He looks at me, and my gut curdles. "Me."

He nods. "You. Your father. He's certain your father arranged his death. And he believes you were complicit."

"*Believes*," I repeat. "Not certain?" Maybe it's silly, but I'm grasping tight to that tiny bit of hope.

Leo shrugs. "Honestly, who knows. But it makes sense to me. He's been focused on the money. The properties. The businesses. Thus, the fucking with your dad. I don't think he'll hurt your father himself, but he'll joyfully raze the Hart businesses to the ground. Because your father without his reputation and power? That's punishment enough."

"He wants to hurt me, too," I whisper, then feel a tear slide down my cheek as Leo nods.

I wipe it away, then tilt my head up so that my eyes meet Leo's. "I hate him," I say. "I hate him for believing for even a second that I could hurt him."

"No," Leo says. "You don't. But you wish you could."

I nod as Harper pulls me close, stroking my hair as Leo shoots me one more sympathetic look, then turns back to the group. "Gabe's a fucking genius, you all know that. Brilliant and strategic. He could always see twelve moves ahead, right?" He glances around the room, and everyone nods. "But this doesn't feel like strategy. It feels like obsession. Stealing a painting? That's an unnecessary risk. Showing up at the engagement party. Actually, taking Bella to his home?"

"So what does it all mean?" Ruby asks.

"First, that he's running on fury." He looks directly at me again. "But he loves you. So this is killing him."

"He hates me."

Leo shrugs. "One coin, two sides."

"But this is Gabe," Harper says. "I mean, I get why he's upset. But he's gone off the rails. Gabe would never in a million years believe that Bella would send someone to kill him."

"Except someone did come to kill him," I say quietly. "He was shot and left to die. That changes a person. The last thing he heard was probably that I betrayed him. And I don't know if he was hallucinating or what, but he swears I was there, too.

I hug myself, stifling a shudder.

Leo turns to me. "If I thought you'd done that, I'd kill you myself. But I don't think it. And he wouldn't either if his head was on straight. Whoever tried to take him out set a pretty convincing stage and fucked him up good. So I get what he's doing. But that doesn't mean he gets to keep doing it."

"The question is whether he can still hear reason." From his corner, Alexander speaks for the first time, his voice low and smooth as silk. "Or whether he's too far gone."

Everyone turns to look at him.

"Gabriel had a mean temper and a fierce sense of loyalty to the family. Father used to play on that. Push him hard. Have Gabe be the one who did the family's dirty work. We all know that. And we know that Gabe did what Father asked."

Alexander pauses, taking a sip of whiskey as his eyes rake over us. "But we also know that in the family, he was always the one who held things together. When Father was at his worst, Gabriel was the buffer. The strategist. The one who kept the rest of us from falling apart.

His eyes lock on mine now. "I think you're the one who kept him from becoming what Father was." He draws a breath. "And all that shattered when something shifted, and he believed—truly believed—that you'd betrayed him."

"But I didn't," I whisper, tasting my tears.

"Moot at this point. Because if Gabe's lost his grounding—if he's become what Father always wanted him to be—then talking him down may not be enough."

"But it has to be enough," I say, my eyes still locked on Alexander's. "You can't hurt him. You can't cage him without breaking him. But I can't give up on him."

For a moment, I see something flicker in Alexander's dark eyes—respect, maybe. Then he simply nods. "In the end, we'll do what we have to and hope you get him back. That we all get him back."

"Okay, then." Leo stands, rolling his shoulders as he looks at me. "Ready to go talk some sense into my brother? Who knows? Maybe today's the day we get him back."

"You're coming with me?"

"Hell, yes." His expression is grim. "He might not let you in alone. But I'm betting he won't keep me out. If he does, we'll find another way in."

Ruby pulls me into another hug. "Go get your man," she whispers in my ear. "Or at least knock some sense into his thick skull."

Harper squeezes my hand. "I'll be here when you get back. With wine. Lots of wine."

Even Alexander unfolds from his corner, crossing to stand near the door. "If reason fails," he says to Leo, "call me. I speak his language."

I'm not entirely sure what that means. I'm not sure I want to know.

Leo and I take the elevator down and step out into the Atlantic City evening. The sun is setting over the ocean, painting the sky in shades of orange and purple. It's beautiful—the kind of light Gabriel would have loved to capture on canvas, back when he still believed in beauty.

Back when he still believed in me.

CHAPTER
SIXTEEN

The Obsidian's lobby bar is packed—the after-work crowd gathered on leather chairs, their cocktail glasses catching the amber light. It's the kind of scene I'd normally enjoy. Tonight, it just feels like yet another gauntlet I have to jump to get to Gabriel.

As Leo and I approach, Anissa's behind the front desk with an array of Tarot cards spread face down in front of her. When she sees me, her lips twitch. Not a smile—but close. "You came back."

"And I'll keep coming." I'm hoping for a reaction from her, but all she does is slide her gaze to Leo. "You're, Leo," she says, her voice shaking a little. "I'm Anissa. It's really good to meet you."

Leo's brow furrows. "And you know me how? "

"Well, one, you're a Grimm, so there's that. But mostly because he keeps pictures in his desk. All of you. His brothers, I mean." She glances at me. "I clean his place sometimes."

Leo goes rigid beside me, and I'm certain he's seeing the same thing I am—Gabriel alone in the dark, pulling out photos of the family he'd abandoned. Grieving them while they grieved him.

"And no one knows this, except you?" Leo says. "Because you snoop?"

She lifts a shoulder, totally unrepentant. "He's downstairs," she continues. "He's been different the last few days." Her eyes flick to me. "Something rattled him."

I tell myself that's good. But what I feel is something closer to grief.

"We need to see him," Leo says firmly.

Anissa reaches for the phone, then pauses, looking at me.

"That painting he just hung in his apartment—it's you, isn't it?"

My stomach tightens. "You spend a lot of time in his apartment?" The words come out more clipped than I intend.

Anissa grins. "I just told you I clean it. Plus, it doesn't have a kitchen. Just a mini-fridge and a microwave, and a coffee maker. I bring his meals sometimes." She shrugs. "And he keeps the door open a lot. Says he likes to hear what's happening in the club."

"The fighting," I say quietly.

"The fighting." Her smile fades. "He's pretty fucked up, you know."

"Yeah," I say. "I've figured that out."

Leo leans on the counter. "You seem to know pretty much everything about my brother."

She laughs. "Don't worry, I'm not fucking him." She leans forward, her eyes shifting to me. "From what I know, he hasn't been with anyone in years."

I draw in a sharp breath, then look away, hoping I look casual, but knowing that I don't. She nods at the cards spread out before her. "Pick one."

"What?" I say. "Me?"

She shrugs. "Why not?"

Why not indeed. But I reach past Leo and flip the card two spaces from the end.

"Two of cups," she says, then looks at me with a sweet little smile. "Yeah, that's a good one."

I just nod, pretending that I know what the card means—and feeling strangely optimistic now, too.

She sends a quick text, then nods toward the elevator. "Head on down to SB2. My dad will meet you."

In the elevator, the descent feels endless. Leo stares straight ahead. "Photographs," he whispers. "The bastard kept photographs."

I don't know what to say. So I just stand beside him, lost in my hopes and fears.

When the doors open, Travis is waiting, and his attention lands on Leo. "He knows you're coming?"

"No, and I don't care if he wants to see me or not."

Travis studies him for a long moment before his gaze shifts to me.

"You came back."

"Why does everyone keep saying that like it's a surprise?"

"Because it is." He uncrosses his arms. "Most people run from Gabriel. Especially people who've gotten on his bad side. Whether deserved or not." I see a hint of a smile and hope that means I'm now on Travis's good side.

We walk a bit together, then pause when his phone chimes. He glances at the text, then frowns before looking at me. "You remember the way?"

I nod.

"All right, then. Don't go wandering."

"You're not coming with us?"

He lifts his phone. "Duty calls." Then he turns and heads in the opposite direction as I lead Leo through the maze of corridors echoing with the distant thuds of fists on flesh and leather. Gabriel's empire, and it was built on pain.

"I'm surprised he let us walk alone," I say, mostly to drown out those pervasive thuds.

Leo just looks up.

Cameras. Duh.

When we arrive, the door is wide open, but Gabe's at his easel and doesn't seem to see or hear us. Leo shrugs, then knocks on the doorjamb. When Gabe still doesn't look up, he steps inside, gesturing for me to do the same. The slight shift in position gives me a view of what he's working on—and it's not much. Just a blank canvas with one long, red brush stroke. I remember what Anissa said—that he only sketches now, but doesn't paint.

Something's changed, and as I feel a twist in. my stomach, I can't help but think that the change is me.

A glass of something that's probably whiskey sits on the nearby desk, apparently untouched.

As for Gabe himself, he's looking past the canvas to the painting that now hangs on the far wall—my face rendered in shadow and longing, trapped behind bars.

Caged.

"That wasn't yours to take," I say, my voice low, as if I'm in a church. "You gave it to me."

He turns, and for just a second, I see something flash across his face, too fast for me to even tell if it's relief or fury or something in between. "I gave it to a woman I loved. Not to a bitch who betrayed me."

His gaze slips over me to land on Leo. "Little brother." His voice is cool, but it cracks at the edges. "What the hell are you doing here?"

"No." Leo's fury explodes out of him. "You don't get to do that. You texted me. Said you were alive, that you were coming to the apartment. Then nothing—just dodging my calls while you played your revenge games."

"I knew you'd take her side."

"Side? There are no sides, you dolt." Leo's voice is level. Cold. "There's just the truth, and you're too much of a coward to hear it."

"Truth?" His eyes flick to me. "I was stabbed in the back by truth."

"I thought you were dead, damn you. I gave a eulogy." Leo's voice breaks, and his hands are fisted at his sides. I tried to figure out how to live in a world without my brother. And you've been alive all along. Alive. Keeping our photographs with you while you let us drown in grief, you goddamn bastard."

Gabriel flinches, but when he speaks, his voice is flat. "Your brother died in Aspen. The man who crawled away from that cabin isn't him. Isn't anyone."

His eyes flick to me, cold and empty. "I'm on a mission now. That's all. And I won't stop until I've destroyed everyone who stole my life from me."

"Bullshit." In two long strides, Leo gets right in his face. "You're hiding behind revenge because you're too afraid to face the possibility that you were wrong about her."

"*No.*" Gabriel's voice is low, as if he's working hard to keep everything about this moment dialed in. "*Hart sends his regards.* And that bitch," he adds with a nod toward me, "she..." He trails off.

"What?" I say, taking a step toward him. "What did *she* do?"

"Looked me in the eyes and destroyed me," he says. "The bullets she fired after were just an epilogue."

"Dammit, Gabe, I didn't." Unwelcome tears clog my throat. "And damn you to hell for not knowing that in your heart."

He scoffs and shakes his head. "I loved you so much. So damn much. I would have given my life for you. I never expected you to take it. *Surprise,* he says, holding his hands up and wiggling his fingers. "Turns out my heart was wrong about a lot of things."

I just stand there shaking my head, wondering what freakish dimension I've crossed into. Before Aspen, I could never have imagined a scenario where Gabe would hurt me. And I can't believe he could have imagined me hurting him. So what really happened that night? And why is he so sure—and so wrong— about me?

"Get the hell out," he says, looking between me and Leo before his gaze lands hard on mine. "I already told you what happened. Why I know what I know. None of it should be a *surprise,* should it?"

I frown. That word again.

"You're not an idiot," Leo says. "You and I both know a motivated PI could have found your cabin. And any jerk can take a pop at you and say it's courtesy of the Pope, much less Bella."

"It's not just that," he says, shooting me a glance so full of hate I almost vomit.

"Then what?"

His eyes narrow. "She knows."

"*No,*" I shout. "*She* doesn't. Dammit, Gabe. *She's* been dead for five years, too." He's gone blurry, and I furiously rub the tears from my eyes. "You have no evidence I did anything. You can't, because I didn't. So there can't be evidence. "You have the word of men who tried to murder you. That's it. That's all you have."

"I saw the truth in your eyes, princess. Just like I do now."

"Bullshit. I told you I investigated. I told you I never stopped looking for answers. Did *you* even check? Did you even try to verify what I said? Or did what we once had mean so damn little to you?"

He doesn't answer. But I see it—or I think I do. The tiniest crack in the armor he's spent five years building.

"Come on, bro," Leo says. "Think. They set you up. And now you're trying to destroy the woman who loves you."

"Loved." The correction is automatic. Bitter. "*Past tense.*"

"No." I step closer. Close enough to see every line that grief has carved into his face. "Present tense. Despite everything. Despite all of your bullshit, I still love you, Gabriel. I never stopped. Believe me, I wish I could."

His breath catches. Just barely. But I see it.

"And I think you still love me," I continue. "Because if you don't—if you've really killed that part of yourself—you wouldn't have kissed me. You wouldn't have stolen Caged." I take another step. "You wouldn't be shaking right now."

"Get the fuck away from me."

"No." I reach out. Touch his arm, then watch in horror as he flinches back as if I've burned him. "I'm not going to hurt you," I say, trying to keep the confusion out of my voice. "I just want to see you. The real you. The one who painted me like I was something precious."

I swallow, then let my voice drop to a whisper. "He's still in there. I have to believe he's still there. Because if he's not—"

My voice breaks. I let it. "If he's not, then I've spent five years mourning a man who never existed. And I don't know how to survive that."

Gabriel closes his eyes.

For a long moment, no one speaks. No one moves. The only sound is the distant thump of leather against flesh from the ring. Pretty damn apropos.

Then he opens his eyes. And the walls slam back into place.

"Get out."

"Dammit, Gabe," Leo starts.

"I said get out." He steps back from both of us, his face gone cold and hard. "I'm not your brother anymore, Leo."

His eyes find mine, and there's nothing there. Nothing I can reach. He reaches out to stroke my cheek, and I have to force myself not to melt on the spot. "Surprise, bitch. You should have finished me when you had the chance, because I don't do things by half-measures."

"So that's it?" Leo's voice is rough. "You're just going to keep destroying yourself? Keep punishing her for something she didn't do?"

"I don't remember you being so gullible, little brother." Gabriel's smile is thin and cruel.

"Gabriel, please." I hate the way my voice breaks. Hate the tears burning in my eyes.

"Leave." He turns his back on us, facing Caged. Apropos, I suppose. Right now, I feel as trapped as that woman in the painting.

Leo's hand closes on my arm. Gentle but firm.

"Come on," he says quietly. "We're done here."

I want to fight. Want to scream. Want to grab Gabriel by the shoulders and shake him until he sees me—really sees me.

But Leo's already guiding me toward the door, and I know he's right. Gabriel's shut us out. Completely.

We're almost to the door when I stop and turn to him.

"I'm not giving up on you," I say to his back. "I don't care how long it takes. I don't care how hard you push me away. I'm going to prove the truth, and when I do, you're going to have to live with what you've done."

He doesn't turn around.

He doesn't say a word.

And I surrender to defeat as Leo pulls me through the door.

The walk back through the corridors feels endless. The sounds of the fight club seem louder now, more brutal. Or maybe that's just how everything feels when your heart's been ripped out.

We ride the elevator in silence, then step out into the lobby, and move in silence past the bar crowd and the soft jazz, until we reach the doors and exit into the cool evening air.

"That was a disaster," I say.

"No." Leo's voice is quiet. "It wasn't."

I stare at him. "Are you bonkers? He threw us out."

"Give it time." Leo's jaw is tight, but there's something in his eyes—not hope exactly, but something close. "Trust me."

The car is waiting. We slide in, and the city blurs past the windows. Something soft builds inside me. It's not hope. Not really.

But Leo saw something in there. And right now, that's all I have.

"So what do we do?" I ask.

"We give him time." Leo stares out the window. "And we find proof. Something he can't ignore. Something that forces him to see the truth whether he wants to or not."

"And if we can't?"

He's quiet for a long moment.

"Then I'll drag him back to the family kicking and screaming," he says finally. "Because I didn't spend five years grieving my brother just to lose him again to his own stubbornness."

"Good," I say. "I'll help you drag him."

CHAPTER
SEVENTEEN

The door closed behind them, and Gabriel was alone.

No. Not alone. Never alone. He was with the ghosts. With her face on the wall. With five years of certainty that was starting to crack like ice in spring.

He crossed to the bar. Poured another whiskey. Didn't drink it.

I still love you, Gabriel. I never stopped.

He closed his eyes, but that just made it worse. Made him see her face when she said it—not defiance, not calculation. Something raw. Something that looked like truth.

But he'd been fooled by that face before. By the daughter who'd turned out to be so very like her father.

Slowly, he moved to sit on the sofa. He tossed back the whiskey, then closed his eyes as the memories pressed against him, pushing forward.

They came whether he wanted them to or not.

Today...well, today maybe he wanted them. Maybe, just maybe, he'd find her in his memories. And maybe what she said would be true. Maybe she hadn't betrayed him.

He didn't believe, but he did still hope.

And so he kept his eyes closed as the tide of memories dragged him back into the deep.

Five years ago.

His apartment in Manhattan.

Morning light streaming through the windows.

Izzy curled against him, her hair spread across his chest, one hand tracing lazy patterns on his skin.

"Your birthday's next month," she murmured. "What do you want to do?"

"Surprise me."

She lifted her head, those mismatched eyes—one green, one blue—sparkling with mischief. "A surprise party? You hate parties. For that matter, you hate surprises."

"I hate parties my father throws. Parties where I have to schmooze investors and pretend I give a damn about quarterly projections." He tucked a strand of hair behind her ear. "But a party you throw? With people I like?" He pulled her closer. "That I could handle. And—this is how sneaky I am—now it won't be a surprise."

She laughed. "Oh, it will be. I just have my work cut out for me." She was already scheming—he could see it in her eyes.

"I'm going to go completely overboard. You know that, right? There will be balloons. Possibly a theme. And," she added in a doomsday voice, "there will be games."

"As long as you're there." He pressed a kiss to her forehead. "That's all I want. Just you."

"You're disgustingly romantic."

"Your fault. You ruined me."

She laughed—that sweet laugh he'd fallen in love with, bright and real and completely unguarded. "Good. You needed to be ruined. You were too broody before. Someone had to fix you."

He rolled her beneath him, pinning her wrists above her head. "Fix me, huh?"

"Mmm." She arched up against him. "Extensive repairs required. Might take years."

"I've got years." He kissed her then—slow and deep and full

of everything he couldn't say. That he loved her. That he wanted those years. That he'd already talked to a jeweler about a ring.

That she was the only person in his life who made him feel like he could be something other than what his father raised him to be.

With a jolt, he opened his eyes.

Beside him, the whiskey was still untouched. And now his hands were shaking.

A surprise party. Their private joke. Just between them.

Until it wasn't.

The cabin in Aspen.

Snow falling outside.

He'd gone there to plan—to figure out how he was going to propose. Had the whole thing mapped out. A weekend away, just the two of them. He'd take her to the overlook where they'd watched the sunset on their first trip to Colorado. He'd get down on one knee and—

The door splintered inward.

Three men. Big. Armed. Faces masked and eyes he didn't recognize.

He fought. Of course, he fought. He was a Grimm—his father had made sure he knew how to handle himself. But it was three against one, and they had guns.

The first bullet took him in the chest before he could get his hands on any of them, and he went down hard.

They were laughing. One of them kicked him onto his back so he could see the cabin's rough-hewn roof. See them standing over him.

"Hart sends his regards." The big one crouched down, grinning. "And his daughter? Guess you know now you've never been more than a plaything to her. She's got a special message for you."

He tried to speak. Tried to tell them they were wrong. Bella would never hurt him.

Then she stepped out of the shadows.

That familiar winter coat. A dark hat pulled to her brows. A woolen scarf wrapped around the lower half of her face so only her eyes were visible. Those beautiful, dual-colored eyes.

"You told her to surprise you," the man who'd kicked him said, sliding his arm around her waist, then squeezing her breast. "So, surprise, fucker."

She looked down at him with nothing in those eyes. No grief. No hesitation. Just cold, flat emptiness.

"It was a good ride, but she's done with you, boy," Kicker said.

That's when she raised the gun, and he saw her mother's gold band on her finger. "Surprise," she whispered, then fired.

Those eyes were the last thing he saw before the darkness took him. Green and blue, watching him die.

———

GABRIEL SLAMMED the glass down on the bar so hard it cracked.

It was her. He saw her. Those eyes. That ring. That word— *surprise*—thrown back at him like a knife. Their private moment weaponized. The party she was supposedly planning, turned into the last word he'd ever hear.

Proof that everything they'd had was a lie. That he'd been a fool. A mark. A plaything, just like they said.

She'd been wearing her mother's ring.

She was the only one who knew about the cabin.

She was the only one who knew about the surprise party.

He'd never told anyone that last part. Not Travis. Not Anissa. Even now, he knew he wouldn't tell Leo.

He'd take that truth to his grave.

Because if he did tell, Leo would kill her. Or drag her to the cops. Either way, it would be over too fast. Either way, he'd lose control.

And he'd spent years making sure he never lost control again.

He wanted to be the one who destroyed her. Piece by piece. The way she destroyed him. Her gallery. Her reputation. Her family's empire. He wanted her to watch it all crumble and know that he was the one turning the screws.

He wanted her to suffer.

But now—

I still love you, Gabriel. I never stopped.

He turned at the soft knock at the door, was about to tell whoever it was to get the fuck away, when the door opened, and Travis leaned against the frame.

"I need to start locking that damn thing," Gabriel said. "They're gone?"

Travis nodded. "Leo looked like he wanted to punch a wall. The girl looked like she wanted to cry." A pause. "And you look like hell."

"I'm fine."

"You're a shitty liar." Travis crossed to the bar, poured himself a drink, and settled into the leather chair. "You want to tell me what that was about?"

"Why? You heard it all."

"I heard you throw your brother and the woman you've been obsessing about for years out of this damn cell you keep yourself locked up in." He took a sip. "I'm asking why?"

"Because she tried to kill me."

"Did she?"

Gabriel turned to face him. "You, too? Christ, Travis. You're the one who fucking saved me. You know these wounds better than I do."

"The wounds, yeah. But I've only just met who you say inflicted them."

"Fucking, hell, Travis." He dragged his fingers through his hair. "You know what happened to me. Don't rewrite history."

"I think we may have us a Columbus situation here."

"A what?"

"We thought the world was flat. Now I'm thinking it's round."

Gabe rubbed his temples, then sat. He knew perfectly well that he wasn't going to get Travis to drop it. Whatever *it* was. "I'm listening."

I've been doing some digging." Travis's voice was calm. Level. The same tone he'd used when he found Gabriel half-dead in a snowbank and told him he was going to be fine, even though they'd both known it was probably a lie.

"You know damn well that woman spent months trying to find out what happened to you." He held up a hand before Gabe could interrupt. "She hired investigators. Bribed cops. Burned through money like she was printing it to chase leads that went nowhere." He set down his glass. "You know it. I know it. When will you get it through your thick skull that those aren't the actions of a woman who wanted you dead?"

"She's playing the grieving princess. Of course, she's covering her tracks—"

"For five years?" Travis shook his head. "Nobody's that committed to a lie. And the grief? People I talked to said she was destroyed. Couldn't eat. Couldn't sleep. Almost fell apart completely."

Gabriel didn't answer. *Couldn't* answer. He remembered those months only too well. The months after Travis pulled him out of that snowbank and drove him to his home in the middle of nowhere. The months Travis spent stitching him back together— literally. At first, with the skills he'd learned during his time as a Texas Ranger, and then figuratively, sitting with him through the nightmares, forcing him to eat when he wanted to starve, talking him down when the rage got so bad he couldn't see straight.

Travis had given up everything to follow Gabe. His store. His quiet life. He'd brought Anissa with him, and they'd helped Gabe build this empire of shadows and violence. Five years of unwavering loyalty, and he'd never once questioned Gabriel's mission.

Until now.

"Why are you telling me this?" Gabriel's voice came out rougher than he intended.

"Because I don't think you're as sure as you pretend to be."

"I saw her, Travis." The words ripped out of him before he could stop them. "I saw her standing over me. I saw her eyes. They're pretty damn unique. I heard her say—"

He stopped. Swallowed hard.

Travis waited.

"She said *surprise*." Gabriel's voice was barely a whisper. "We'd talked about her throwing me a surprise party. A private conversation. Just the two of us. And she stood over me in the that cabin and said *surprise* before she pulled the trigger."

Travis was quiet for a long moment. "You never told me that."

"Never told you that she was wearing her mother's gold ring, too. It gleamed in the lamplight. I think that's the last thing I saw before I blacked out."

"Why hold that back?"

Gabriel laughed—harsh, broken. "You're still a lawman at heart, buddy, and with evidence like that, you might have called in a friend. But I don't want the law. I want—" He stopped. Pressed his palm against the bar, steadying himself. "I wanted to do it myself. I wanted to be the one who destroyed her."

"Wanted," Travis repeated. "And now?"

Gabriel stared at the painting on the wall. At her face, rendered in shadow and longing. At the woman reaching for light she couldn't touch.

"Now I don't know what I want."

"Yeah." Travis moved to Gabriel's side, then clapped a hand on his shoulder. "That's what I thought."

He headed for the door. Paused with his hand on the frame. "You know what I think? I think you've been so focused on revenge that you never stopped to ask if you were right."

"Her eyes," Gabriel said. "Her ring. *Surprise.*"

Travis just shrugged. "Someone wanted you dead. Maybe they wanted to set her up, too."

Gabriel scoffed. "She's gotten under your skin."

"She has. And I'm a damn good judge of character. I chose to save you, didn't I?"

Gabriel flashed an ironic smile. "Not sure that supports your case."

"It does," Travis said softly. "All those conversations we'd had before the fire whenever you came into the store? You're a good man, Gabe, whether you believe it or not. Usually level-headed, too. But about her? She's your kryptonite, son. You love her too much to see straight. And you love her enough that if you hurt her, it's going to kill you when you finally realize you're wrong."

"And if you're the one who's wrong?"

"Then I'll eat my words. But if you find out she didn't do those things, well, you might just have to remember how to be happy."

He paused at the threshold and turned back to Gabe. "By the way, ever heard of contact lenses? They come in a variety of colors. And in case you're wondering, *surprise* is a pretty common word."

Then he left, the door clicking shut behind him.

Gabriel sat still for a long time, staring at the painting. At her face. At the eyes—one green, one blue—that had haunted him for five years.

Surprise.

His gut twisted. *Had he really gotten it wrong?*

He'd been so certain. The eyes. The word. The money. The cabin. Every piece fit together like a puzzle designed to destroy him.

But tonight, standing in front of him, her voice had been different. Raw. Desperate. *I still love you, Gabriel. I never stopped.*

The same voice that said "surprise" in that low-almost whisper before shooting him?

Or not?

For the first time in five years, Gabriel let himself ask the question he'd been running from—*What if it hadn't been her?*

What if it wasn't a puzzle he'd been trying to put together? What if he'd really been dismantling a trap?

The thought was so terrifying that he had to sit down. If it wasn't her—if he'd spent years planning revenge against an innocent woman—then everything he'd done, everything he'd become...

He reached for his phone. His hands were still shaking.

He knew a guy. Former FBI, worked private now, owed no one anything. Expensive as hell and mean as a snake, but good. More importantly, honest. He'd find the truth whether Gabriel wanted to hear it or not.

He pulled up the number. Stared at it.

Then he put his phone down.

An investigator wouldn't solve this. Gabriel knew that. No one was going to hand him proof on a silver platter. If there was a bug in his apartment that caught them talking about a surprise party, it was long gone. If someone had hired that woman to wear contacts and play a part while she joined the team that killed him, the trail was cold by now.

At some point, he was going to have to decide—was he the man who trusted what he saw? Or the man who trusted what he knew—what he'd known for years, before Aspen, before the bullets and the blood and the word surprise echoing in the frozen air?

He'd loved her. God, he'd loved her so much it had terrified him. She was the only person who'd ever made him feel like he could be more. The only one who looked at the darkness in him and didn't flinch.

Even now, she looked at him tonight the same way she used to. Like he was worth saving. Like she still believed the man she'd loved was buried somewhere under all this scar tissue and rage.

He's still in there. I have to believe he's still in there.

Gabriel pressed the heels of his hands against his eyes.

He didn't know if that man existed anymore. Didn't know if he'd ever really existed, or if he'd just been a performance—a version of himself he'd created because she made him want to be better.

But he knew one thing.

He couldn't keep doing this. Couldn't keep destroying her

while this doubt gnawed at his gut. He'd kept the doubt pushed back behind thick walls, but she'd been chipping away. Weakening them.

Then Travis had gone into full-on demolition mode. And, dammit, the man was right.

He usually was.

Gabriel couldn't keep pretending he was certain when everything she said, everything she did, made him wonder if he'd gotten it wrong.

It wasn't forgiveness. It wasn't trust. It wasn't even a decision, not really.

It was just the first step toward finding out if he'd wasted five years hating the wrong person.

And if he had...

Gabriel stared at the painting of the woman he'd loved. The woman he might have destroyed for nothing.

If he had, he didn't know how he'd ever make it right.

But he was starting to realize he'd have to try.

CHAPTER
EIGHTEEN

Despite last night's clusterfuck with Gabe, I feel surprisingly normal this morning.

Honestly, it's a welcome change.

David and I are having breakfast in the suite's dining area—coffee and croissants from room service, sunlight streaming through the windows, no crisis demanding immediate attention.

It's almost peaceful. Almost like the life I thought I might have, before Gabriel walked back from the dead and set everything on fire.

"These sausages are incredible," David says, reaching for his second one. "Remind me to tip whoever's running the kitchen this week."

"That would be Marcel. He's been here since before I was born."

"Ah, a lifer." David grins. "Smart man. Job security and unlimited breakfast food."

I smile, and for a moment, everything feels easy. Simple.

"I'm sorry." I blurt out the words without thinking—apparently, I'm not happy without things being awry.

David's brow furrows. "Whufer?" he says with his mouth full, and which I translate into *what for.*

"You know..." I gesture vaguely between us. "Everything. This. You."

He swallows. "Bella."

"You deserve better." Now that I've started, I can't seem to stop. "You deserve someone who lights up when you walk into a room. Someone who isn't still in love with a ghost. Or whatever Gabriel is now."

"Zombie. I mean, he's back from the dead."

"I'm serious."

He sighs. "I know." For a moment, he's quiet. Then he leans back in his chair, studying me with those kind brown eyes. "You think I don't know that?"

"I think you keep hoping I'll change."

He shrugs, but there's pain underneath the casual gesture. "I keep hoping Global Warming will stop, too. But strangely, I don't have as much control over the world as I'd like." He tilts his head, looking like a mischievous kid as he says, "At the very least, I hope you noticed that I'm a big boy now."

I roll my eyes and force myself not to laugh. "I'm trying to have a serious conversation with you."

"I know," he says. "But come on, Bella—do you think I've got such a huge ego that I can't wrap my head around not being the guy for you?"

"I—no. It's just..." I trail off, not sure how to finish.

"Am I worried? Yeah. Gabe's a ticking time bomb as far as I'm concerned. That's what you should worry about. Let me worry about me." He reaches across the table, and I let him take my hand. His grip is warm, steady. "I knew what I was signing up for, Bella. I've always known."

"David."

"No. "Hear me out. "I'd rather have you in my life as a fake wife and real friend than not have you at all. Even if it means watching you pine for a man who doesn't deserve you." His voice hardens slightly. "Not anymore. Maybe not ever. The Gabriel you loved? That man might have deserved you. But this version? The one who runs fight clubs and stalks you and accuses you of trying to murder him?" David shakes his head, then leans back, pulling his hand free of mine. "That man's dangerous."

"You think I don't know that?"

"I think you know it here." He taps his temple. "But here?" He moves his hand to his chest. "Here, you're still hoping he'll turn back into the man he used to be."

I don't have an answer for that. Mostly because he's right.

I hear the lock turn, then the door opens, and Harper wanders in, oversized mug in hand. "Well, this looks heavy. Should I come back?"

"No." I sit up straighter, grateful for the interruption. "It's fine."

She drops into the chair beside me, utterly unrepentant. "Don't mind me. I love awkward emotional conversations over breakfast. Really sets the tone for the day."

David snorts. "Your timing is impeccable as always."

"It's a gift." She takes a long sip of coffee, eyeing us both over the rim. "For what it's worth, pushing Gabe out of her mind isn't going to cement you any closer to her heart. The heart wants what it wants, and all that poetic bullshit."

I meet David's eyes, relieved when he rolls his.

"Thanks for the input," I say dryly.

She grins. Anytime. I'm like a fortune cookie. Full of unsolicited wisdom and occasionally stale." She stands, grabbing a banana from the bowl on the table. "I'm gonna get more coffee. Back in a sec."

"She's right, you know," David says as Harper disappears into the kitchen. "I'm not trying to push Gabriel out of your mind. I just..." He exhales. "I worry about you. What he's doing to you. What he might do."

"I can handle Gabriel."

"Can you? Because from where I'm sitting, you're barely sleeping, barely eating, and every time someone mentions his name, you look like you're about to shatter."

I want to argue. I can't.

"I do love you," I say instead. "You know that, right?"

"Just not that way."

I hold his gaze, letting the silence speak for me. An acknowledgment. An apology. Everything I can't put into words because the words would be too cruel.

David nods slowly. "Yeah. I know." He manages a small smile that doesn't quite reach his eyes. "Can't blame a guy for trying, though, right?"

"You'll find someone." The words feel inadequate. "Someone who deserves everything you have to give."

"Sure." He stabs some hash browns with his fork. "Or I'll die alone, surrounded by cats."

"You're allergic to cats."

"Then it'll be a very short, sneezy death."

Harper breaks the tension by popping out from the kitchen. "Well, hey. I'm available."

David laughs—a real laugh this time. "Careful. I might take you up on that."

"Don't threaten me with a good time, Mercer."

And just like that, the heaviness lifts. We're all laughing, the three of us, and for one perfect moment, there's no Gabriel, no bullshit gaming commission investigations, no father lurking in the shadows. Just friends enjoying the morning together.

Then the door bursts open.

My father storms in like he owns the place—which, technically, he does. At least for a little while longer. His face is flushed, a vein pulsing at his temple. I recognize the signs immediately. I've seen this version of him my whole life. The barely contained rage. The way his hands clench at his sides. The cold fury in his eyes that promises pain for whoever caused his displeasure.

He's beyond angry. He's volcanic.

My body reacts before my mind catches up. Shoulders drawing in. Spine curving slightly. Making myself smaller, less of a target. Twenty-eight years of conditioning kicking in like muscle memory.

I force myself to straighten. To sit tall. To not give him that satisfaction.

"Out," he snaps at David and Harper. "Both of you. Now."

David is on his feet instantly, his body angling between my father and me. "I don't think so."

"I said *out*." My father's voice drops to something low and dangerous. "This is family business."

"Bella is—"

"Not your concern." Father steps closer, and I see the calculation in his eyes. He's assessing David. Deciding how much of a threat he poses. "You may technically be her fiancé, but you're not yet her husband. All you are right now is a guest in my hotel. Don't make me reconsider my hospitality."

David's jaw tightens, a war playing out on his face—the desire to protect me versus the knowledge that escalating this will only make things worse.

I catch his eye and shake my head slightly. Whatever this is, it'll be worse if he stays. My father doesn't like being challenged, especially not in front of witnesses. If David pushes, Father will push back harder. And the person who pays the price will be me.

That's always how it works.

David hesitates, every line of his body rigid with reluctance. Harper is already gathering her things.

"We'll be in the bedroom," David finally says, the words clearly meant for my father as much as for me.

Father doesn't even acknowledge him. Just stands there radiating fury, eyes fixed on me until the door clicks shut. For a moment, neither of us moves. We just stare at each other across the sun-drenched room—father and daughter, predator and prey. I can hear my own heartbeat, loud and fast.

Then he breaks the silence. "Do you have any idea what you've done?" His voice is low. Almost a hiss.

I stay seated. Force myself to take a calm sip of coffee, even though my hands want to shake. "Good morning to you, too, Father."

"Don't." He stalks toward the table, plants his hands on the surface, and looms over me, getting so into my face I can see the broken capillaries in his cheeks. He looks older than he did a week ago. Older and meaner.

"Gaming commission investigations," he says. "Twelve Hart properties over three continents, including the Monarch. Do you have any idea how much money this is going to cost us? How much damage control?"

"It's going to be a nightmare, of course. But I've got a handle on the Monarch. It's my responsibility now, not yours.

"Goddammit, you little bitch."

"I didn't file the damn complaints," I snap, the outburst surprising both me and my father.

For a moment, he's speechless. I think that may actually be a first. "No," he says, his voice so low that tiny word sounds like a threat. Your psychotic ex-boyfriend did. The one holed up in a pathetic hotel. The one you've been sneaking off to see."

"That's none of your business."

"Everything about you is my business." He straightens, starts pacing. "I've spent decades building this empire. Protecting this family. And you're going to let some dead man walk back in and destroy everything because you can't keep your legs closed?"

The crudeness shocks me, even from him. "That's none of your business."

"I don't care what it is or isn't." He wheels on me, and I flinch before I can stop myself. I see him register the reaction. And I see the flash of satisfaction in his eyes.

He likes that I'm afraid. He's always liked it. Not for the first time, I think about what my mother must have endured. I think the cancer that killed her when I was a toddler was probably sweet relief.

"You're going to fix this," he continues. "The gaming commission complaints need to go away. The merger needs to stay on track—if that falls through because of your lover's vendetta, we lose everything."

He takes a breath. "Most of all, Gabriel Grimm needs to disappear back into whatever hole he crawled out of."

"Or what?"

The question surprises us both. I'm not sure I've ever challenged him so directly.

My father goes very still. "Excuse me?"

"You heard me."

"You ungrateful little bitch."

"What did you do to him?" The words come out sharp. Fierce. I push back from the table and stand. "Five years ago. In Aspen. What really happened?"

Something flickers in my father's eyes. Just for a second. A crack in the mask. And that tells me everything.

"I don't know what you're talking about."

"I think you do. He was shot. Beaten. Left in a burning cabin to die." I step closer, searching his face for more cracks. "Someone made sure he'd believe I was involved. Wanted him to go to his grave believing the woman he loved wanted him dead. Why, Father? Why the hell would you do that?"

"Don't be absurd. If Gabriel Grimm crawled out of a fire with brain damage, that's not my problem."

"That's not an answer."

"It's the only answer I have. You're talking nonsense." He moves toward the door, then pauses, looking back at me. The fury in his eyes has gone cold. Calculating. This is the version of my father that terrifies me the most—not the volcanic rage, but the icy control. "Fix the gaming commission problem. Keep the merger on track. And stay away from Gabriel Grimm." His voice drops. "That's not a request, Isabella."

"And if I don't?"

He holds my gaze. "Don't test me, child. You should know better by now."

He strides out, the door slamming shut behind him.

I stand there for a long moment, my hands shaking, my heart racing.

I was right about Aspen. I'm certain I saw fear on his face. Fear of being caught. Fear of being exposed. Fear of whatever truth he's been hiding for five years.

I move to the window, then stare out at the Atlantic City skyline without really seeing it. Somewhere out there, Gabriel is fighting his own war. Planning his next move. Trying to decide if I'm his enemy or his salvation.

And somewhere in the past—in a fire that was supposed to destroy all evidence—lies the truth about what really happened that night.

My father knows. Maybe he ordered it. Maybe he just knows who did. But he knows.

I think about Gabriel. The web of scars on his shoulders. The bullet wounds that should have killed him. The rage that's lived in him all those years.

Five years of planning and building and waiting, all because he believed the woman he loved had betrayed him.

Because someone made sure the last thing he'd ever believe was that I wanted him dead.

That's not just murder. That's salting the earth. Making sure that even if he survived, Gabe would never trust me again.

My father operates like that. Not just destroying his enemies, but making sure nothing can ever grow there again.

The door to David's bedroom opens behind me, and I whip around to face David and Harper.

"Are you okay?" Harper asks.

"No." I wrap my arms around myself. "But I'm going to be."

"What did he want?"

"He just popped by to threaten me. To control me." I look at each of them in turn. "To feel me out and make sure I don't suspect the truth."

Harper and David exchange a glance. "Truth?" David asks.

"About Gabe."

Harper sucks in a breath. "You think your father was involved back then." It's not a question.

"I *know* he was involved." The certainty settles into my bones, cold and heavy. "I just have to prove it."

David frowns. "How?"

"I don't know. But I'm going to figure it out."

CHAPTER
NINETEEN

He shouldn't be there.

Gabriel stood in the recess of a service alcove that was conveniently located where he could stay mostly hidden but still see the door to Isabella's suite. He'd been there ever since he'd followed her father's angry march through the casino to Isabella's door. And even from across the hall, he'd heard the bastard's shouts.

He told himself he didn't care what Sterling had said to her behind that closed door. Whatever vitriol her father wanted to dole out, Isabella deserved.

But that satisfaction curdled into something else as the minutes ticked by. Something that felt uncomfortably like concern.

He told himself he was here for intelligence. To observe. To gather information that might be useful in his campaign against the Harts.

He was a goddamn liar.

Her door flew open, wrenching him away from his thoughts as he watched Sterling Hart storm past, face purple with fury, fists clenched.

Gabriel felt a twinge of dark satisfaction. Whatever had happened inside that suite, Sterling wasn't winning.

But had he hurt Isabella?

He pushed the worry down. Bella wasn't his problem. Not now. Not anymore.

He told himself that, and here he was, lurking near her door, seemingly unable to walk away.

She was still inside, probably alone now. Probably shaking. Probably trying to put her armor back together after whatever her father had just done to her.

He should leave. There was nothing to gain by staying. Nothing except—

The door opened again.

Harper emerged first, her face tight with worry. David Mercer was at her side, also worried, though he hid it better.

Gabriel stepped out of the shadow as they passed.

"Harper."

She spun around, eyes wide. David moved instantly, putting himself between Harper and Gabriel.

"What the hell are you doing here?" David's voice was low and dangerous. Not the smooth businessman Gabriel had seen at the engagement party. This was something rawer. More primal.

Interesting.

Gabriel ignored him, his focus on Harper. "I need to talk to you."

"She doesn't have anything to say to you." David didn't move. Didn't back down. "And you need to stay the fuck away from Bella."

"This doesn't concern you, Mercer."

"Everything about Bella concerns me." David stepped closer, and Gabriel saw something in his eyes that he recognized. Something that went beyond friendship. Beyond the engagement he'd believed to be nothing more than a business transaction.

The man was in love with her.

The realization hit Gabriel like a fist to the gut. Of course he was. Of course, this handsome, wealthy, safe man was in love with the woman Gabriel had spent five years hating. The woman he still dreamed about, still woke up hard and aching for, still wanted so badly it made him sick.

And she'd been with him—probably fucking him—for five years while Gabriel rotted in his self-imposed grave.

Five long years when he'd craved her—and all the while, she'd been building a life with someone else.

The jealousy was irrational. He knew that. She'd been the one who'd announced his death based on the teeth and blood and ring the authorities had found by the cabin, all planted by him.

And then he'd done everything in his power to make the world believe Gabriel Grimm really was dead. He'd stayed hidden, hadn't he?

So he had no right to feel betrayed. No right to want to tear David Mercer apart with his bare hands.

But he wanted to anyway.

Goddamn him to hell. He'd literally seen the bitch point the gun at him, but he was still jealous that she could have fallen for another man.

Ever heard of contact lenses? And in case you're wondering, surprise is a pretty common word.

He pushed the memory down as he looked Mercer in the eye. "Get the fuck out of my way."

"Make me."

Gabriel scoffed. He was bigger, stronger, trained in ways Mercer couldn't imagine. He could put the man on the ground in seconds.

But that wasn't why he hesitated.

He hesitated because Mercer wasn't backing down. Wasn't flinching. Was standing his ground despite knowing exactly who and what Gabriel was.

That took guts. Or stupidity. Or love.

Probably all three.

"I don't want to hurt you," Gabriel said, and was surprised to find it was true.

Mercer laughed bitterly. "No, you just want to hurt her. That's so much better."

"I want the truth. I want to know why she tried to kill me."

Mercer's eyes widened, and he glanced at Harper, who looked equally befuddled.

"She didn't."

Harper shot David a grimace, then crossed her arms and turned her focus to Gabriel. "You know I love you, but you are seriously out of line. She was fucking broken for years after you died. Do you understand that? _Broken_. Couldn't get out of bed. Couldn't eat. Couldn't function."

She took another step closer. "I grieved for you, Gabriel. Big time. But Bella? She was the walking dead. And now that she's finally come back to life, you show up and try to knock her six feet under again? Fuck that."

"Actually," she added, giving his chest a shove. "Fuck you."

Gabriel's jaw tightened, but he said nothing. This was Harper laying into him. The girl who'd been his closest friend for years. One third of The Trio. And he wanted to believe her. So help him, he wanted it to be true...even though the truth would make him more reprehensible than he already was.

"She went to Aspen after the fire," David said, his voice low and tentative. "Did you know that? Even though the investigators said there was nothing left to find, she went anyway. Spent a week in that frozen hellhole, walking the grounds, talking to local cops, determined to prove you had to be alive because no body was found."

He paused as if gathering himself. "She came back broken," David said. "Ripped to bits. But she went again and again and again. And you have the gall to stand there and say she didn't care? Didn't love you? Fuck that. You don't deserve her love."

Gabriel went still.

"It's true," Harper said softly. "She hired private investigators, too. Three different firms over two years. Spent a fortune trying to find answers because she couldn't let go. And when she finally learned about some men who bragged about killing you, the teeth, the fire…It nearly destroyed her all over again. Especially when she could never track them down."

Some men who bragged about killing you…

Fury cut through him at the words. Not at Harper. Not at David. Not even at his killers. This fury he had to carry on his own shoulders.

"Go," he said.

"Fuck you," David retorted. "If you think—"

Gabe turned and walked away himself.

"What a fucking shame she wasted so much time loving you," David said, his words seeming to echo in the hall. Gabriel tensed, fighting the urge to whip back around. To snarl that David didn't know what it was like to be left for dead, pain ripping through you as life oozed out.

But he didn't turn back. David was right. Gabriel deserved the harsh words. The torment. The torture.

Every goddamn scar.

She'd searched for him.

The eyes hadn't been hers.

It had all been part of the ruse his killer had set up to make him believe the woman who loved him had betrayed him.

And it had worked.

God help him, it had worked

CHAPTER
TWENTY

The back showroom is quiet, which isn't a surprise as it's well past three in the morning. But I couldn't sleep. I'd only intended to take a quick walk and clear my head. Instead, my feet carried me here, the only place that's ever truly felt like mine.

Now, I'm curled up on the old velvet couch, shoes kicked off, a glass of whiskey in my hand as I stare at a canvas I haven't looked at in months. *Stillwater,* he called it. Swirls of blue and green and silver that look like water caught mid-motion. Like a lake holding its breath.

I remember the day he painted it.

We'd driven upstate for a weekend away from the city, away from our families, away from everything that made our relationship complicated. We'd rented a cabin by a lake so still it looked like glass. We spent most of our first morning in bed, our bodies sated and tangled.

I can still remember the way the sunlight had streamed through the curtains, painting golden stripes across his face as he moved above me. The way he'd laughed when I pulled him back down for one more kiss. The way everything had felt possible, like the world was ours and nothing could ever touch us.

Then he'd led me outside, a blanket around my shoulders, and we'd sat on the dock watching the water.

"That's what you are to me," he'd said after a few moments. "Still on the surface. But underneath..." He'd pulled me closer, pressed his lips to my temple. "Underneath, you're a whole world I want to explore."

He'd started the painting that afternoon, then worked late into the night while I'd dozed on the couch. When the sun urged me awake the next morning, he was still at the easel, and the canvas was alive with motion and muted colors.

"Hey."

He'd looked up, clearly startled. I grinned, certain I'd just pulled him from what I called his artistic trance. I nodded toward the canvas. "It's beautiful."

His eyes met mine. "It is," he said. "It's you."

Now, I close my eyes as the memory washes over me, both sweet and painful.

I take a long swallow of whiskey, letting the burn chase away the softness. I can't afford softness right now. Can't afford to remember the man he used to be when the man he's become is systematically trying to destroy me.

I take another sip of whiskey and let my eyes drift to another canvas. This one is smaller, more intimate—a study of hands intertwined, painted in shades of gold and shadow. My hands and his. I'd watched him paint it one lazy Sunday afternoon, sitting across from him in his studio while rain streaked the windows.

Memories. Each of these canvases comes complete with memories. And right now it feels like torture being here. Loss and longing and only the tiniest bit of hope because at least he's alive.

But he's no longer mine.

How do I live with that?

I'm about to stand and force myself back to my suite when I hear footsteps, and my heart picks up tempo. Not Chris—he'd have called out when he realized the alarm's disabled. Not David —once he's asleep, it takes a marching band to rouse him. Not

Harper, she'd have texted first. And definitely not my father. I'd have felt the air turning to ice.

Gabriel.

"The gallery's closed," I say flatly. "And I'm not in the mood."

He doesn't respond. Doesn't leave, either. I can feel him standing there, watching me the way he's been watching me for days. Like I'm a puzzle he can't quite solve. Like I'm prey he's not sure he wants to devour.

"Are you here to torture me some more?" My voice is hard, and I still don't turn around. "Because I've already had a lovely conversation with my father, so I've met today's quota for emotional abuse."

Silence.

Then, quietly, "Isabella."

Something in his voice makes my heart skitter. Something broken. Something raw.

And, dammit, before I can order myself not to, I turn.

Gabriel stands in the doorway, looking completely destroyed. There's no other word for it. The cold mask he's been wearing since he walked back into my life is gone, shattered into a thousand pieces, and underneath it is devastation. His eyes are bloodshot. His posture tense, his arms stiff at his sides. He looks like a man who's just watched his entire world collapse around him and doesn't know how to stand in the rubble.

Good.

But the thought rings hollow. Because even now—even after everything he's done to me—seeing him in pain makes something hard twist in my chest. Some stupid, stubborn part of me still wants to go to him. Still wants to smooth the anguish and tell him everything will be okay.

I hate that. Hate that I still care. Hate that some treacherous corner of my heart still loves this man who's made it his mission to ruin my life.

"Get the hell out of here." I turn back to the painting, gripping my whiskey glass tighter.

"No."

"Fine." I stand up. "Then I'll go."

I take a step, and he moves to block my way. "Dammit," I snap. "What the hell do you want from me? I know you think I'm an evil bitch. You've told everyone who matters that I tried to have you killed, and you're doing your best to rip the world out from under me. So what now? What new torture are you here to inflict?"

Silence.

"Tell me. Tell me what else you could possibly want?"

His eyes meet mine, then dart away. "I was wrong."

I take a step back, fear bubbling. This is a trap. Somehow, this is a trap.

"I'm sorry," he says, his already wrecked expression shattering even more as the words hang between us, heavy as stones. "I'm so goddamn sorry."

I don't move. I don't even breathe.

"David told me," he continues, his voice rough as gravel. "More like read me the Riot Act. He and Harper both. The investigations. Aspen. Everything you did after...after I died."

A bitter laugh escapes him. "Except I didn't die. I let you believe I did, and you spent years trying to find out what really happened. Trying to find out who killed me. Trying to find justice for a dead man who was alive the whole time, hiding in the shadows, planning his revenge."

I swallow, then open my mouth to speak, but I have no words.

"I should never have believed what I believed," he says, the words barely a whisper.

He moves closer. Close enough that I can see the wreck of emotion playing across his face despite the armored shell he's built.

"They said they'd been hired by your father, but that you wanted to come personally." He shakes his head. "I still believe the part about your father."

He swallows, his eyes dipping to the ground. "The woman

who was with them—all I could see were her eyes. One blue. One green. And before she pulled the trigger," I saw her ring." He nods to my mother's ring. The one I always wear.

I start to speak, but my throat's too clogged with tears.

"She said *surprise*," he adds. "And then she pulled the trigger."

"Oh, god." I realize with a start that I'm sitting on the couch again.

"I should have known." His voice is low. Wrecked. "I *did* know. I knew you would never do that. And yet you did. You were there. Your eyes. Your ring. The only one who knew about the cabin. Who knew we'd been talking about a surprise party. It all made a horrible kind of sense." He draws in a long breath, then meets my eyes. "It still does."

I frown, then hug myself tighter as a shiver runs up my spine. "If it makes sense, why are you here?"

He turns to face Stillwater, but doesn't say a thing.

I stand, then take a single step toward him. "No, really. Walk me through it."

When he stays quiet, I fill the silence. "There you were, all psyched to kill me. But then I put on the show of the grieving girl-friend. I spent years trying to find answers."

I hear the bitterness creep into my voice and don't bother to hide it. "That's where your mind should go, right? That's what the SOB who doesn't trust me would think. *She's just covering her tracks.*"

"I guess it is," he says.

"Then why are you here?" I have to hug myself to keep from shaking. Not with fear. Not with smug redemption. Not even with joy. Honestly, I don't know why. Maybe because whatever happens next, this, at least, is an ending.

Trouble is, I can't quite see the new beginning that comes next.

"Why am I here?" he repeats, turning to face me. "Because I was an idiot."

The words are flat. Simple. And as they hang between us, I feel something break open inside me. *Hope*, tentative and terrified, but stirring back to life.

"I should never have believed what I knew in my heart was a lie."

He breaks off, then presses the heel of his hand against his eyes like he can force the tears back through sheer will. "I'm sorry. I'm so goddammed sorry."

I should feel vindicated. Should feel triumphant that he finally sees the truth. But all I feel is tired. So desperately, bone-deep tired.

He draws a breath, then meets my eyes. "I can't prove it wasn't you," he says, his voice flat. "The woman with the dual-colored eyes. I have no proof. All I have is what I know in my heart—what I should have always known. But I do know it. And I'm so, so sorry."

"Sorry," I repeat, the word bitter on my tongue.

How many times have I prayed for this, dreamed of it—Gabriel finally seeing the truth, finally understanding that I never could have hurt him?

A thousand times? A million?

But never did I imagine it would feel like this. Like a wound being reopened just as it was starting to scar over.

I set my whiskey glass on the small table beside the couch, then make finger quotes. "You *know* it? After everything? After the accusations and the stalking and the public humiliation, *poof*, you just know it?"

His brow furrows, but he says nothing. Smart man.

I take a step toward him. "And I'm supposed to—what? Fall into your arms? Forgive you? Pretend you haven't fucking tortured me ever since you slid into that damn Town Car beside me?"

"No." He shakes his head and takes a step closer, and I breathe in the familiar scent of sandalwood and vanilla. The scent of *my* Gabe. Except maybe he's not anymore.

"I don't expect forgiveness," he says. "I don't deserve it."

"You're right. You don't."

"I know."

"You destroyed me, you prick." The words lash out before I can stop them, all the pain I've been holding back finally breaking free like water through a crumbling dam. "Not five years ago—*now*. This week. You walked back into my life and accused me of killing the person I loved most in the world. Do you have any fucking idea what that felt like?"

"Yes." His voice is barely a whisper. "I know exactly what that's like."

The words stop me cold.

Because of course he does. That's what he's been living with for five years. Believing the woman he loved had tried to kill him. Carrying that betrayal like a knife in his chest, every single day, with every breath.

We've both been living in that same hell. Just different corners of it.

"I hate you," I say, but the words come out wrong. Too soft. Too broken. Too much like the opposite of what they mean.

"I know."

"I should tell you to leave. That I never want to see you again."

He takes a step toward me. "You should. You should kick me out. Push me away." His eyes meet mine. "I don't deserve a second chance. Not after what I let myself believe."

I cross my arms. "Then why the hell are you here?"

He looks toward *Stillwater*. "Because I can't stay away." His voice is a whisper, so low I can barely hear him. "I've tried. God, I've tried. But every time I close my eyes, I see your face. Every time I see something beautiful, I want to share it with you. Dammit, Bella, I hate that you still have this power over me. I hate that even when I believed you wanted me dead, I still—"

He stops. Swallows hard.

"You still what?"

"I still loved you." The confession tears out of him like it costs him everything he has left. "Even when I hated you, I loved you. Even when I was planning your destruction, I loved you. And now, knowing the truth, knowing what I almost did." His voice breaks completely. "I don't know how to stop loving you."

I stare at him. This broken, beautiful, infuriating man who put me through hell. I should walk away. Should protect myself from any more pain. Should make him grovel and beg and prove himself worthy before I give him anything.

But I've never been able to protect myself from Gabriel Grimm.

"I hate you," I say again. And then—before I can talk myself out of it—I close the distance between us and kiss him.

It's not a gentle kiss. It's brutal. Punishing. Years of fury and grief channeled into something that feels like war.

Gabriel makes a sound against my mouth—something between a groan and a sob—and then his hands are in my hair, fisting tight, pulling me closer with a desperation that steals the breath from my lungs. He kisses me like he's drowning and I'm air. His tongue warring with mine, his lips claiming, his hands holding me close as if they'll never let me go.

Heat blooms through me, immediate and devastating. My body remembers him—remembers this—even after all this time. Remembers the way his mouth moves against mine, the way his tongue slides past my lips, the way his hands grip my hips hard enough to bruise.

I should stop. Should slow down. Should make him work for this instead of giving him everything he wants.

But I don't want to stop. I want to burn. I want to consume and be consumed. I want to destroy us both so completely that there's nothing left but ash—and then rise from the ruins as something new.

"Izzy—" he gasps against my lips.

"*No*," I snap. "*Bella.*"

"Bella," he murmurs, then kisses me harder, deeper, in a way that makes my knees go weak. His hands slide down my back, then curve over my ass to pull me against him. I feel the hard length of his cock, and a bolt of pure need races straight to my core.

I tear at his shirt, fumbling with buttons, fingers clumsy with desperation. When they won't cooperate fast enough, I grip the fabric and pull. Buttons scatter across the gallery floor like tiny casualties of war. Gabriel breaks the kiss long enough to yank what's left of the shirt off, and I freeze, shocked into immobility by the sight in front of me.

His chest is a roadmap of suffering. Burns and cuts and three puckered bullet wounds that tell me just how close I came to losing him for real.

Scars that weren't there five years ago, written on his skin in brutal, permanent ink. Evidence of everything he survived while I was mourning him. Everything he endured while I was crying into my pillow, wishing I could hold him one more time.

"Gabriel." His name comes out broken, barely a whisper.

He tenses. Something guarded flickers across his face, and he starts to turn away, but I catch his arms and hold him in place with a grip that surprises us both.

"Don't." I press my palm flat against his chest, right over his heart, and feel it hammering under my hand. "Don't hide from me."

He swallows. "I'm not the man you remember."

"I'm not the same woman." I hold his gaze, letting him see the truth in my eyes. "I'm not the girl who fell in love with you all those years ago. She died when you did. What's left is...someone else. Someone harder."

"Someone stronger," he says quietly.

"Maybe." I trace my fingers along a scar that curves across his ribs, and he shivers under my touch. "Or maybe just broken in different places."

His hand comes up to cover mine, pressing it harder against his chest. "Bella." His voice is wrecked, raw as an open wound.

"Every single day. I told myself I hated you, but I never stopped missing you. Never stopped wanting you."

I kiss him again, hard and demanding. I don't want words right now. Words are horrible misunderstandings and lies and wasted years.

Bodies don't lie. And right now, I want to speak in the only language that's ever been completely honest between us.

I push him backward onto the couch and then we're a tangle of limbs on the cushions, his body hard and hot beneath mine.

He reaches for my shirt, his fingers trembling as he tugs it over my head. I'm not wearing a bra, and when he tosses my shirt away, he stares at me like he's seeing something holy. Like I'm a miracle he never expected to witness.

"Christ, Bella." His voice is reverent. Worshipful. "You're so beautiful. I used to dream about this. Even when I was trying to hate you, I dreamed about touching you. Tasting you. I'd wake up reaching for you, and you were never there, and I thought it was because you'd betrayed me. But it was because I was too fucking stubborn to question the lies I'd been fed." He pulls me down and kisses me softly. "I'm so goddamn sorry."

"I know." I frame his face with my hands. "I know you are. Now stop apologizing and really touch me."

Something sparks in his eyes—that familiar heat I remember from a thousand nights in his bed. His hands find my breasts, cupping, kneading, thumbs brushing across my nipples until they peak and strain against the fabric.

I arch into his touch, a moan slipping past my lips before I can stop it. It's been so long since I felt his touch. Tender and desperate all at the same time, yet mixed with a wildness that is almost primal. As if I'm sustenance. As if he'll die if he can't have me.

Sparks race to my core as his mouth closes over my breast, hot and wet and devastating. He traces his tongue around one nipple, teasing, before drawing it into his mouth and sucking hard enough to make me gasp as liquid heat races through my veins.

"Gabriel." His name is a plea, a prayer, a curse.

He switches to the other breast, lavishing it with the same devoted attention, and I thread my fingers through his hair—longer now than he used to wear it—and hold him against me. Every pull of his mouth sends sparks cascading through my nervous system. Every brush of his teeth against a nipple makes me squirm and writhe.

I need more. Need everything. Need to feel him inside me, filling the emptiness that's lived in my chest for years.

I reach between us, fumbling with his belt, and Gabriel groans against my skin, the vibration traveling through my body like an electric current.

"Bella, wait—"

"No waiting." I get the belt undone, work open the button of his pants with fingers that won't stop shaking. "We've waited five years. I'm done waiting."

"He pulls back enough to meet my eyes, and what I see there makes my heart stutter. Vulnerability. Fear. Hope so fragile it looks like it might shatter at the slightest touch.

"Are you sure?" His voice is a whisper. "After everything I've done?"

I press my palm against his chest, feel his heart racing against my hand. "All I'm sure of is that if you don't fuck me right now, I'm going to lose my mind."

Amusement fires in his eyes. And while the vulnerability doesn't disappear, something else rises alongside it—something dark and hungry and utterly male. Then, without another word, he flips us so I'm beneath him, pressed into the cushions with his body covering mine.

The rest of our clothes disappear in a frenzy of pulling and tugging and desperate hands. And then there's nothing between us—no fabric, no lies, no five years of misunderstanding. Just skin against skin, heat against heat, breath mingling with breath.

He settles between my thighs, and I can feel his cock, hard and ready, pressing against me, and the anticipation is almost unbearable. I'm wet. Aching. Empty.

And I so desperately want to be filled.

"Bella." His voice is wrecked, stripped down to nothing but need. "I need to hear you say it."

"Say what?"

"That you want this. Even if you hate me. Even if you never forgive me. I need to know this is what you want."

I look up at him. This man I loved. This man I lost. Who completely broke me.

And who I want right now more than anything in the world.

"I already told you," I whisper. "Please, Gabe. I want you inside me."

He pushes inside me with one long, relentless stroke, and I cry out—from the stretch, the fullness, the overwhelming sensation of having him inside me again after so long. I moan, arching up. Wanting more. Wanting all of him. "More." I dig my nails into his back, feel the raised ridges of scars beneath my fingers. "Please, Gabriel. Please fuck me harder."

He does.

It's not gentle. It's not tender. It's five years of grief and rage and desperate longing channeled into something primal, something elemental. He drives into me with a ferocity that borders on violence, and I meet him thrust for thrust, our bodies crashing together like storms colliding.

The pleasure builds like a wave, like a wildfire, like something too big to contain. Every stroke hits that spot deep inside me that makes stars explode behind my eyes. Every roll of his hips grinds against my clit, sending shockwaves rippling through my body.

"Christ, Bella." His voice is ragged, desperate.

"I know." I pull him closer, wrap my legs around his hips, so he sinks even deeper. "I know. Me, too."

He buries his face in my neck, and I feel his breath, hot and ragged, his body tense and tight, like he's holding back the explosion to come.

"Bella." My name on his lips, over and over, like an incantation. Like a spell to ward off all the darkness that's lived between us. "Bella, Bella, Bella."

I don't know who's destroying whom anymore. Maybe we're destroying each other. All I know is that I want to rip him apart. To shatter him. To break him down completely. Not as punishment, but as repentance. So that somehow we can move forward past the pain.

And then I'm not thinking at all. I'm just feeling. Hot and wild and deliciously used.

"Gabe." My voice is rough with need. "I'm close. I'm so close."

He hooks one of my legs over his shoulder in a stretch that makes me cry out, then drives deeper than I thought possible. I arch up, groaning as pleasure rolls through me, making me forget everything except the feeling of him inside me and the impossible pleasure that's building to a wild and desperate crescendo.

"Come for me," he demands.

And I do.

The orgasm rips through me like an earthquake. Like the end of the fucking world. I scream his name—actually scream, loud enough that security might come running—and my body arches off the couch as wave after wave of pleasure crashes through me.

Gabriel follows a heartbeat later, crying my name as if it's been ripped out of him. I feel him pulsing inside me, feel his body shudder, feel the moment he completely lets go before finally, collapsing, his weight on me like the most real thing I've felt in five long years.

Time means nothing as we lie there, tangled together on the couch, both breathing hard, hearts racing in tandem, sweat cooling on our skin.

Eventually, he lifts his head and looks at me, his face awash with love and grief and hope and fear. "I'm sorry."

"For that?" I tease, though I know that's not what he means.

He brushes a strand of hair off my face, then presses a finger to my lips. "Let me say this. Let me say I'm sorry, even though that's not enough. Even though words can't erase what I did. What I believed. But I am sorry. For all of it. For every moment of pain I caused you."

"I know you are," I say.

"Does that mean you forgive me? *Can* you forgive me?"

I look away, then force myself to meet his eyes again. "I don't know. You believed the worst about me. You truly thought I could do that to you, and you came back to destroy me. You believed the lie while I spent five years in agony missing you."

He closes his eyes, then gives a brief nod when he opens them again. "I understand." The word is barely a whisper.

I draw a deep breath, then let it out slowly as I look him in the eye. "But I want to try," I say. "I want to find out if whatever this is between us can survive what we've been through."

"*Whatever this is,*" he repeats. "Once upon a time, you would have called it love."

"For what it's worth, I do still love you. Apparently, I'm as foolish as my father's always telling me. But that's not enough."

"No," he agrees. "But maybe we can call it a start?"

I see the hope that flickers in his eyes, but I stay silent. I have hope, too. But I'm holding it close, shielding it like a candle flame.

"I'll do whatever it takes," he says. "Whatever you need. However long it takes.

I should tell him to go now. Promise that we can talk more tomorrow. But his body is still warm against mine, and even though I don't know if I still want him forever, I know that I want him for now.

"Stay," I whisper. "Just for tonight. Stay here with me."

It's not forgiveness. It's not trust. It's not anything close to the happily ever after I used to dream about for us.

But it's a start.

And right now, a start is everything.

CHAPTER
TWENTY-ONE

I wake up slowly, drifting up from sleep like a swimmer rising toward light.

For a moment, I don't remember where I am. The surface beneath me is velvet, not cotton. The air smells like old wood and something else—something warm and male and achingly familiar.

Gabriel.

Memory floods back. The confrontation. The confession. The desperate, devastating sex on this couch, surrounded by his paintings.

I open my eyes.

He's propped up on one elbow, watching me. The cold mask is gone, replaced by something softer—something that looks almost like the man I fell in love with years ago. His free hand is tracing lazy patterns on my bare shoulder, feather-light touches that send shivers across my skin.

"Hi," he says quietly.

"Hi."

"You're beautiful when you sleep." His fingers drift up to my hair, tucking a strand behind my ear. "You always were. I used to watch you for hours."

"That's creepy."

"Probably." A ghost of a smile touches his lips. "I was creepy about a lot of things when it came to you. Obsessive. Possessive." The smile fades. "Turns out those tendencies didn't go away when I thought you'd betrayed me. They just got darker."

I should respond to that. Should say something meaningful about last night and the impossible tangle of emotions sitting heavy in my chest.

I don't.

Instead, I sit up, covering myself with the throw blanket. "What time is it?"

Gabriel checks his watch. "Almost four in the morning."

"We should..." I trail off. Should what? Go back to my suite, where David is probably waiting with questions I don't know how to answer? Pretend last night didn't happen, even though I'm wildly glad it did?

"Come back to my place," he says, sitting up. "We can talk. Get some real sleep."

I should probably say no. It's going to be light in just a few hours, and I have things to do here at the Monarch. But I just spent hours in Gabriel's arms. A Gabriel who loves me—not a Gabriel who's been tormenting me.

So I say yes, and soon we're both dressed and in his Porsche, then tumbling out into the Obsidian's parking garage before hurrying through the sub-basement hallways to the rhythm of men pounding each other in the ring, even at this hour.

I glance sideways at him, but he just shrugs as if to say *You know who I am now, and you came. Deal with it.*

So, yeah. I'm dealing.

Unlike the hall, his apartment—quarters?—is quiet. Familiar, even. But now, I'm looking at it through different eyes.

The thought reminds me of my first time here, and my eyes dart to where I'd seen the crumpled photo of me and David and that kiss.

It's gone.

I glance at Gabe and find him looking back at me. "I tossed it," he says. "Yesterday, actually."

"Oh?" I try to sound casual, but inside, I'm gleeful. Before, this apartment had felt like enemy territory. Now, it feels like hope.

"I can make coffee," he says. "And there's a real bed, if you want to sleep. And a shower."

"Coffee," I say, both because it's so freaking normal and because I could use some. "Coffee would be good."

He grins, and some of the tension he's still carrying eases. "Coming right up."

Exhaustion catches up with me, and I settle onto the sofa as he moves around the kitchen. The space is warm despite being underground, with the only natural light coming from four high windows.

"How long have you been living down here?" I ask.

"Since I came back. A little shy of four years." He sets a mug of coffee on the table beside me, then sits on the opposite end of the sofa with his own cup.

"Before that, I was with Travis and Anissa in Aspen. They're the reason I'm alive."

"The reason? What do you mean?"

He'd been looking straight at me. Now he seems focused more on my chin. "Travis found me," he says softly. " In the woods, barely alive. He took me back to his place—I managed to stay conscious long enough to beg him not to call the cops. He'd been a medic in the military, then a Texas Ranger after that, and he'd taught Anissa what he knew. Between the two of them, they kept me alive. Well, them and my dreams of vengeance."

"Against those men," I whisper. "And me."

"Just you," he says. "The men were nothing to me. Not then. Not while I was trying to hang on." He flashes an ironic grin. "So, yeah, I'm alive because I loved you enough to truly hate you."

I blink back fresh tears. "I'm so sorry."

He takes my hand. "Don't be. We've danced this one already.

It wasn't you. But, hey, the fact that I thought it was really did give me something to live for, dark though that might be."

I bite my lower lip, hesitate, then plow forward. "About Anissa. Was there ever—" I cut myself off with a shake of my head, feeling like a seventh-grader. Gabe, however, looks delighted.

"I love her," he says, his voice completely serious.

"Oh."

The corner of his mouth twitches. "Like a sister."

I scowl and suppress the urge to whack him with a pillow. Then I say *fuck it* and smack him anyway. Because this is what I missed. Talking with him. Being close to him. Sharing all sorts of gooey emotional stuff with him.

As if he can read my mind, he reaches over and twines his fingers with mine. Hell, maybe he *can* read my mind.

"What about your brothers? I mean, you texted Leo, but why didn't you reach out before? To him or any of them? They could have been searching for the men all this time."

He shakes his head. "No. Those men. You. Your father. They were my prey, not my brothers'."

"But still. Just for them to know you were alive."

"Couldn't risk it. Couldn't risk anyone being dragged into my war with your father. And I couldn't face them." He stops, then looks down at the floor. "I couldn't tell them what had happened, what I believed you'd done. Leo loved you like a sister. If I'd told him..." He trails off with a shudder and a very harsh sound.

"No," I say. "Leo would have defended me."

"And I would have thought he was compromised. Fooled, the way I'd been fooled." He drags his fingers through his hair, then reaches for my hand again.

"I wasn't thinking clearly," he says, his fingers twining with mine. "Wasn't capable of it. After what they did to me, I can't—I *couldn't*—trust anyone.

"And now?" The question comes out softer than I'd intended, and for a moment, I feel like I'm made of glass.

"I guess that part of me's healed up," he says, just as softly. "I trust you, Bella. Looking back, I'm ashamed I ever didn't."

"It hurt," I tell him. "I won't lie. But I get it. And I'm so sorry you had to go through all of that. That my own father put you through all of that. Sorry," I repeat, "but not surprised. I have no illusions about that man."

"He managed one good thing."

I frown. "Seriously? What?"

"You."

My heart literally flutters, and I lean over to kiss him on the cheek, his beard tickling my lips. A kiss that turns much hotter and wilder when he shifts, capturing my mouth with his in a kiss that's wild and desperate and needy. The kind of kiss that heats skin and melts bone and sends need running through your veins instead of blood.

His fingers twine in my hair, and his palm cups my head, holding me in place while he devours me with his kisses, wilder than I remember and full of a desperate need that matches my own, making me want and crave, my body begging for more. It's wild and wonderful. Familiar and yet not. This is the man I love—the only man I've ever loved, and the memories flood back with each touch, each stroke, each claiming, brutal kiss.

When we finally break apart—both of us breathing hard—I expect him to rip my shirt off. To slide his fingers into my jeans. To tell me to stand up and strip. Or just to pull me close in one of those long, deep kisses that almost feel like fucking.

Instead, he squeezes my hand and whispers, "We should get some sleep."

For a moment, I sit there, as startled as if he'd dumped a pail of cold water all over me. "Oh. Yeah. I guess we should."

"I'll take the sofa. There's an actual bed back in the storage area I use as a bedroom."

"Oh. Okay." I shouldn't be disappointed, but I am. "Well, goodnight, Gabriel."

"Goodnight, Isabella."

I nod and head down the short hall, then I open the door across from the bathroom to reveal the tiny space with only a twin-sized mattress bed and a single painting on the wall.

It's me.

I'm sleeping, my face peaceful, my hair is longer, like I used to wear it, and spread across a pillow. The brushstrokes are looser than his usual style, almost impressionistic, like he painted it from memory rather than life.

Because he did.

He must have painted this after he thought I'd betrayed him. After he believed I wanted him dead.

And still, he painted me like this. Soft. Beautiful. *Loved.*

I stand there for a long time, staring at that painting, feeling something crack open in my chest.

Then I step back into the hallway and stand where I can see him still sitting on the sofa. "Gabe?"

He looks up.

"Will you—I mean, not sex. But will you come sleep with me?"

His smile is slow. "Yeah," he says. "I'd like that."

CHAPTER
TWENTY-TWO

Morning comes too soon.

I wake to the smell of coffee brewing and bacon sizzling, and I stay under the covers for a moment, staring at the painting of myself and taking stock of all the things that have shifted in the cyclone that has been these last few days.

Gabriel is alive.

Gabriel believes me.

Gabriel painted me like something precious, even when he hated me.

All of these things are true. All of these things should make me feel something—joy, relief, hope, anything.

And I do. I feel all of that.

But somehow I feel hollow, too. As if all his confessions and kisses and apologies will never be enough to fill the ache that looms inside me like some dark, empty, hungry place.

But hungry for what? His apology? He's already given that. His love? I truly believe I still have that. His trust?

Maybe.

Because no matter how much he might have loved me five years ago, he still didn't trust me.

He had good reason. The little voice in my head is right. But I'm done thinking about it. Instead, I push the thoughts aside, then pad to the bathroom in my shirt and underwear.

I find a robe hanging there and put that on before heading to the main room and the scent of breakfast.

He's at the counter, shirtless, wearing only a pair of low-slung sweatpants. The scars on his back are as brutal as the ones on his chest—long, raised welts that crisscross his skin like a roadmap of suffering. He must have heard me because he turns, and his face softens when he sees me.

"Morning." He gestures to the counter. "Coffee's ready. No kitchen, but we can go up to the hotel restaurant. Or I can ask Anissa to bring something down."

I know there's nothing between them, but just the idea that she takes care of him like that makes me unreasonably jealous. "The Gabriel Grimm I knew wouldn't be without cereal."

He laughs. "Kashi it is. I can even manage a banana cut up on top."

I laugh. "Such refined taste."

"That's me. A born aristocrat."

I pour myself coffee, then follow him to the tiny table for our breakfast. It's surreal, this domestic scene. Gabriel making me breakfast like we're a normal couple. But that's not the real surprise. No, that's the way being here *feels*. Comfortable. Relaxed. Both casual and intimate.

It's as if the last five years didn't happen. Like we didn't spend part of last night fucking out our grief on a velvet couch surrounded by paintings of our lost love.

"You saw the painting," he says quietly. Not a question.

I pause, a spoonful of cereal frozen in mid-air. "The one by the bed? It would have been hard not to."

"I painted it about a year after Aspen. Couldn't stop myself. I tried to destroy it a dozen times. Couldn't do that either."

"Gabe."

"I hated myself for still wanting you despite what I believed you'd done."

He shakes his head. "Anyway. We should eat before this gets soggy."

He's deflecting. Protecting himself before the conversation gets too real. I recognize the tactic because I use it too.

"Okay," I say, letting him have this one.

As soon as I finish my cereal, I take the bowl back to the sink, then lean against it, watching him eat.

His eyes narrow. "What?"

"Just thinking. This place—it's you, but it's not. I guess it makes me realize I don't really know you anymore." The words come out before I can stop them. "That five years is a long time, and we're both different people now, and I don't know how we bridge that gap."

He's quiet for a moment. "Do you want to?"

"Yes." The answer comes immediately, without thought. "Yes," I repeat, meaning it with all my heart. "I'm just afraid we don't know how."

Gabriel leaves his bowl on the small table, then comes to stand beside me, both our backs to the sink. He stands close, his arm sliding around my waist, and I lean against him, warm and solid and *here*. That's what's overwhelming. That he's here. I'd gotten so used to him being gone that every touch, every glimpse feels like both surprise and celebration. "Yes," I say again. "I want to get back what we lost."

"Then we figure it out," he says. "Day by day. Conversation by conversation. We learn each other again."

"And if we don't like what we find?" I'd spoken the words without thinking, and now I wish I could call them back. They seem to hang in the air between us, and I see the flicker of fear in his eyes—the same fear that lives in me.

The fear that we've been through too much. That the people we've become can't fit together the way we used to.

"Then at least we'll know," he says finally. "But I don't think that's going to happen."

"Why not?"

"Because when I look at you, I still see my Izzy. And I have to believe that means your Gabe is still in here somewhere, too. We'll find each other again," he says. "I know we will."

I want to believe him. God, I want to believe him. But there's still that empty place that his words can't soothe. That place inside me that cries out that he believed me capable not just of murder, but of murdering *him*. And, yeah, I get that he was tortured and manipulated and broken into believing it.

But understanding isn't the same as healing.

And healing takes time.

I'm willing to give it all the time in the world. I hope to hell that he is, too.

"Okay," I finally say. "We've got this. Day by day."

He smiles then, a real smile, wide and toothy. The first one I've seen since he came back from the dead.

It transforms his face, makes him look younger, softer. And even with the beard, it makes him look more like the man I fell in love with.

I try to smile back, and almost manage it this time.

It's not everything. Not yet. But it's a start.

WE SPEND THE AFTERNOON APART—ME at the Monarch, putting out fires and dodging my father's calls, him doing whatever it is he does in that underground world of his. But when I slip back into his apartment as the sun sets over Atlantic City, he's waiting.

Not at his easel. Not on the couch. He's standing beneath the high window, staring up at the sliver of sky, and when he turns to look at me, there's something raw in his expression. Something hungry.

"Everything okay?"

"No." He crosses to me in three long strides, and before I can ask what's wrong, his hands are cupping my face and his mouth is on mine.

This kiss is different from last night, both at the gallery and when we came back here. That was wild desperation. This is slower. Deeper. Like he's trying to memorize the shape of my lips, the taste of my tongue, every small sound I make against his mouth.

"Gabe." His name is as soft as breath.

"I spent all day thinking about you," he murmurs, his forehead pressed to mine. "Couldn't focus. Couldn't paint. Couldn't do anything except remember how you felt in my arms last night."

Heat pools between my thighs. "And?"

"And I realized something." He pulls back just enough to meet my eyes. "Last night was about anger. About grief. About trying to fuck away five years of pain on that damn slippery velvet."

I laugh. "It worked," I whisper.

"I guess it did. His thumb traces my lower lip, and I shiver. "Because I woke up this morning and I still wanted you. But not to punish. Not to prove anything. Just...to have you. To be inside you. To watch your face when you come apart."

Oh god.

"So that's what I want now." His hands slide down my arms, leaving goosebumps in their wake. "I want to take my time. I want to learn your body again—every curve, every sound, every place that makes you gasp." His lips brush my ear. "I want to make you come so many times you forget your own name. And then I want to do it again."

My knees actually wobble. "That's...very specific."

"I've had all day to think about it." He's smiling now—that wicked smile I remember from before, the one that always meant I was in for a very long, very satisfying night. "Any objections?"

"Not a single one."

He kisses me again, and this time there's no hurry. Just the slow, devastating exploration of his mouth on mine, his tongue sliding past my lips like he has all the time in the world. His hands find the hem of my shirt, then slip underneath to trace the curve of my waist with agonizing patience.

"Bedroom," I manage against his mouth.

"Eventually."

He walks me backward until my shoulders hit the wall, then drops to his knees in front of me. My breath catches as he looks up, those ice-blue eyes burning into mine while his fingers work the button of my slacks.

"Gabe—"

"Shh." He tugs the silk down my hips, taking my underwear with it. "I told you. I'm taking my time."

And he does.

His mouth finds the inside of my thigh first—soft kisses, the scrape of his beard, the hot press of his tongue against sensitive skin. I'm already trembling by the time he reaches the apex, already wound so tight I might shatter.

Then his mouth is on me, his tongue teasing my clit, and I stop thinking entirely.

He knows my body. Even after five years, even after everything that fell down around us, he knows exactly how to take me apart. Slow, devastating strokes of his tongue. The press of his fingers inside me, curling just right. The way he groans against my flesh like I'm the best thing he's ever tasted.

I come with his name on my lips and my fingers fisted in his hair.

He doesn't stop.

"Gabe," I gasp as he works me through the aftershocks and straight into another climb. "I can't."

"You can." His voice vibrates against me. "Again."

The second orgasm hits harder than the first, a wave that crashes through me and leaves me boneless. My legs give out entirely, but he catches me, rises, presses me back against the wall with his body while I remember how to breathe.

"Bedroom now?" I manage weakly.

"Now," he agrees.

He carries me there—actually carries me like I weigh nothing —and lays me on the bed with a gentleness that makes my chest ache. Then he strips off his shirt, and I watch the scars ripple across his skin as he moves. Beautiful and brutal.

Mine.

"Your turn," I say, reaching for him.

He lets me undress him. Lets me trace each scar with my fingers, then my lips. The bullet wounds. The burns. The raised welts that crisscross his back. I kiss every one of them, feeling him shudder under my touch.

"Izzy." He catches himself. "*Bella.*"

"You can call me Izzy." The words surprise me, but they're true. "When we're like this. When it's just us."

Something cracks open in his expression. "Izzy."

"Yeah." I pull him down to me. "Now stop talking and fuck me."

He does.

But not fast. Not rough. He slides into me inch by devastating inch, watching my face the whole time, drinking in every gasp and moan like he's dying of thirst and I'm water. When he's all the way inside, he goes still.

"I missed this." His voice is wrecked. "Missed you. Every single day."

"Show me."

He moves then—long, deep strokes that hit places I'd forgotten existed. His mouth finds mine, swallowing my cries. His hands are everywhere, touching, claiming, worshipping.

We build together, slow and steady, a fire that burns rather than explodes. I feel another orgasm coiling in my core, and from the way his rhythm falters, he's close too.

"Together," I whisper. "Please."

"Always." He drives deeper, harder, and I shatter around him just as he groans my name and follows me over the edge.

Afterward, we lie tangled together, sweat-slicked and

breathing hard. His hand traces lazy patterns on my hip. My head rests on his chest, right over his heartbeat.

"Day one," he murmurs.

I smile against his skin. "Day one."

It's a beginning. And right now, with his arms around me and his heart beating under my ear, it feels like it's enough.

TWENTY-THREE

Three days later, I'm having coffee with Harper and Anissa at the small cafe on the east side of the Obsidian's lobby. It's quiet and lovely with the feel of a European cafe. It's not quite four, so Anissa's still technically working, but it's a slow time, and she's letting a trainee run the front desk while she keeps an eye on him from afar.

"I still can't believe how lucky Gabe is that your dad found him," Harper says. "It's like a miracle."

Anissa nods. "I guess it kind of was. He wanted to do some hunting over behind Gabe's cabin, so he was heading that way to ask if Gabe minded. Turns out Gabe had managed to drag himself a good ways, so Dad found him in the woods near the cabin. Nick of time, too," she says, with an apologetic look to me. "He was seriously fucked up. I mean, you've seen the scars, right?"

I nod.

"Well, I haven't," Harper says. "But I'll take your word for it until I'm sure that showing them to me won't throw him into a funk."

I reach over and take Anissa's hand. "I owe you big-time," I tell her.

"You don't. Neither does Gabe. He's family now. Besides, you're really good for him."

"Yeah?" I feel my cheeks go pink with pleasure.

"At first—well, you know. I really thought he was going to kill you. After I met you, though, I was sure it wasn't you. The bitch who was with those murderous pricks, I mean."

"He told you? About how she must have faked my eyes?"

She nods. "That was the deepest wound. You, I mean. Now that he knows it wasn't actually you—well, now that he believes it —It's like he's getting back to how I imagine he was before all of that happened. When he was with us…

She trails off with a shudder, then takes another sip of coffee.

"Will you tell me?" I ask.

She frowns, then looks between Harper and me. "I probably shouldn't, but he loves you both. And you should probably know. In case—well, honestly, in case he goes off the rails."

I meet Harper's eyes. "Yeah," she says. "We probably should."

Anissa nods but doesn't speak right away. Instead, she just traces her finger around the rim of her mug. "Broken," she finally says. "I mean, you both know that, but I'm talking shattered into tiny shards, broken. Psychically and physically. I mean, he was more wound than man for those first few months. That was his body. As for the rest, it was like the part of him that knew how to be human had just switched off."

Harper and I exchange a glance, and I can see the horror and heartbreak in her eyes, and I'm sure she sees the same in mine.

"He didn't talk for the first three weeks," Anissa continues. "Not a word. Just stared out at nothing. Dad thought maybe the fever had damaged his brain. But then one night I heard him screaming—nightmares—and when I ran in, he grabbed my arm so hard he left bruises." She shrugs. "That's when I knew he was still in there. Just…buried under a lot of pain."

"Gabe," Harper's voice catches. "Oh, god."

"The rage came later. He made a promise to catch and kill

whoever did that to him. And as soon as he made that promise, he started training. Like obsessively. Like if he stopped moving, the darkness would swallow him whole."

She finishes off her latte, then shrugs. "That's how he coped," she says with a shrug. "Still does, when it gets bad. The fighting, the training—it's not about violence for him. It's about…I guess you'd say he's trying to burn it out.

"He never talked to anyone?" Harper asks. "A therapist?

Anissa laughs, but there's no humor in it. "Gabriel Grimm, talk about his feelings? Please. Dad tried. I tried. But he just shut down every time. I think painting was his only therapy. "We've got a shit ton of his canvases in storage in Aspen. For a while, he barely ate. Just painted. And he'd go days without even speaking. And when he finally finished a canvas, he'd be a little more human. Like he was *there*."

She pauses, then looks at me. "He painted you the most, even though he said he hated you."

I sip my coffee, trying to swallow the lump in my throat.

"The thing is," Anissa continues, "I've never seen him like he's been lately." She tilts her head, studying me. "He's still fucked up. But he's lighter, too. Like he's remembered what hope looks like, you know? And his cards have been lighter lately, too. Less swords, more cups. And his energy isn't so jagged anymore. Still a mess, but a healing mess."

"I'll take whatever I can get," I tell her. I down the final sip of my coffee. "Speaking of, I'm going to go see him." I look at both of them. "Coming?"

Harper shakes her head. "Give him a hug for me, but I have to go hop on a video call with Elliott and—honestly, I don't even know what it's about. He's probably just sick of London and wants company."

"I can't either," Anissa says when I glance her way. "Front desk duty. I can't leave the ducklings alone yet."

Having thus been blown off by my friends, I make my way

down to the corridor that leads to Gabe's place. And as I do, I realize I'm smiling. It's nice to have Anissa's perspective. It makes clear that he's already come a long, long way.

But when I step through the door and see him pounding the shit out of a punching bag, my gut twists, and I know there's still a long, long way to go.

For a moment, I just stand there. He hasn't seen me yet. He's too far gone, lost in whatever demon he's battling, fists slamming into the bag with a fury that makes the chain rattle and groan.

I should announce myself. Should clear my throat or say his name.

Instead, I watch.

There's something hypnotic about it. The coiled power in his shoulders. The way his muscles flex and release with each strike. The raw, primal energy rolling off him in waves.

This is the Beast. The thing he's been trying so hard to keep leashed around me. The darkness he's terrified will swallow us both.

And I realize, watching him, that Anissa had it pretty much right. This is how he survives it. This is how he's survived it for five years. Not by healing. Not by processing. But by beating it out of himself, blow by blow, until his knuckles split and his muscles scream and there's nothing left but exhaustion.

"Gabe."

His head snaps toward me, and for a split second, I see it—the wildness in his eyes, the predator surfacing before he shoves it back down.

"Bella." He's breathing hard. "I didn't hear you come in."

"Clearly." I set my bag on the counter, but don't move toward him. Not yet. "What's going on?"

"Nothing." He grabs a towel, wipes his face. His knuckles are red. Battered. "Just...burning it off."

"Burning what off?"

He doesn't answer. Just stands there, chest heaving, the towel clenched in his fists like he's fighting the urge to go back to the bag.

"Gabe. Talk to me."

"You don't want to hear it."

"Yeah, I really do."

His jaw tightens. When he finally speaks, his voice is low. Rough. Like the words are being dragged out of somewhere deep and dark.

"It never stops." He stares at the bag, not at me. "The rage. The fear. The fucking darkness that lives inside me. I wake up and it's there. I go to sleep and it's there. Every time I close my eyes, I'm back in that cabin, and I can smell the smoke and feel the ropes and hear them laughing."

His hand slams into the bag once, hard. "It never fucking stops."

My heart cracks open. "Gabe."

"This is how I survive it." Another punch, then another. "This is how I keep from destroying everything around me. I beat it out until there's nothing left. Until I'm too tired to feel anything."

"And does it work?"

He laughs—a hollow, broken sound. "For a few hours. Maybe. Then it all comes back."

I cross to him slowly. He tenses when I get close, like he's afraid of what he might do.

"Don't." His voice is strained. "I'm not...I'm not safe right now, Bella. I need to get this under control."

"Or what?"

"Or I might lose it completely." He finally looks straight at me, and what I see in his eyes steals my breath. Not anger. *Desperation.* The look of a man drowning in his own darkness and terrified he's going to drag me under with him. "I don't want to hurt you."

"You won't."

"You don't know that. You don't know what I'm capable of when I'm like this."

"Then show me."

He goes very still.

"Use me," I say quietly. "Instead of the bag. Use me."

"That's insane."

"Is it?" I step closer, close enough to feel the heat radiating off his skin. "You need to burn it out? Burn it into me. You need to lose control? Lose it with me." I reach up, cup his face in my hands, and force him to meet my eyes. "I'm not afraid of your darkness, Gabriel. I'm not afraid of the beast. So stop trying to protect me from it and just let go."

"I could hurt you." The words are barely a whisper.

"You won't."

"You can't know that."

"I can. I know you." I hold his gaze, steady and sure, and in that moment, I realize it's not an act. Maybe I should be scared, but I'm not. Whatever it is he needs, he can get from me—I'm certain of it. More, I'm certain he can get it without hurting me.

I take his hand. "I trust you. I know you," I repeat. "I know that even when you hated me, you couldn't bring yourself to truly destroy me. I know that the man who painted me reaching for light would never snuff that light out. I know that the Beast isn't separate from you—it's part of you. And I love all of you."

I press my forehead to his, my arms sliding around his waist. "So stop fighting it," I say. "Stop fighting yourself. Just be with me. All of you. Even the parts you're afraid of."

For one endless moment, nothing happens. He just breathes, ragged and harsh, his whole body trembling with the effort of holding himself back.

Then something in him breaks, like a dam finally giving way after years of pressure.

His mouth crashes into mine, and there's nothing gentle about it. It's teeth and tongue and raw, desperate hunger—not for sex, but for release. For absolution. For someone to hold all the broken pieces of him and not flinch.

I don't flinch.

I grab his shoulders and pull him closer, meeting his intensity with my own. When his hands tear at my clothes, I help him. When he lifts me and pins me against the wall, I wrap my legs around him and hold on.

"Tell me to stop," he gasps against my throat, his voice wrecked. "Tell me this is too much."

"Don't stop. Don't ever stop."

He yanks my knit skirt down, then pushes my panties aside to enter me in one hard thrust. I cry out—not from pain, but from the sheer overwhelming rightness of it. This is what he needs. What we both need. Not careful lovemaking, but this raw, primal claiming.

He moves like a man possessed, driving into me with a force that shoves me up the wall with every thrust. And I take it. Take all of it. Take his rage and his fear and his five years of darkness and meet it with my own.

"Harder," I gasp against his ear. "Give me all of it."

He groans—a sound torn from somewhere deep—and obeys. One hand fists in my hair, the other grips my hip hard enough to bruise. The pleasure and the pain blur together into something transcendent.

"Izzy." My name is like a prayer. "God, Izzy."

"I've got you," I whisper, even as my body hurtles toward release. "I've got you. Let go."

He does.

I feel the moment he stops holding back. Stops trying to control the beast and just surrenders to it completely, trusting me to survive the storm.

We shatter together.

The orgasm rips through me, and I hear myself scream his name as he roars mine, his whole body shuddering as he pours everything—the rage, the grief, the darkness, all of it—into me.

We stay there for a long time, pinned against the wall, breathing hard. His face is buried in my neck. His shoulders are shaking.

It takes me a moment to realize he's crying.

"Hey." I stroke his hair, his back, anywhere I can reach. "Hey. I'm here. I've got you."

"I'm sorry." His voice is muffled, broken. "I'm so sorry. For all of it. For everything.

"Shh." I tilt his face up, make him look at me. His eyes are red, wet, devastated. "You don't have to apologize. Not for this. Not for any of it."

"I could have hurt you."

"But you didn't." I kiss his forehead, his cheeks, the salt tracks of his tears. "You didn't. And you won't. Because the beast isn't separate from you, Gabe. It's not some monster waiting to break free. It's just you. The parts of you that learned to survive. And I love those parts too."

He stares at me like I've just handed him something precious. Something he never expected to hold.

He kisses me then. Soft and achingly tender after what we just did. And I taste his tears and his relief and something that feels like hope.

We make it to the bathroom, and he cleans us both up with hands that have finally stopped shaking.

"You're okay?" he asks quietly. "Really?"

"I'm perfect. That was hot as hell and exactly what we both needed." I catch his hand, then press a kiss to his split knuckles. "You don't have to fight alone anymore. You have me. You'll always have me."

Something settles in his expression. As if some weight he's been carrying since he crawled out of that burning cabin has finally started to lift.

He leads me to bed, and as I lie in the circle of his arms and let sleep draw me under, I finally let myself believe for the first time since he's come back from the dead that we'll really, truly make it.

———

I'M SIPPING coffee when his phone buzzes on the counter, and whatever he sees when he reads the text makes him go still. He snatches it up, presses a speed dial button, and says, "You're sure? No, don't do anything yet. I want to be there."

I set down the mug I'm holding. "What is it?"

Gabriel ends the call, his expression caught between disbelief and something darker. Like hunger mixed with fury. "They found one of the men from Aspen. Carl Dekker."

My heart stutters. "Dekker's dead. My investigators almost nailed him years ago. Then, before we could verify he had anything to do with you, he slipped away, and then got himself dead."

Gabe's mouth twists. "Apparently, it didn't stick."

Gabe's already moving. "He got picked up in Reno two weeks ago. Bar fight. Ran his prints and got a hit. Guess he got sloppy," Gabe adds as he shrugs on his jacket. "Leo's people grabbed him last night. He's being held outside the city."

"And the one he worked with? Webb?"

"Still in the wind. But I bet Dekker knows where he is." His expression grows darker, and I watch as he transforms from the man who made me breakfast into something harder. More dangerous.

"I'm coming with you."

"The hell you are."

"Do not play that game." My words are slow and measured. "I spent years looking for these men. I hired the investigators, I followed the leads, I hit the dead ends. You don't get to cut me out now."

"This isn't going to be pretty."

"And you don't get to play babysitter just because you're the big, strong man." I close the distance between us, forcing him to look at me. "These men tortured you. They stole you from me. I deserve some goddamn answers. And, dammit, I hope it's not pretty. I want a goddamn front row seat."

I watch his face. The resistance doesn't disappear, but it softens around the edges.

"It's dangerous."

"Yeah? Well, guess what. So is loving you, but I'm standing right here. I'm going," I say again. "Just say okay."

A moment passes. Then another. And just when I think we're going to really have it out, he nods. "Okay. We do this together."

CHAPTER
TWENTY-FOUR

The drive takes almost an hour.

Gabriel is silent behind the wheel, his jaw tight, his eyes fixed on the road. I watch the city give way to industrial sprawl, then to empty stretches of nothing—warehouses, abandoned lots, the kind of places people go when they don't want to be found.

"How long has Leo had him?" I finally ask.

"Since last night."

"Has he talked?"

"Not yet." Gabriel's hands flex on the steering wheel. "Leo's people softened him up, but they're waiting for me."

Softened him up. My stomach turns, even as another part of me —darker, angrier—thinks *good.*

"What are you going to do?" I ask.

He doesn't answer right away. When he does, his voice is flat. Completely devoid of emotion. "Whatever it takes."

I should be horrified, but all I can see are the bullet holes, burns, and scars that mar the man I love. All I can think of is how close he came to death. And about the lies that broke the man I loved.

"Good," I say quietly.

Gabriel's head turns sharply, his brow furrowed.

197

"Bella."

"I'm not the girl you left behind." The words come out harder than I intended. "Five years changes a person. So does grief. So does being accused of murder by the man you love."

The silence that follows is thick with everything we haven't said.

"I know," Gabriel finally says. "You have sharp edges now, too." His voice drops. "I hate that I put them there."

"You didn't. Life did. My father did. The men we're about to see did." I stare out the windshield at the empty road ahead. "You just made it worse for a while."

It's not absolution. We both know that. But at least it's honest.

Gabriel reaches across the console and takes my hand. After a moment, I twine my fingers with his.

For now, that's enough.

THE LOCATION IS a warehouse on the outskirts of the city—nondescript, industrial, the kind of place that could be anything or nothing. Leo's waiting outside, leaning against a black sedan with his arms crossed.

He straightens when we pull up, his eyes moving from me to Gabriel. "You brought her."

"She's good at getting what she wants when she puts her mind to it."

I'm not sure, but I think Leo almost grins. "I know the type," he says, turning to look at me. "And you've earned it."

"How's Dekker?" Gabriel asks.

"Scared. Angry. Not talking yet." Leo pushes off the car and heads toward the warehouse entrance. "But he will."

Inside, the warehouse is what I expected—vast concrete floors, exposed beams. Basically, an industrial skeleton. Leo leads us through a maze of corridors to a room at the back. The door's closed and there's a guard stationed outside. At least I assume he's a guard since he's got a holstered gun.

"Ruby's in there with him," Leo says. "She's good at reading people. Says he's close to breaking."

Even though I know that Ruby and Leo's business has a Black Ops vibe, it's still a bit of a shock to learn that Ruby's in there for the purpose of getting info from a guy probably tied to a chair.

Gabriel's hand finds the small of my back—a grounding touch, though I'm not sure if it's meant to steady him or me.

"Ready?" he asks.

No. Not even close. "Sure," I say.

Leo opens the door, and the three of us head in.

The room is like something out of a mob movie. Small, windowless, lit by a single bulb. There's a chair in the center, and in it sits a man with a scar through one eyebrow and his wrists zip-tied to the chair arms. He's also bloodied and bruised, with one eye swollen nearly shut.

Ruby stands in the corner, arms crossed, watching him with an expression of cold patience.

The man—Dekker, I presume—looks up, his head turning slowly as he takes us all in, then backtracking to stop at Gabe.

He makes a scoffing sound, and something shifts in his expression. Fear, I think. But he's trying to disguise it as mirth.

"You look pretty good for a corpse."

Gabe doesn't respond. Just walks slowly toward the chair, each step deliberate. Predatory.

"You know who I am," Gabriel says quietly. "Which means you know why you're here."

Dekker spits blood onto the concrete floor. "I don't know shit."

"You shot me three times and left me to burn." Gabriel's voice is almost conversational. "You made sure I'd die believing the woman I loved had betrayed me." He leans down, bringing his face close to Dekker's. "I remember every second. Do you?"

Something flickers in Dekker's expression. Not guilt—I doubt men like him even feel guilt. But recognition. Maybe fear.

"You survived," Dekker says. "Congrats. Most don't."

"Who hired you?"

Silence. Gabriel straightens, then looks at Leo, and I see some unspoken communication pass between them.

"Isabella," Gabriel says, not turning around. "You should step out.

He's right. Every civilized instinct I have is screaming at me to walk out that door, to preserve some shred of the person I used to be.

Instead, I step forward. Past Gabriel. Until I'm standing directly in front of the man who tried to murder the love of my life.

"My investigators found you three years ago," I say, my voice steadier than I feel. "You faked your death to avoid them. Why?"

Dekker's good eye slides to me. Takes in my designer clothes, my manicured nails. The soft girlie things he probably thinks define me.

"Lady, I don't know what you're talking about."

"I'm so sorry," I say sweetly. "I forgot to introduce myself. I'm Isabella Hart." I watch his face carefully. "Sterling Hart's daughter."

There it is.

A flicker. Surprise, maybe, or calculation.

"You know my father."

"Never heard of him."

"Liar." The word comes out sharp, vicious. "You tortured Gabe in my name, you fucker. *The Hart bitch.* Isn't that what you said?"

Dekker's expression shutters closed. But that doesn't matter. I know what I know.

"My father hired you." It's not a question anymore. "He hired you to torture the man I loved and make sure Gabriel believed I was responsible."

"I told you. I don't know what the fuck you're talking about."

I lean closer—close enough to smell his foul breath. "Then let me make this very clear. The man standing behind me spent five years planning revenge against me because of what you told him. Five years believing I'd betrayed him. Five years of both of us in hell."

My voice drops to something cold. Something I barely recognize.

"So you're going to tell us who hired you, or I'm going to walk out of this room and let him do whatever he wants. And believe me, after what you did to him, I won't lose a single night's sleep."

Silence.

Then, slowly, Dekker starts to laugh. A wet, rattling sound that ends in a cough.

"Damn," he wheezes. "Hart's little princess has teeth after all." He looks past me to Gabriel. "You picked a good one, rich boy. Cold as ice under all that pretty."

"Last chance," Gabriel says, moving to stand beside me. "Who hired you?"

Dekker's laughter fades. He looks between us, and something in his expression shifts. Resignation, maybe. And why not? He must know that his options have run out.

"You want answers?" He leans back in the chair. "Fine. But you're not gonna like what you hear."

"Try us," I say.

Dekker's smile is bloody. Broken. "You're right, Princess. Daddy hired us. Paid top dollar, too."

Even though I expected it, hearing the confirmation feels like a punch to the gut. *My father.* My own father hired men to torture and kill the man I loved.

"Why?" Gabriel's voice is tight. Barely controlled. "What did Hart want?"

"Fuck if I know." Dekker shrugs like we're discussing the weather. "I was just the hired help."

"You're going to have to do better than that," Gabriel says. "If you value your life, anyway."

"Hey, swear to God. What the fuck reason have I got to cover for the SOB? Not like he sat me down and told me a bedtime story. But, okay," he adds as Gabe takes a step closer. "Maybe I heard some tidbits might help you."

"What tidbits?" I ask."

"Something about a big deal he had going down with Elias Grimm. Wanted the old man distracted. Off his game." He grins, bloody teeth flashing. "Killing the golden boy seemed like a good way to do that."

Gabriel goes rigid beside me. I can feel the rage rolling off him in waves.

"Maybe that's true," I say, forcing my voice to stay steady. "But it's not all. If it was only business, you'd have just killed him. But you didn't. You planted lies about me. Things to make him hate me before he died. Why?"

"Daddy said the bastard wasn't good enough for his little princess. Thought you were too stupid to see it."

He laughs again, the sound wet and ugly. "Wanted the last thing your boy here ever thought to be that you wanted him dead. That you were glad to be rid of him. Honestly, I thought that was too fucked up. Didn't want to do it, you know? But he had a way of negotiating that my bank account loved."

I have to look away. My own father. I've always known he was vile. Now I'm starting to see how deep it runs.

Dekker cocks his head, studying me with something like amusement. "Gotta say, Princess, your old man's a real piece of work. All high and mighty about those Grimm bastards, but he's got no problem paying guys like me to do his dirty work."

I don't answer, but he's right about the irony.

"Where's Webb?" Gabriel asks. His voice is ice. Controlled in a way that scares me more than rage would. "Your partner. Where is he?"

"Webb's got a place outside Carson City. I'll give you the address." Dekker leans forward. "But I want something in return."

"You're not in a position to negotiate," Leo says from behind us.

"Maybe not. But I got more information than just Webb's address." Dekker's good eye gleams. "I got names. Dates. Details of other jobs the little girl's daddy commissioned. Real nasty shit. The kind of stuff that would put Sterling Hart away for the rest of his miserable life."

I look at Gabriel, and I'm certain he realizes it, too. My father's crimes extend far beyond what he did to Gabriel and me.

"Talk," Gabriel says. "Tell us everything. And maybe—*maybe* —you leave this place alive."

Dekker smiles that bloody smile. "Now we're negotiating."

An hour later, we emerge from that room with Webb's address, a list of my father's crimes that turns my stomach, and the beginnings of a plan. Leo and Ruby are staying behind, waiting for their liaison at the FBI to send a team to take the vile prick away.

We walk back to the car in silence, and I don't push Gabe. I figure he's got as much to think about as I do. Not just the confirmation that Sterling Hart ordered his torture—but the why. The casual cruelty of it. The way my father wanted to destroy not just Gabriel's life, but his last moments of consciousness.

After a few moments, I reach for his hand. He lets me take it, but his fingers don't curl around mine.

"Gabe."

He stops walking. Turns to face me. And the shattered look on his face just about breaks my heart.

"Talk to me," I whisper, forcing the words past the tears gathering in my throat.

"He did this because of me," he says, his voice low and wrecked. "Because I loved you. Because I wasn't worthy of you." His laugh is bitter, hollow.

"My father is a monster." I step closer. "What he thinks about worthiness means nothing. Less than nothing."

"But he's right, isn't he?" Gabriel's voice cracks. "I spent five years believing you betrayed me. I came back to destroy you." He pulls his hand from mine, then runs it through his hair. "How am I any better than him?"

"Because my father never bothered to know you. He saw Elias Grimm's son—a name, a threat—and decided you were the enemy. He never saw *you*."

He makes a scoffing sound and starts walking again. I grab his sleeve and pull him to a stop. "Dammit, listen to me. You believed the lie he told you. But you had evidence. It was fucked up and fake and horrible, but it was tangible. My father played you. It's not even close to the same."

He says nothing. He doesn't have to. The pain on his face says it all.

"Dammit, Gabe." I grab his face and force him to meet my eyes. "Don't you get it? When you saw the truth, you *chose* to believe me. And now you're standing right here, hurting for what was done to both of us."

"I want to kill him." The words are raw, torn from somewhere deep. "Your father. I want to watch him suffer the way I suffered."

"I know." I press my forehead to his. "I know. And we'll figure out what to do with him. Together. But not like this. Not while your soul is bleeding."

Gabriel's breath shudders out of him. For a long moment, we just stand there—foreheads touching, breathing together, two broken people trying to figure out how to be whole.

"Day by day," he finally whispers.

"Day by day."

When we pull apart, Leo is waiting by the car, giving us space but clearly ready to move.

"Webb?" Gabriel asks.

"Ruby's coordinating with our people. We'll have him within forty-eight hours."

Gabriel nods. Then he looks at me—really looks, the way he used to before everything went wrong.

"Let's go home," he says.

Home. His underground apartment beneath the city. The place where we're trying to rebuild something from the ashes.

I take his hand. And this time, his fingers curl around mine.

CHAPTER
TWENTY-FIVE

The first few days after Dekker are almost normal.

We fall into an easy rhythm—mornings in Gabe's apartment, coffee and conversation before I hurry to the Monarch to deal with the gallery or the casino. I've told him to come with me, to hole up in the back room and paint. But he just shakes his head and says he's not ready.

I don't push.

It would be easier to move him into my suite, but that could put him on a collision course with my father, and neither of us wants that. Not until we have enough evidence to bury Sterling Hart for good.

And so our days stay separate.

Chris has a tight hand on the gallery, so I can mostly cross that off my plate. But between putting out fires at the casino and dodging my father's calls, I'm ridiculously busy. At least Gabriel pulled the Gaming Commission complaints. That's one less battle for me. Plus, it's proof he's done trying to destroy me.

Not that I still need proof.

He's busy, too. Tracking Webb with Leo, building the case. Anything and everything they can find to nail my father to the proverbial prison wall.

Evenings, though…

Well, evenings are ours.

We cook together. Talk. And inevitably end up with our bodies tangled together on his couch, or in that tiny closet of a bedroom, and for a few hours at least, it almost feels like us again.

Almost.

Because something's shifted. Since Dekker. Since Gabriel watched me watch him beat the truth out of a man. Since he came face to face with what was done to him—and what he's capable of doing in return.

The beast that had finally started to trust me is back in its cage.

Gabe touches me like I'm breakable now. Like I might shatter. Like one wrong move will undo everything we've rebuilt.

Except, no. That's not quite it. He touches me like a giant holding a baby bird, terrified that he'll somehow accidentally crush the life out of the little thing. And knowing that he's more than capable of doing that.

I tell myself he needs gentle. After everything, we both do.

Except I don't need gentle. Hell, I don't want gentle.

What I want is him. The real Gabe. The man who pinned me against that wall and growled my name like it was sacred. The beast, not the penitent.

But every time the heat rises between us, I feel him pull back. Slow down. Check himself. Like he's afraid that if he lets go, he'll prove he's the monster he saw reflected in Dekker's terrified eyes.

He's punishing himself.

It takes me a while to realize it, but now that I do, there's no denying it. The careful touches, the restrained passion—it's not tenderness. It's penance.

But I don't want his guilt. I want his fire.

I want the man who told me to use him instead of his demons. The man who let me see all of him—the darkness and the light— and trusted me to love him anyway.

That man is still in there. I know he is. But Dekker dragged him back underground, and I don't know how to reach him.

So I wait. I give him space. I let him set the pace, even when my body screams for more.

Because pushing him now would only make it worse. Would only confirm his fear that he's too broken, too dangerous, too much.

And I refuse to be the reason he retreats further into himself.

Day by day, I remind myself. We promised each other that.

Day by day.

I just hope he remembers it, too.

————

THE NIGHTMARE COMES THAT NIGHT.

I wake to the sound of screaming.

Not mine. His.

Gabe's thrashing beside me, tangled in the sheets, his face contorted in an expression of pure agony. The sounds coming from him aren't words—just raw, animal noises of terror and pain.

"Gabriel." I sit up, reaching for him. "Gabriel, wake up. It's a dream. You're safe. You're—"

His hand shoots out and catches my wrist in a grip like iron. Before I can jerk free, he's rolling, pinning me beneath him, his other hand closing around my throat.

I gasp, but I get no air. *I can't breathe.*

Panic washes over me, cold. Hard. I struggle, trying to cry out. Trying to get through to him. But I can't.

His hand is a vice around my throat, crushing, killing, and I claw at his fingers, but they don't move, don't even twitch. My lungs burn. My chest heaves, but nothing gets through.

His eyes are open. He's looking right at me. But he doesn't see me.

I try to say his name, but nothing comes out. Just a wet, airless rasp. Black spots bloom at the edges of my vision.

I'm going to die.

The thought is clear. Calm.

Terrifying in its stillness as my body thrashes beneath him, his weight pinning me down, and his hand tightening.

I can't breathe, I can't breathe, I can't breathe.

I go limp. Not a choice. Not a decision. I just—stop fighting. My body goes soft. My mind fuzzy.

I'm limp beneath him. "Gabriel." It's my voice. Somehow, it's my voice.

Something flickers in his eyes. A crack in the nightmare's hold.

"Izzy." My name on his lips, confused. Lost. "Izzy, I—"

His gaze clears. Focuses on my face. On his hand around my throat.

The horror that floods his expression is worse than the choking.

He releases me like I've burned him, scrambling backward off the bed, hitting the wall hard enough to knock a painting loose. It crashes to the floor, but neither of us looks at it.

"No." The word is barely human. *"No, no, no,"*

I sit up, sucking in air, one hand pressed to my throat. I can already feel the bruises forming.

"Gabe."

"Don't." He holds up a hand, warding me off. His whole body is shaking. "Don't come near me."

"It was a nightmare. You didn't know what you were doing."

"I could have killed you." His voice cracks. "Do you understand that? I had my hands around your throat, and I was squeezing, and I didn't even know it was you."

He makes a wailing noise, then presses the heels of his hands against his eyes. "I thought you were one of them. I thought I was fighting back."

I stay on the bed, giving him space even though every instinct screams at me to go to him. "But you stopped. You heard me, and you stopped."

"This time." He laughs—a horrible, hollow sound. "What about next time? What about the time I don't wake up fast enough?"

"Gabe. I'm okay."

"This is why I go to the gym. Why I fight until I can barely stand, until every muscle in my body is screaming. Because if I'm exhausted enough—if I'm broken down enough—I can sleep without dreaming. He gestures at me, at the bed, at the space between us. "Without this."

I touch my throat, and though I don't' mean to, I wince at the tenderness there.

Gabriel sees it, and his face crumples.

"They broke something in me, Izzy." His voice is raw, scraped hollow. "I came out of that cabin wrong. I'm always on edge now. Always waiting for the next attack. I can't trust myself. And if I can't trust myself, how can you?"

"I can. I do."

"I'm going to hurt you." The words come out flat. Certain. Like he's pronouncing a death sentence. "Maybe not tonight. Maybe not tomorrow. But eventually, I'm going to lose control, and you're going to be the one who pays. And then I'll lose you." His voice breaks. "Either you'll run—which you should—or I'll..."

He can't finish. Can't say the words.

Or I'll kill you.

I should be afraid. Some part of me is—some primitive survival instinct that remembers the pressure of his hand on my windpipe. My body knows it came close to death tonight.

But I look at Gabriel—at this man who survived something unimaginable, who crawled out of hell only to find himself trapped in a different kind of prison—and all I feel is heartbreak.

"Come here," I say softly.

"Didn't you hear what I just said?"

"I heard you. Come here anyway."

He doesn't move. Just stands there against the wall, broken glass glittering around his bare feet, looking at me like I'm speaking a language he doesn't understand.

"Gabe." I keep my voice steady. Calm. "You can get through this. Yes, you're struggling. Yes, you have triggers and nightmares and reactions you can't always control. But that doesn't mean you're doomed to hurt me. It doesn't mean we can't figure this out."

"I almost killed you." Each word is precise. Brutal. "The woman I love. I had my hands around your throat, and I was going to squeeze until you stopped breathing. That's not a struggle, Isabella. That's a ticking time bomb."

I flinch at the use of my full name. At the distance it creates.

"So what's your solution?" I ask quietly. "You leave? Go back to the fight clubs, the underground empire, the life you had before? Spend the rest of your days alone because you're afraid of what you might do?"

"At least you'd be safe."

"I'd be miserable." I slide off the bed, ignoring the way he tenses as I hurry to his side. "You'd be miserable, too. We spent five years apart, Gabriel. Five years of grief and rage and loneliness. I'm not doing that again."

"Even if staying with me could get you killed?"

"Even then. But it won't."

I stop about a foot away from him. "I'm not afraid of you."

"You should be."

"Maybe. But I'm more afraid of losing you again."

His composure finally cracks. A sob bursts out of him—raw and broken and completely unguarded. And then his arms are around me, crushing me against his chest, and he's shaking so hard I can feel it in my bones.

"I'm sorry," he gasps into my hair. "I'm so sorry, Izzy."

"I know." I hold him just as tightly. "I know."

We stand there in the wreckage of the bedroom—fallen painting, sheets tangled on the floor—and just hold each other.

It's not a solution. It's not healing. But for now, in this moment, we're choosing each other.

Then his phone buzzes. I hurry to get it so he doesn't slice up his feet, then take him the phone and some slippers.

"Leo," he says after he hangs up. "Webb's in custody. We should get going."

And just like that, the walls are back.

CHAPTER
TWENTY-SIX

Gabriel won't touch me.

It's been two days since the nightmare. Two days since his hands closed around my throat. Two days since he looked at me with horror and called himself broken.

He sleeps on the couch now and won't even discuss sharing the bed.

"Not until I figure this out," he'd said, and the finality in his voice left no room for argument.

So I lie alone in sheets that still smell like him, staring at the ceiling, listening to him pace the apartment at three in the morning. Sometimes I hear the punching bag he set up. Sometimes, the familiar sound of his brush on canvas.

He's busy. Always battling demons. Always moving.

And each move takes him further from me. I can feel it—the distance growing, the walls going back up. Every time our hands accidentally brush, he flinches. Every time I move toward him, he finds a reason to step back.

It's his bullshit way of protecting me.

And it means I'm going to lose him all over again.

When I finally call Harper, it's not because I have a plan, but because I'm at my wits' end.

"You sounded terrible on the phone," she says when she rushes into the gallery, then pulls me into a hug. "How bad is he, really?"

"Not good," I say, then signal to Chris that I'm escaping to the break room. Normally, I'd go into one of the showrooms, but right now, I don't want even a hint of Gabriel keeping me from thinking straight. And the showrooms are pretty much odes to the man and his work.

We sit at the small round table, each with coffee, mine going cold as I try to articulate the width and breadth of the wall that's gone up between Gabe and me.

"I can't even talk about it. He just *won't*."

Her brow furrows, then she leans back, her eyes going wide. "*Oh*. You mean…"

"Touch me. Yes." I glance at the door, as if I'm afraid the words will escape and tarnish the ears of someone browsing the gallery.

"Ever since that horrible nightmare," I continue, then gesture vaguely at my throat. The bruises have faded to greenish-yellow, easily hidden with concealer, but we both know they're under there.

"He's convinced he's too broken to be close to anyone, let alone me."

"And you think he's wrong?"

"I think he's scared." I pull my knees up, wrapping my arms around them like a child. "I don't know how to reach him. What magical words will bring him back to me. I've had him back for like thirty seconds, and I'm losing him all over again."

"Oh, sweetie." She squeezes my hand. "He'll get past it."

I shake my head. "Maybe. I don't know. He won't talk to anyone. And every time I try to get close, he pulls away. God forbid I suggest he talk to a professional. I've done that twice, and he just sort of slips away inside himself. "It's like he's built this wall between us, and I can see him through the glass, but I can't get to him."

"Have you tried just talking to him? Telling him how you feel?"

"Only a zillion times. He won't hear it. He's convinced that he's dangerous—that being close to me puts me at risk."

I laugh, but there's no humor in it. "The irony is that it's the distance that's killing me. Not the fear of what he might do."

"What about..." Harper hesitates, clearly choosing her words carefully. "What about showing him? Instead of telling?"

I shake my head, completely clueless. Show him what?"

"That he has more control than he thinks." She leans forward, her expression intense. "Look, I've known Gabriel since we were kids. He's always been about control—controlling his image, his emotions, his father's expectations. When he lost that in Aspen—I mean, when those assholes took everything from him—it broke something fundamental inside him."

"Well, yeah. I know that."

"But here's the thing." Harper's voice drops. "He didn't lose control with you during the nightmare. Not really. He stopped. Some part of him heard your voice and pulled back. That's not a man who's lost control—that's a man whose control runs deeper than he realizes."

I consider this. She's right—he did stop. Even in the grip of that horrible dream, something in him recognized me and let go. "You may be on to something, but he won't think so. He didn't stop right away. And he was close to truly hurting me. I'm not scared of him—I'm really not. But a few seconds longer..."

I look up at her. "That's what he's scared of."

"Except he *did* stop. That's what you have to focus on. And what he has to focus on, too."

She's probably right. And god knows I don't have a better idea. "So what do I do?"

"Make him see it." She shrugs. "I don't know how. That's your territory, not mine. But if anyone can reach him, it's you."

"Great. You're a big help."

"Yeah, well, you get what you pay for."

The door to the break room opens, and we both turn. David stands in the doorway, looking apologetic.

"Sorry—Chris said you were back here. I wanted to check in." He looks between the two of us, then frowns. "Bad time?"

I exchange a glance with Harper. There was a time when David's presence would have made this conversation impossible. When the awkwardness of discussing my love life with a guy— even one who is top of the friend zone—would have shut me down completely.

But things are different now. We're different.

"Actually," I hear myself say, "I could use a guy's perspective."

David's eyebrows rise. "On what?"

"Sex. And Gabriel."

He chortles—that's really the only word for it—then takes a seat. "This should be interesting."

"And how to convince a stubborn man that he's not as broken as he thinks," I add.

He leans back in the chair, his expression somewhere between amused and wary. "You really want me to be part of this pow-wow?

"Sure," I say. "That's what friends do, right?" I hold his gaze. "Share perspectives?"

A beat passes, then he nods. "Yeah," he says quietly. "That's what friends do."

Harper looks between us with barely concealed amusement, but she doesn't comment. Smart woman.

"So," David says, leaning the chair back onto two legs. "Gabriel won't touch you because he's afraid of losing control. And you want to show him he won't. Am I tracking?"

"Wow. Psychic much?"

He tilts his head toward the door. "Here's not the best place to discuss anything gossip-worthy. Just fyi."

I exchange an amused glance with Harper. "Noted."

David leans forward, bringing the chair back down. He clears his throat, starts to say something, then stops again.

"Close your eyes," Harper says. "Then picture yourself naked and spit it out. Or picture Bella naked. Whatever works."

"*Harper!*" She looks at me and shrugs, utterly unrepentant. "Just lightening the moment. Nobody thinks clearly when they're stressed.

She's right. My newly arrived stress headache is definitely clouding my judgment.

"Look," David says, the word bursting out as if he's trying to shut us up. Which, frankly, he probably is. "This is weird for me, but—have you considered taking control yourself? Not giving him the option to retreat?"

"Sort of," I semi-admit. I twist my fingers together in my lap. "But what if it goes to hell? I mean, what if I push too hard and he breaks?"

"Then you'll deal. But you deal with it together." David's voice is gentle but firm. "I mean, come on, Bella. You're not fragile. You survived losing Gabriel—not to mention surviving his miraculous return. You survived a lifetime of your father's bullshit. You're seriously fucking strong. "If Gabriel breaks, you'll help him put the pieces back together. That's what love is."

The word hangs in the air between us—*love.* From another man, it might sound bitter. From David, it just sounds true.

"He's right," Harper says. "And for the record, I'm impressed." She nods at David. "That was very emotionally intelligent of you."

"I have hidden depths." He turns to me with a grin, and there's no pain in his eyes. Just warmth. And that's when I know for sure. We're fixed now. Just friends. No lust. No benefits. No romancy goo.

At least one relationship in my life is on even ground.

Now to get there with Gabriel.

———

I FIND him in front of his easel that evening.

He's been there all day, from the looks of it. Paint smears his forearms, his shirt. One streak across his cheekbone looks like war paint. Canvases surround him—all unfinished. All fragments of whatever he's trying to exorcise.

But there's something different about this one.

It's me. Or the suggestion of me—curves and shadows, the impression of a woman reaching toward something. Unlike the others, this one has depth. Layers. It's not finished, but it's closer than anything else he's painted since he came back.

"You were working on that one this morning," I say as the door clicks shut behind me, blocking the sound of tonight's first fight at The Beast.

Gabriel doesn't look up. "Couldn't sleep."

"You never sleep anymore."

"I sleep."

I suppose he must, but not enough. Never enough.

I cross the room, stepping over discarded brushes and crumpled paper towels stained with color. When I reach him, I don't touch. Just stand close enough that he can feel my presence.

"Gabriel. Look at me."

He doesn't move for a long moment. Then, slowly, he sets down his brush and turns.

The exhaustion in his face makes my heart ache. Dark circles deep beneath his eyes. His beard wild and untrimmed. The haunted look of a man who's fighting a war he doesn't believe he can win.

"You can't keep doing this," I say softly. "You can't keep running from me."

"I'm not running. I'm being realistic."

"You're being a coward."

The word lands like a slap. Something flickers in his eyes— anger, maybe, or hurt.

"You think I want this?" His voice is rough. "You think I enjoy sleeping on the couch while you're not even twenty feet away? I can hear you breathing, Bella. I can smell your shampoo on the pillows. Every part of me wants to be in that bed with you, but I can't.

"Can't what? Can't trust yourself? Can't risk hurting me again?"

"Yes." The word comes out like it's been torn from him. "Exactly that."

"So your solution is to torture us both indefinitely? To live in the same apartment but never touch? To watch each other from across a room for the rest of our lives?"

"My solution is to keep you alive."

"I don't want to just be alive, you idiot. I want to *live*. With you. All of you—including the parts you're afraid of."

He turns away, running a hand through his paint-streaked hair. "You don't know what you're asking."

That's it.

I grab his arm and spin him back toward me. Before he can react, I'm pushing him—hard—until his back hits the wall. My hands fist in his paint-stained shirt, holding him there.

His eyes widen, and before he can say a word, I kiss him. Not gentle, not tentative—I crush my mouth against his, pouring every ounce of frustration and want and fury into it. Five years of grief. Five years of loneliness. Five years of aching for a ghost who turned out to be flesh and blood after all.

He freezes for a heartbeat. Then his hands come up—not to push me away, but to grip my hips, pulling me closer. His mouth opens under mine, and the kiss turns desperate, hungry. *He's back. Once again, he's back.*

"Bedroom," I gasp against his lips. "Now."

He doesn't argue.

We stumble down the hallway, shedding clothes as we go—his ruined shirt, my blouse, a tangle of fabric left in our wake. By the time we hit the bedroom doorway, I'm in my bra and he's bare-chested, and the sight of him—scarred and beautiful and mine—makes my breath catch.

I push him toward the bed. He goes willingly, sitting on the edge, looking up at me with something like wonder.

"We're doing this my way," I tell him, climbing onto his lap. "You don't get to take over. You don't get to bail."

He kisses me.

And for a moment, everything is perfect. His hands in my hair, his mouth hot against mine, the solid warmth of his body beneath me. I can feel how much he wants this—wants me—and I rock against him, drawing a groan from deep in his chest.

I reach between us, working at his belt. He's shaking—I can feel the fine tremor running through him—but he doesn't stop me. Doesn't pull away.

I free him from his pants. He's hard, straining, and when I wrap my hand around his cock, he makes a sound like something breaking.

"I need—" His voice is ragged. "I need to—"

"No." I stroke him slowly, watching his face contort with pleasure. "You don't need to do anything. Just feel."

"You don't understand." His hands clamp down on my hips, fingers digging in hard. His eyes have changed. Gone hard in a way that should frighten me. The beast is there, pacing just behind his gaze, and I can see him fighting to keep it caged.

"Let go," I whisper. "I trust you."

Something snaps.

One second, I'm straddling him, in control, setting the pace. The next I'm on my back, his weight pinning me to the mattress, his hand wrapped around my throat.

Not squeezing. Not yet. But the threat is there—along with the memory of the nightmare. Of waking up to his fingers cutting off my air.

"Gabriel."

His hips jerk forward, driving into me without warning. I cry out—part pleasure, part shock—and his hand tightens reflexively.

"Gabriel."

He freezes, staring down at me with horror blooming in his eyes.

Then he's gone—scrambling backward off the bed, hitting the floor hard, retreating until his back hits the wall. His chest heaves. His whole body shakes.

"No." The word is barely human. "No goddammit, no."

I sit up slowly, my hand going to my throat. He didn't squeeze hard—barely touched me, really—but the intent was there. The instinct.

I reach for him.

"Don't." He holds up a hand, warding me off. "Don't come near me. Don't touch me. He draws in a breath. "I told you." His voice is low. Hard. "I fucking told you this would happen."

"You stopped."

He meets my eyes, his hard. "I almost didn't."

"Fuck almost," I snap. "You. Stopped."

But he's not hearing me. He's on his feet now, pacing like a caged animal. "Another second and I would have—I was going to—"

He can't say the words.

"But you didn't."

"That's not good enough." The anguish in his voice breaks my heart. "Don't you get it? I can't control it. When I'm with you, when I want you that much, the beast takes over. He shakes his head violently. "I become something that hurts people. That hurts you."

"Gabriel, no."

"It's done." His voice has gone flat. Empty. "We're not doing this again. I'm not risking you again. Not ever."

He grabs the blanket and walks out of the bedroom. A moment later, I hear the creak of the couch springs.

I sit alone in the wreckage of our attempt, my throat tender, my body still humming with unfulfilled need. And I watch the empty doorway where he disappeared.

He thinks I'm looking at him like he's broken.

He's not wrong.

But not for the reason he thinks.

He's broken because he won't let anyone help him heal. Because he's so convinced he's a monster that he won't give himself the chance to be anything else.

I lie back on the pillows, staring at the ceiling. My body aches, still craving the connection that shattered before it could form.

How do you save someone who refuses to be saved?

How do you love someone who thinks love is a weapon that will destroy you both?

I don't have answers. All I have is a cold bed and the growing certainty that if I don't find a way around his walls, I'm going to lose him for good.

Not to death this time, but to fear.

And somehow, I think that's worse.

CHAPTER
TWENTY-SEVEN

David helps me unpack the last of the new inventory—prints of LaBete's most popular works, and originals from curated artists around the country who paint in the same style.

Chris is off today, and I'd been looking forward to some alone time, but this is better. After all the weirdness stemming from our still-technically lingering engagement, it sometimes seems like our friendship has gotten lost in the shuffle.

We both know our arranged marriage isn't happening now. And not just because Gabe's back, but also because my father is soon to be a monkey who doesn't live on my back. And that, frankly, makes me giddy.

Even now, Leo and Ruby and Gabe and Travis are working with investigators to find the evidence to nail my father to the wall.

I've known the Grimms most of my life, and when they set their mind to something, it happens.

How lucky for me they're looking to destroy my dad.

And the bonus cherry on that yummy sundae? The Monarch will be mine even without the farce of marrying David. Because the corporate documents make clear that once Daddy Dearest is arrested for what he did to Gabe, then Monarch goes to me, even before my trust officially kicks in.

"Where does this one belong?" David asks, holding up a painting in greens and browns and reds that evokes wine and bonfires and cool Autumn nights.

"The east wall in the main showroom," I say. It'll look amazing with the afternoon light from the skylight."

"You've said that about three different paintings now."

"And they'll all look amazing."

David laughs, the sound loosening something in my chest. We've been dancing around each other ever since Gabriel came back and everything went sideways. Polite. Careful. Neither of us willing to address the giant neon elephant in the room.

But today feels different. Today feels like maybe we can finally get it all out there.

"Actually," I say, setting down the painting I'm holding. "Can we talk first?"

Something wary flickers across his face as he puts the piece down. "That sounds ominous."

"No, not really. I just think we need to talk about that night."

The wariness deepens, but he nods, then pulls out a chair and sits down. "Okay," he says. Go for it." And, dammit, I can't read his face at all.

I sink onto the small settee that is this room's only place to sit. After a moment, David sits beside me, both of us slightly sideways so that we're more or less face to face.

"I just wanted to say that I'm sorry for—well, for that night. And when I bolted. You know that wasn't about you, right? I got Leo's text about Gabe, and I didn't even think. I just ran. And then I was a total ass and never explained, or apologized, or anything."

"Bella." His voice is gentle. "It's okay. I was a little freaked at first, but when I learned why you bolted, I totally got it."

"But see? You're proving my point. You're probably the nicest guy on the planet, and I rushed out without even the courtesy of a text from the car."

"You found out the love of your life was alive. I would have done the same thing."

"Would you?"

"In a heartbeat." He meets my eyes. "It wasn't a real engagement, remember? And you're my best friend."

"I know," I say. "But David…" I trail off, then bite my lower lip as a reminder that I have to go on. "That deal. I never should have agreed." I look down at my hands, then rub sweaty palms along my jeans. "I know how you felt about me. The whole arrangement. It wasn't fair to you."

"It wasn't fair to you, either. We talked about it, remember? And I'm a big boy. I knew what I was agreeing to. And I knew you didn't feel the same way about me that I felt about you. Did I hope that you'd let go of Gabe's ghost once we were married? Maybe that we'd even end up with a real happily ever after? Sure, I did. But I never bet on hope."

I swallow a throat full of tears. "David."

"I always knew you weren't over him. And I also knew that if you ever did get over him, I might not be the guy you wanted to fill that empty hole. Even if we were technically married, I still might not have been that guy. I wanted it—hell, I prayed for it. But I never expected it."

I press my lips together and blink like mad. "Would it help if I told you that I've wished on a million stars that I felt that way about you?"

"Maybe a little."

"How about if I tell you that sleeping with you really was good. I mean, you have mad skills, my friend."

That gets a real laugh out of him.

When we both quit laughing, we're holding hands, smiling at each other.

"For the record," he says quietly, "I'm glad you found him again. I want you to be happy, even if it's not with me. Even if your happy is currently complicated because your dad fucked with that boy's head. You'll get him back, Bella. And when you do, I'm going to be cheering the loudest for you two crazy kids."

I laugh, and as I do, he puts an arm around my shoulder and leans in to kiss me, soft and gentle. A kiss that's not about romance, but a toast to what we've shared and the friendship still to come.

His lips have barely grazed the corner of mine when he's gone.

One second, David is there, leaning toward me. The next, he's stumbling backward, Gabe's fist twisted in the collar of his shirt, Gabe's face a mask of cold fury.

"What the fuck do you think you're doing?"

"Gabriel, dammit!" I'm on my feet, heart pounding. "It's not what it looks like!"

"It looked like he kissed you." Gabriel's voice is ice. "In a gallery full of my work.

"We were talking."

"I heard you talking." His grip on David's collar tightens. "I heard him tell you he's glad you're happy despite distance and worries. Sounds like a pretty intimate conversation to me."

"Gabriel, please. "

"Is this what you do when I'm not around? Run to him? Tell him all our problems so he can comfort you?"

"That's not fair."

"Life's not fair. I learned that the hard way."

He shoves David back, hard enough that David stumbles into the wall. For a terrible moment, I think Gabriel's going to hit him —really hit him, with the full force of five years of rage.

But he doesn't. He just stands there, chest heaving, hands clenched into fists.

"I think I should go," David says quietly.

"Yes." Gabriel's voice is flat. "You should."

"No." I step between them, facing Gabriel. "He doesn't have to leave because you can't control your jealousy."

"My jealousy?" Gabriel's laugh is sharp. "I'm not jealous. I'm furious. There's a difference."

"Is there? Because from where I'm standing, it looks like you're punishing me for something I didn't do. Just like before."

The words land hard. I see Gabriel flinch.

"This is different."

"The hell it is." I press my fingers to my temples. "Dammit, I thought we were past this. I thought you trusted me."

"I do trust you."

"Then act like it."

The silence that follows is suffocating.

Gabriel stares at me, his chest heaving, and I can practically see a beast clawing at the inside of his skin, fighting to burst out. For a long moment, I think he might actually apologize. Might admit he was wrong.

Instead, he turns and walks out.

The door slams behind him, and I'm left standing in the middle of my half-unpacked break room, shaking with anger and something that feels terrifyingly like grief.

"Bella." David's voice is gentle. "I'm so sorry.

"You didn't do anything wrong." I sink back onto the settee, suddenly exhausted. "He did."

David sits beside me, careful to leave space between us. "Do you want me to go?"

"No." The word comes out fiercer than I intended. "No. He doesn't get to chase my friends away because he can't control his jealousy." I draw in a long breath, then another. Then one more for good measure.

"I can't keep doing this," I finally say. "I can't keep walking on eggshells, wondering when the next explosion is going to happen. I love him, but I can't live like this."

"So what are you going to do?"

I shoot him a half smile. "Good thing I have a permanent suite in a kickass Atlantic City casino. Any chance you want to hang out? We could snag Harper, then order pizza and drink wine."

"You had me at pizza," he says as we walk out together, and I try not to think about the man headed back to The Beast to spend a long night alone with his rage.

CHAPTER
TWENTY-EIGHT

The pizza arrives at eight, and Harper tips the delivery guy with a twenty she pulls from my wallet.

"I'll pay you back," she says, dropping the box onto my coffee table and flipping it open. The smell of garlic and melted cheese fills my living room, mixing with the salt air that drifts in through the balcony doors I'd left cracked. From forty-seven floors up, the Atlantic is a dark ribbon beyond the boardwalk lights, and the distant crash of waves is just audible beneath the hum of the city.

"You won't," I say from my perch on the sofa. "And I don't care."

"Good. Because I definitely won't." She grabs a slice, ignoring the plates I'd set out, and folds it in half the way she's done since we were kids. Grease drips onto her silk blouse. She doesn't seem to notice.

"Eat something," she tells me. "You look like you're about to fall over."

"I'm sitting down," I say, "so falling isn't an issue. And if you bring me a slice, I'll eat it."

She does, and my stomach growls the moment she puts the plate in my hand.

"See?" she says. "Don't argue when I'm mothering you. Oh,

good!" she adds, as David emerges from the kitchen with an open bottle of wine and three glasses.

I'm already settled in the middle of the sofa, and now they take a seat on either side of me. As they do, I say a silent *thank you* for the No Talking About Gabriel rule we'd laid down before we ordered the pizza.

"Anything else," Harper had said. "But no Gabe. And," she'd added, with a narrow stare aimed at both me and David, "no talking about running a casino. Some of us are only interested in the betting side of things."

I'd met David's eyes and we'd both shrugged. "No problem," I'd said. "We can talk about Tarot cards. Anissa's been teaching me."

"Or we can just sit around and drink and watch TV," David had countered.

Since that sounded both fun and easy—and required very few brain cells—David's plan won, and just over two hours later, we've done significant damage to the pizza, watched a movie that was either a very bad comedy or a darkly comedic drama, and have moved on to a reality show about people buying tiny houses.

Harper's moved to the recliner and is providing running commentary on the tiny house folk and how they must be better people than her, who thinks ten thousand square feet is really, really cramped.

By the time nine o'clock rolls around, I've polished off three slices of pizza and two glasses of wine and am nicely buzzed and comfortably settled long-ways on the couch with my feet in David's lap as I sip wine and suck up the awesomeness of simply spending a non-productive evening at home with friends.

The knock at the door comes at nine-fifteen.

We all freeze. Harper's hand tightens on mine, and David straightens in his seat, suddenly alert.

"Expecting anyone?" Harper asks.

"No."

"Probably your father wanting another photo of our happy engagement," David says.

For the first time ever, I hope he's right, and it is my dad at the door.

The knock comes again. Louder this time. More insistent.

David stands. "I'll get it."

"You don't have to."

"I know." He crosses to the door, then checks the peephole. His shoulders stiffen. When he turns back, his expression is carefully neutral.

"It's Gabriel."

Yeah. Father's never around when I want him. Which, considering that's pretty much never, works out well.

Except that now I have to deal with Gabriel.

"You don't have to let him in," Harper says. "You don't owe him anything tonight."

She's right. I know she's right. I could tell David to send him away, then deal with this tomorrow when I've had time to sleep and think and rebuild my defenses.

But the truth is, I need to set some freaking boundaries. To tell him very firmly that today was bullshit.

And if I'm going to do that, I need to at least have the balls to do it in person.

"Let him in," I say.

David hesitates. "You sure?"

"No. But do it anyway."

He opens the door, and Gabriel steps inside.

He looks terrible.

That's my first thought.

He looks even worse than he looked earlier, which shouldn't be possible.

His dark hair is disheveled and could use a wash, his beard is a mess, and his eyes are red-rimmed like he's either been crying or rubbing the shit out of them. He's still wearing the same clothes from the gallery, which makes me wonder if he's even gone home. Or has he spent pretty much the whole day wandering? Pacing. Maybe punching things?

No matter what the details, I think it's a safe bet that this man I love—this man who is driving me batshit crazy—has been stewing in his own misery for hours.

His gaze sweeps the room. The way Harper and David stand there like bodyguards. Two wine bottles and a pizza box. Reality TV playing silently on the big TV screen.

All evidence of a night spent trying to forget him.

When his eyes finally land on me, something in his face cracks. "Izzy—"

"Don't." The word comes out sharper than I intended. "You don't get to 'Izzy' me right now. You don't get to walk in here with those eyes and expect everything to be okay."

He flinches. Actually flinches as if I've struck him.

Good.

No, not good. I don't want to hurt him. I just want him to understand.

"I'm sorry," he says. The words are rough, scraped raw. "I know that's not enough. I know I keep saying it, and then I keep fucking up." He shakes his head. "And I did it again. I saw David leaning toward you, and I didn't think. I just reacted. Like a goddamn animal."

"Yeah, you did."

He looks across the room. "For what it's worth, David, I'm sorry."

David looks utterly befuddled, but he tilts his head in acknowledgment as Gabe turns his attention back to me. "I know you weren't doing anything with him. I know David is your friend. I know—" He runs a hand through his hair, a gesture so familiar it makes my chest ache. "I know all of that. But when I walked in and saw you together, all I could think was that I was losing you. That you'd finally realized I'm too broken, too fucked up, too much work. That you were already moving on."

"So your solution was to prove me right? To storm in and act like a possessive asshole, confirming every fear I might have about whether you can actually handle being in a relationship?"

Another flinch. But he doesn't look away.

"Yeah. Pretty much. I told you—I didn't think. I just reacted."

"That's the problem." I stand up, needing to be on my feet for this, needing to not feel so small. "You keep reacting. You keep letting whatever's broken inside you take the wheel, and then you apologize afterward like that makes it okay. But it doesn't. It doesn't make it okay."

"I know."

"Do you? Because this isn't the first time. You did the same thing when you first came back—decided I was guilty without ever giving me a chance to defend myself. So how many times is this going to happen? How many times am I going to forgive you, only to get blindsided by the next explosion?"

He's silent for a long moment. Harper and David are silent too as they watch this play out, not interfering but very clearly ready if they need to.

"I don't know," Gabriel finally says. And the honesty in his voice, the raw, bleeding honesty, makes something twist in my chest. "I want to tell you it won't happen again. I want to promise you I'll be better. But I've made those promises before, and I've broken them. So, I don't know what to say that you'd actually believe."

"Then don't say anything." I move closer to him, stopping just out of arm's reach. Close enough to see the details I missed before —the redness around his eyes, the tension in his jaw, the way his hands are trembling slightly at his sides. "Show me. Show me you're willing to actually deal with your shit instead of just apologizing for it."

"How?"

"I don't know. Therapy? Support groups? Hell, even talking to Travis or Leo or literally anyone who might be able to help you figure out why you keep self-destructing?" I throw my hands up in frustration. "I can't be your only lifeline. I can't be the only person standing between you and your worst impulses."

The words land hard. I watch them hit, watch him absorb them, watch something shift in his expression.

"You're right," he says quietly.

I cross my arms, wanting to hug him, but needing to stand firm. "I know I'm right. The question is whether you're going to do anything about it."

He's quiet for a long moment. Behind me, I hear Harper move to sit on the couch, and David shift his weight from one foot to the other. The tension in the room is thick enough to cut.

"I will," he says, his voice low but firm. "Dammit, I will."

I feel a squeeze around my heart. "Good. Because I love you. But I can't keep being the collateral damage when your demons take over."

"Izzy—"

"*Bella.*" The correction comes out hard. Maybe too hard. But I'm too tired to soften it. "Izzy was something a man I used to know called me." I look up at him, hoping he can see the love in my eyes. "I'm hoping to find him again someday."

Something breaks in his expression, and he nods. "Yeah," he says. "I hope so, too."

He starts to turn away, and without thinking, I reach out and grab his sleeve.

"Stay." The word surprises me as much as him. And God only knows what David and Harper think about it. "Just for a glass of wine. Just to hang with us for a bit."

"You sure?"

"I'm not sure about anything right now," I admit. "But I know I don't want you to leave. Not like this. Not with everything still broken between us."

He nods. Slowly. Like he's not sure he deserves the reprieve, but he's going to take it anyway. "If it's okay with…" He trails off.

David, to his credit, is already pouring another glass of wine.

He crosses to Gabriel and holds it out—a peace offering. Or maybe a test.

"I'm not entirely convinced you're not going to punch me at some point," David says, "but so long as it's not tonight, you should join us."

I seriously want to kiss him. But under the circumstances, that would probably be a mistake.

Gabriel takes the glass. "I'm not going to punch you. And I'm sorry for earlier. For the whole caveman routine. I was an ass."

David surprises me by nodding. "Apology accepted. This time. But don't pull that shit again."

"I know." Gabriel almost smiles. "You'll have Harper hold me down while you give me a strongly-worded lecture."

"I was thinking more like I'd let Harper handle the whole thing. She's scarier than me."

"True," Harper says from the couch. She hasn't moved, but some of the defensive tension has left her shoulders. "Come sit down. All of you. I switched the channel over to watch *Friends*, and I think something's going to go completely awry in this episode."

We settle back onto the sofa—me in my corner, Gabriel beside me with a careful few inches of space between us, and Harper curled up in the other corner. David settles into the armchair. The wine gets passed around. We laugh at the antics and the monkey on the screen. And when Harper says she's craving cookies, Gabriel gets up to get them without even being asked. It's a small thing. A tiny thing. But it feels right.

Around eleven, Harper stands and stretches. "I should go. Early meeting tomorrow." She leans down to kiss my cheek. "Call me in the morning. And you," she points at Gabriel. "Don't make me regret giving you another chance."

"I'll try not to."

"Try harder than that."

David blows off my earlier suggestion that he stay in his old room—for which I'm grateful. He leaves a few minutes after

Harper, but first making me promise to eat the leftover pizza for breakfast and extracting a handshake from Gabriel.

Now it's just the two of us, alone in my living room with the ocean dark beyond the patio doors and everything still uncertain between us.

"I should go too," Gabriel says. But he doesn't move.

"I meant what I said," I tell him. "About finding someone to talk to. About doing the work if you want us to have any chance at all."

"I know," he says. "I have to earn you back."

I shake my head. "It's not about earning me. It's about healing yourself." What I don't say is that I'm afraid the damage goes too deep. And yet, that thing called hope still flutters.

He moves toward the door, but I take his hand before I can talk myself out of what might be a very bad idea. "Will you stay with me?" My voice is barely a whisper. "Just to sleep. To be here."

He studies my face, as if looking for some hidden meaning. "You know I can't. The nightmares—" He shakes his head. "I don't trust myself. What if I hurt you?"

"You won't."

"You don't know that."

I hold his gaze. "Stay. Please."

A long silence. Then something in him surrenders. "If that's what you want."

"It's what I want."

I take his hand and lead him to the bedroom, and we undress in the dim light—separately. Just two people getting ready for sleep.

When we climb into bed, he stays on his side, and I stay on mine. But after a moment, his hand finds mine under the covers. And I let him hold it.

It's not forgiveness. It's not even trust, not really.

But it's a start. A tiny, fragile start.

CHAPTER
TWENTY-NINE

Morning light filtered through Bella's curtains, soft and golden, the kind of light that made everything look gentler than it actually was.

Gabriel hadn't slept. He'd been too afraid of what might happen if he did. Instead, he'd lain there all night, her hand in his, staring at the ceiling while his mind churned through everything she'd said.

Hell, everything she'd demanded.

Find someone to talk to. Do the work.

He knew she was right. But the thought of sitting in some therapist's office, spilling his guts to a stranger with a notepad and a degree...He shuddered.

Everything in him rebelled against it. He'd spent five years building walls, learning to survive on his own, trusting no one. The idea of tearing all that down for some shrink who'd probably never even thrown a punch felt like walking into enemy territory with a water pistol.

But he'd promised her that he'd try. And Gabriel Grimm kept his promises.

Even the ones that terrified him.

Beside him, she stirred, stretching like a cat in a patch of sunlight. When she opened her eyes and found him watching her, something soft flickered across her face.

"Hey," she murmured. "Did you sleep?"

"Some," he lied.

She studied him for a moment, and even though it was clear she didn't believe him, she didn't push. Just squeezed his hand once before letting go and sitting up.

"I have a meeting at the gallery in an hour," she said. "You could come with me. If you want."

He should say yes. Should spend the day with her, prove he could be normal. The man she deserved, instead of the monster he kept becoming.

But he couldn't. Not yet. Not until he figured out how to fix what was broken inside him.

"I've got some things to handle at The Beast."

He thought he saw disappointment flicker, but it was gone so fast he couldn't be sure. "Will I see you tonight?"

He cocked his head. "Do you want to?"

Her slow smile started a fire inside him. "Yeah," she said softly. "I do."

He reached out and brushed a strand of hair from her face. "Then I'll be here."

After she left for the gallery, Gabriel sat on the edge of her bed as his mind circled back to the nightmarish idea of therapy. Of professional help. God, he felt like making finger quotes around the words. He just wasn't wired that way.

Then he thought about Travis.

Travis, who'd pulled him off the floor more times than he could count in those first brutal months. Who'd listened without judgment when Gabriel raged about Isabella's betrayal. Who'd watched him fight his way through five years of pain and never once told him to stop, just made sure he didn't kill himself in the process.

Travis wasn't a shrink. But he'd been friend, counselor, and priest all rolled into one. He'd seen more broken men than any therapist—and he'd helped some of them find their way back.

If Gabriel was going to talk to anyone, it should be him. If nothing else, Travis was a place to start.

———

THE CLUB WAS QUIET NOW—THE monthly day off with no crowds, no fights, just the cleaning crew and a few staff prepping for the next day's fights. Gabriel moved through the corridors on autopilot, past the locker rooms and storage areas until he came to Travis's office. The door was half-open, and Gabriel could hear sports radio playing from inside.

He stopped in the doorway. Knocked on the frame.

Travis looked up, surprise flickering across his weathered face before his eyes narrowed. "You look like shit."

"So I've been told."

"Anissa keeps sending you food. You eating any of it?"

"Some."

"Liar." Travis closed his laptop and leaned back in his chair, propping his feet on the cluttered desk. "You want to come in and tell me what's wrong, or are you just going to stand there looking like a man who's about to jump off a bridge?"

Gabriel stepped inside, then closed the door behind him. The office was cramped—barely bigger than a closet, with cinder block walls and a single flickering fluorescent light.

He'd given Travis his choice of offices, most of which had room to stretch both arms to the side while also expanding your chest to breathe. But his friend had chosen this tiny interior room. Had said it was cozy.

Cozy.

"Is that a grin?" Travis asked as Gabriel took a seat in the battered guest chair.

"If it is, it's an outlier," Gabriel admitted. "Not much to grin about these days."

Travis nodded, but didn't say anything. Just put his hands on his desk, watched Gabriel, and waited.

Travis waited. That was one of the things Gabriel had always valued about his friend—the man understood silence. Understood that some things took time to surface. A long career as a Texas Ranger and almost five years of managing underground fighters had given Travis a patience that most people mistook for indifference.

It wasn't indifference. It was respect. The understanding that a man would talk when he was ready, and not before.

"I'm going to lose her," Gabriel finally said.

"Isabella?"

The name sent a spike of want through him. Even now. Even here, in this cramped office that smelled like old coffee and sweat. Just her name was enough to make his body respond.

"She reamed me out for being a jealous prick."

"Was she right?"

"She's rarely wrong."

Travis nodded slowly. "Solution's easy. Stop being a jealous prick."

Gabriel forced himself not to laugh. "Yeah," he said. "I got there on my own. I'm working on implementation."

"Life's a bitch. What's the real reason you're here?"

Gabriel drew a breath, then let it out slowly. "I almost fucking killed her."

Travis went very still. "All right. You have my attention."

"A nightmare," Gabe said. "I almost killed her while I was having a fucking nightmare. And when we tried to—"

He couldn't finish. The memory of his hand around her throat —twice now, once asleep and once awake—was too raw. Too shameful. "They may not have killed me, Trav, but they damn sure broke me."

Travis leaned back. His expression didn't change, but his eyes held both compassion and understanding.

"You talk to anyone about this yet?" Travis asked, his voice as soft and measured as Gabe had ever heard. "Professionally, I mean."

"No."

"Maybe you should."

"I'm talking to you."

Travis snorted. "I'm not a shrink, Gabe. I'm a guy who runs a fight club. Your fight club."

"You're also the closest thing I've had to a father since mine decided empire-building was more important than his kids." Gabriel dropped his hands and met Travis's eyes. "You've seen more broken men than any shrink I know. Guys who came back from combat and couldn't... Couldn't be normal anymore. Couldn't be with their families." He shook his head. "How did they fix it? The ones who did. How did they come back?"

Travis was quiet for a long moment. His feet came off the desk, and he leaned forward.

"Some of them didn't," he said. "Some of them ate their guns or drank themselves to death or just disappeared. Couldn't find a way back. And the ones who did come back..." He shook his head, "Gabe, man, I was just a friend to them. Just like I am to you."

"You're more than a friend. Hell, you're a savior."

"Your body, maybe. When I found you that day in the snow, I didn't think you'd survive. Neither did Anissa, and that child of mine is the world's foremost wide-eyed optimist. You say I rescued you, and maybe I rescued your body. Got you out of the cold. Got you stitched up. But you rescued yourself, buddy. You did the work. You can do this work, too."

Gabriel's vision blurred, and he cringed, realizing the cause was tears.

"It wasn't anything I did," Travis said softly. "But the ones who made it—they had a few things in common. They had people who wouldn't give up on them. Who they could talk to. You've got me. Anissa. And I think you have Isabella, too."

"That's it?" That's the solution?"

"A part of it. Mostly, I think they came through because they had something to live for. And they figured out what was actually broken, instead of just trying to beat it into submission."

That last part landed hard. Because that was exactly what Gabriel had been doing for five years. Trying to beat the beast into submission through violence and exhaustion and sheer force of will.

But what the hell else was he supposed to do? Offer it tea and crumpets? Whatever the fuck a crumpet was.

"Honestly, boss, I don't know if I can help you, but I'll be your sounding board. So go ahead. Tell me what happens. Walk me through it."

Gabriel's jaw tightened, pride warring with need.

Need won out. And so he told him. About wanting her. About the tender bits falling to the side, as if the beast that lived inside him kicked them away. About the way everything in him would shift, like he was readying for a fight, when that wasn't what he wanted. He wanted her. Not to hurt, but to have. Except it was as if his body didn't get that. His mind didn't get it. He'd end up overcome by a horrible need to strike first. To protect himself.

He shivered. "It doesn't make sense. She's not a threat. She'd never hurt me. But my subconscious is a scared pansy-ass with one hell of a right hook."

Travis nodded slowly, like pieces were clicking into place. "When they shot you in that cabin, you told me they had you tied to a chair?"

The question caught Gabriel off guard. "What? Yeah. Why?" He shook off the unwelcome memory. They'd burst through the door. He'd fought—but three against one, and they had guns. The first bullet took him down before he could land a punch. He came to bound to the chair, ropes on his wrists and ankles. One around his chest.

"You were helpless," Travis said, his voice as soft as a kitten.

The word made Gabriel's stomach turn. "Yes."

"Couldn't fight back. Couldn't defend yourself. Just had to sit there and take whatever they decided to do to you."

He squirmed. Fighting the urge to bolt. "Yes." His voice came out hard. Brittle.

"And then they shot you again."

"The woman did. She had Izzy's eyes." He shuddered. "And she walked up and put a bullet in my chest like she was swatting a fly."

"You barely survived," Travis said, as if Gabe needed to be reminded. "You swore you'd somehow find and kill every one of them."

"Damn right."

"And the one who shot you had eyes like the woman you love."

"He closed his eyes, nodding, hating the memory of how he'd treated Bella when he'd come back. That he'd even for a moment believed that she'd been that bitch in the cabin.

Except some part of him still believed it. Some terrorized part of his subconscious. That's the point. That's where Travis was leading him.

"But it wasn't her," Gabe said. "I know it wasn't. No doubt, no question. Not anymore."

Travis shrugged. "Your nervous system learned a lesson in that cabin—vulnerability equals death. And it's been keeping you alive ever since. Problem is, it doesn't know the war's over. It doesn't know how to turn off. And add her eyes into the equation...."

Gabriel sat with that for a moment, his gut churning. "But I love her. I don't want to hurt her."

"Survival instinct," Travis said. "Sex makes you vulnerable. You let your guard down, you stop thinking, you give yourself over to sensation. For most people, that's the whole point. But for you?" He shook his head. "For you, that vulnerability feels like being tied to that chair again. Like the bullet's coming. So your body does the only thing it knows how to do—it fights."

"I can't just turn it off," Gabriel said. He dragged his fingers through his hair. "*Fuck.* I've tried, Trav. God, I've tried to make it stop. I can't."

An eternity seemed to pass in silence.

Finally, Travis drew in a breath. "Like I said, boss, I'm not a shrink. But hear me out. Seems to me that when you feel vulnerable, every instinct screams at you to attack. To take control. To make sure you're never helpless again. Sound about right?"

Gabe nodded.

"So what if you couldn't?"

"Couldn't what?"

"Couldn't fight. Couldn't attack. Couldn't take control." Travis held his gaze. "What if you took that option off the table entirely?"

The implication hit Gabriel like ice water. "You're saying what, exactly?"

"I'm saying maybe you need to be tied down." Travis's voice was matter-of-fact. Practical. Like he was discussing fight strategy, not Gabriel's fucked-up sex life. "Let her run the show. Let her be the one in control. Your body can scream at you to fight all it wants, but if you physically can't move, you've got no choice but to ride it out."

"And then what?"

"And then maybe—*maybe*—your subconscious learns that letting go doesn't mean getting shot." Travis shrugged. "It's the same principle we use with fighters who flinch. You can't think your way out of it. You've got to retrain the reflexes."

Gabriel wanted to argue. Wanted to say it was too simple, too risky, too much to ask of Isabella. But the more he turned it over in his mind, the more it made sense.

His body had learned that vulnerability meant death. The only way to unlearn that was to be vulnerable and survive. And the only way to guarantee he wouldn't hurt her in the process was to make sure he couldn't.

"And if it doesn't work?"

"Then you try something else. Find a real shrink, do actual therapy, work through it the slow way."

Travis stood, grabbed a half-empty bottle of water from his desk, then took a long swallow. "Or go talk to a real shrink right now. But you've got to try something, Gabe. Because what you're doing isn't working. And that woman isn't going to wait forever. Not because she doesn't love you, but because she can't save you if you won't let her try."

Gabriel stood too. His legs felt unsteady, his mind still churning. But for the first time in weeks, he felt something other than despair.

He felt hope. Terrifying, fragile, dangerous hope.

"Thanks," he said.

"Don't thank me yet. Go home. Talk to her." Travis dropped back into his chair, already reaching for his laptop. "And Gabe?"

Gabriel paused at the door.

"Eat a goddamn muffin. You look like death warmed over."

CHAPTER
THIRTY

He found her in her suite at the Monarch, curled up on the couch with a glass of wine and a book. She looked up when he walked in, tucking the key she'd given him into his back pocket, and the hope in her eyes nearly broke him.

"Hey."

Gabriel crossed the room, then took the wine glass from her hand and set it on the table.

"Come with me."

She laughed. "And hello to you, too."

He pulled her to her feet and led her to the bedroom. "Tie me up."

One brow lifted, clearly intrigued. Then she frowned. "Gabe, are you sure?"

"The scarves in your closet." He was already pulling his shirt over his head, toeing off his shoes. "Tie my wrists to the headboard. Tie them tight."

"Really?"

"Trust me." He caught her face in his hands, then kissed her hard, the kind of kiss that had her moaning and him hard and ready. "Trust me," he said, his voice rough.

For a moment, she just looked at him, her nipples hard under her thin tee. Then she nodded once and crossed to the closet.

Gabriel stripped off the rest of his clothes and lay back on the bed, arms stretched above his head. His heart pounded. Every chatty little instinct screamed at him to stop this, to take control, to protect himself.

He beat the little fuckers back.

Bella returned with two silk scarves, and although she bit her lip as she bound his wrists to the bed frame, her hands were as steady as a surgeon's.

"Too tight?"

He shook his head.

She tested the knots. Tugged. Then sat on the edge of the bed and looked at him. "This is new to me. I mean, I liked it when you used to tie me up, but we never..." She trailed off, gesturing to his naked body, laid out like a present for her.

"Equal opportunity bondage."

She grinned. "I like it. But," she added, tilting her head. "Why?"

"Hello? I'm naked and tied to your bed." He glanced down at his rock-hard cock, then saw her grin when she followed his gaze.

"Fair point. We'll have the debriefing after I have my way with you." She shimmied out of her leggings, then straddled him, still in her tee. "If you need me to stop?"

"Stillwater. I say that, you stop."

"Yeah," she said, her voice soft. "That works." Then she bent forward and kissed him, gentle but intense. At the same time, she started to rock her hips, rubbing her bare cunt against his abs.

"Oh, holy fuck," he murmured, then drew in a breath that was more like a gasp.

"Close your eyes," she whispered. "I've got you. Just let yourself go."

He didn't need much persuasion. The knots were tight. She was safe.

And damn, but this felt good.

Her hands stroked his ribs, moving up slowly, as those hips kept undulating. A brush of her thumb against his nipple.

Then she pulled off her shirt and bent forward, starting slow as she pressed kisses along his jaw, his throat, the ridge of his collarbone. Her hands traced the scars on his chest—the bullet wounds, the burns, the map of everything he'd survived. And Gabriel lay there, bound and helpless, and let himself feel it.

She rose up, now sliding her hands higher, finding his shoulders, teasing the soft skin of his neck, so vulnerable there.

The beast woke up.

It prowled through his chest. Snarling. Straining. His wrists jerked against the ties, twisting at the waist as her hands clung to his shoulders, his head whipping sideways and back as every nerve screamed at him to break free, to fight, to take control before something terrible happened.

But the bonds held. And Bella kept touching him. Kept kissing him. Drawing a line with her tongue down his torso, teasing his cock in a way that had him wanting to scream in fear and desperation, even while crying out in absolute, pure pleasure.

"It's okay," she murmured over and over. "I'm fine. I'm safe. And so are you."

She bent forward again, her breasts brushing his skin as her lips teased his nipples. As her mouth closed over his, hard and demanding. As she rocked her hips so that her ass stroked his cock until he wasn't sure anymore if this was torment or pleasure, heaven or hell. All he knew was that he wanted her. That he needed her.

That maybe—just maybe—this was working.

When she finally stripped off the rest of her clothes and straddled him, he nearly lost his mind.

"Stay with me," she breathed, sinking down onto him. "Right here."

"Izzy." Her name tore out of him.

"I've got you." She started to move, slow and deliberate. "Let go. I've got you."

The beast howled.

He opened his eyes, saw her dual-colored ones, and arched completely off the bed, straining toward her, pushing against the bonds. Lust and fear and desire and need all mixing together like a whirlwind inside him. But he couldn't fight. Couldn't take control. Could only surrender to the sensation, to her, to the terrifying vulnerability of being completely at her mercy.

And somewhere in the white-hot center of the pleasure, something broke open.

Not the beast. Something older. Deeper. The wall he'd built in that cabin five years ago, the one that said vulnerability meant death. It cracked. Crumbled. Let in light. Not completely gone. Not yet. But finally fading.

And when that white hot pleasure ripped through him—when his entire body exploded with his release—he knew that this was it. Not a cure, but a path. A well-lit path to lead him back to his Izzy, and to the man he'd buried deep inside himself.

She untied him afterward, pressing kisses to his lips, his chest, his wrists. Then she curled against his side, her head on his chest.

"How did you know?" she finally asked.

He pulled her closer, pressed his lips to her hair.

"Travis," he said. And then, slowly, haltingly, he told her everything. The conversation. The realization. All of it. "I'm not cured," he said. "Not yet."

"But it's a path," she said, her choice of words making him smile.

"Will you walk it with me?"

"You know I will." For a moment, she was quiet, her fingers tracing patterns on his chest. "I love you."

"I know." He kissed her forehead. "I love you, too."

They lay there in the quiet, wrapped around each other, breathing together. And for the first time in years, Gabriel's mind was still.

His phone shattered the silence.

He tensed, old instincts surging. But Bella's hand pressed flat against his chest, grounding him.

"It's just the phone. And it might be important."

With a groan, he reached for the damn thing, then sat up the second he saw Leo's name on the screen.

"You're on speaker. I'm with Bella. What's up?"

"We found it." Leo's voice was tight with controlled excitement. "The three-hundred thou that got funneled to Dekker and Webb to finance their little party. The one that supposedly traced back to Bella. We know who really owned it."

"Tell me," Gabriel said.

"Two entities co-owned the account. Bella's trust fund and another entity set up to look like a corporation only to skirt some tax laws."

"What was it really?" Bella asked, holding tight to his arm.

"A twisting web of shell companies on top of shell companies, the whole thing set up twenty-six years ago in Isabella's name, but with Sterling Hart buried down deep, the grand master of all that corporate bullshit."

"And you can prove all of this?" Gabe asked.

"Hell, yes. And more. Five days before you left on your Aspen trip, someone walked into a branch bank in Manhattan and withdrew three hundred grand in cash from that account. The teller even remembers. Hell, that much cash, a woman alone. Not something that happens often. She showed ID, signed the paperwork. Everything checked out. As far as the bank was concerned, she was Isabella."

Beside him, she squeezed his hand. "And I'm betting you've found proof of who it really was."

"I'm just that awesome," Leo said. "I had a buddy hack the archive to pull the security footage. We lucked out that the policy was to retain it all on a hard drive." Leo paused. "It's not Isabella. Similar build, similar features. But it's not her."

"Who?"

"Mina Panov."

"That bitch," Bella snapped.

"Yeah, well, can't argue there," Leo said. "And we know she's been fucking Sterling on and off for at least five years. And guess whose account got fifty-K richer that same week?"

"Send us everything," Gabriel said.

"Already done, but here's the problem—Sterling's in the wind. Mina, too."

Gabriel shut his eyes, tamping the fury down. "Of course he is. The bastard's been planning this for years. He's not going to stick around and wait for us to nail him."

"I've got people on it," Leo said. "He can't hide forever."

"Fine." Gabe forced the fury and frustration back down. "I'll check in with you later." With a groan, he hung up, then turned to Bella.

For at least two minutes, she said absolutely nothing. Then she laughed—sharp and brittle. "My whole life," she said. "I've never been his daughter. A tool, that's all. Just someone he can manipulate at his convenience."

"Gabriel cupped her face. "You're here. I'm here. And we're going to take him down. Justice, I promise. Not vengeance."

She flashed a sideways smile. "Honestly, I'm okay with a little vengeance." Then she kissed him—fierce and wild and desperate. When she pulled back, her eyes were bright.

"He can't hide forever," she said. "We'll find him. And then we'll finish this."

CHAPTER
THIRTY-ONE

We're tangled together in his bed, my head on his chest, his fingers tracing lazy patterns on my back. The apartment is quiet except for our breathing and the hum of The Beast through the corridors.

It's been three days since I tied him to this bed and demanded his trust. Three days of learning each other again—not just our bodies, but the people we've become. The sharp edges, the soft places, and all of our scars, visible and otherwise.

"Can I ask you something?" My voice is barely a whisper.

His hand stills on my back. "You can ask me anything."

"Anissa told me some of it. How Travis found you. The months of recovery." I press my palm flat against his chest, feeling his heartbeat quicken. "But she wasn't there for the beginning. Only you were."

He's quiet for so long I think he's not going to answer. Then his chest rises and falls with a deep breath.

"You don't have to," I add quickly. "If it's too much."

"No." He pulls me closer. "You should know. You deserve to know." He draws in a breath, then another. Then he looks away. When he speaks, his voice is so soft at first that I can barely hear him. "They kept me in the cabin for three days, tied to a chair."

His voice is flat. Detached. "They wanted information about various Grimm holdings. Access codes. Account numbers. Weaknesses they could exploit."

"Did you give them anything?"

"No." I hear a ghost of dark pride in that single word. "They would have killed me no matter what. But they didn't do it fast. First, they tried everything to get me to break. Beatings. Burns. They used pliers on my teeth." His jaw tightens. "Yanked out two of them."

My stomach lurches, and I press closer to him, as if I can somehow protect him from the horrors of the past.

"And then she came in," he says quietly. "The woman with your eyes."

I go still.

"I know it wasn't you," he continues. "But in that moment, tied to that chair, beaten half to death—I believed it. I truly believed you'd come to finish what they started." He lifts his head, looking right at me. "I'm so, so sorry."

"Gabe, no. I understand. You know I do." I squeeze his hand. "You don't have to tell me the rest."

He only glances at me, then says, "She raised the gun. She shot me."

His hand finds mine, and he laces our fingers together. "How the hell she missed everything vital, I'll never know. Either she was a bad shot, or..."

"Or my father wanted you to suffer," I finish when he goes quiet, my voice hollow.

"Yeah." He exhales slowly. "After that, everything's in fragments. But I remember they left me bleeding on that cabin floor, walked out, and set the place on fire."

"But you got out."

"Barely." His voice is rough now, the detachment cracking. "The chair was old. Wooden. I managed to break it against the floor and got my hands free."

I shudder as I picture it. Gabriel, shot and beaten and burned, crawling through flames because he refused to let my father win.

"They'd left the door open, and I managed to crawl out. Spat out some more broken teeth. Left my ring. Then I passed out. I remember thinking it wasn't sleep calling me, but death, and no way was I following death home. I had to stay alive. Because if I was dead, I couldn't get revenge."

"Against me," I whisper, and he nods.

"I don't know how long I slept. But when I woke up, I crawled. Into the woods. Down into a ravine. That was as far as I got before my body gave out."

"And Travis found you there."

"The next morning. I don't remember it—I was out of my mind with fever and blood loss by then. He said I was half-dead, barely breathing. He thought I was a corpse until I grabbed his ankle." A small, grim smile. "Scared the hell out of him, apparently."

"I would imagine."

We're quiet for a moment. I think about all of it—the torture, the woman with my eyes, the fire, the desperate escape.

"That's what I found," I whisper. "When I went to the cabin. Your ring, melted in the ashes. Your teeth. Blood everywhere." Tears slip down my cheeks. "I thought you were dead. I mourned you."

"I know." He pulls me closer, presses his lips to my forehead. "I know, Izzy. And I'm sorry. For all of it. For believing you could do that to me. For staying dead when I should have found a way back to you."

"You didn't know. You thought I betrayed you."

"I should have known." His voice cracks. "I should have known you could never hurt me like that. Even though they set me up— even though they had someone starring in the role of Isabella Hart —I should have known it wasn't you. I should have seen through the haze and known it was Sterling Hart. Not you. Never you."

"Gabe." I squeeze his hand.

"I believed the lie, and I kept believing it. And I have to live with that forever."

I kiss his forehead. "Does it help knowing I forgive you?"

His smile is soft. "That's the only thing that does help. That you forgive me. That by some miracle, you're still mine."

"Always," I promise, then grin. "Just don't do it again."

As I'd hoped, he laughs. "Deal," he says, then kisses my hand. "I don't deserve you."

"You do."

"Maybe. But I'm going to spend the rest of my life earning it anyway." He kisses me then, soft and slow. "Day by day."

"Day by day," I whisper against his lips.

And for now, that's enough.

CHAPTER
THIRTY-TWO

My morning at the Monarch is grueling as I deal with enough paperwork to wallpaper the Louvre. When I finally escape, the sun is high in the sky, and I find Gabriel at his easel, taking advantage of the light filtering through the high windows of his underground apartment. The canvas in front of him is different from the chaotic fragments he's been producing—this one has structure. Intent.

I mentally cross my fingers. *Progress.*

I look closer and see a woman's silhouette emerging from shadows, reaching toward something I can't quite make out.

My breath hitches. *Me.* He's painting me again.

I lean against the doorframe, watching him work. The tension that's lived in his shoulders for days is softer this morning. Not gone—I'm not sure it will ever be completely gone—but manageable. Like a tide that's finally started to recede.

Now, as I watch him paint, I see the difference in every brushstroke. Less frantic. More deliberate. Like he's finally creating instead of just exorcising demons.

"I know you're there," he says without turning around.

"I know you know." I push off the doorframe and cross the room, stepping over discarded sketches and dried paint rags.

When I reach him, I rest my chin on his shoulder and study the canvas. "She's beautiful."

"She's you."

I press a kiss to the side of his neck. "When did you start this one?"

"This morning. Couldn't sleep after you left for work." He sets down his brush and turns, pulling me into the circle of his arms. His eyes search my face, looking for something—damage, maybe, or regret. "Are you okay? After last night?"

"Better than okay." I trace my fingers along his jaw, feeling his beard rasp against my skin. "Are you?"

He doesn't answer right away. I've learned to wait him out instead of rushing to fill the silence.

"I don't know what I am," he finally admits. "Different. Less fractured, maybe." His arms tighten around me. "You shouldn't have had to…fuck. You know."

I smile. "We're not keeping score."

"Maybe we should be. The tally's pretty one-sided at this point." There's a darkness in his voice—the familiar self-loathing that rises up whenever he lets himself think too hard about every-thing he's done.

I catch his face in my hands, force him to look at me. "Stop. Day by day, remember? No more drowning in the past."

"Some days the past feels pretty fucking present."

"I know." I brush my thumb across his cheekbone and catch the edge of the scar that extends from under his beard. "That's actually something I want to talk to you about."

Something shifts in his expression. Wariness creeping in at the edges. "That sounds ominous."

"It's not. I promise." I take a breath, organizing my thoughts. "I've been thinking about The Beast. The fight club."

His whole body goes rigid. "What about it?"

"You go there to burn off the fury. The pain. That's why you fight—because the violence helps you sleep without nightmares." I hold his gaze. "I'm right, aren't I?"

He's silent for a long moment. Then his shoulders drop, just slightly. "It's not exactly the picture of the normal man I want to be. But since you already know the answer, then yes."

"We skipped over normal a long time ago," I say, then step even closer—close enough that our bodies are almost touching. "You've never actually shown it to me. Not really. And the bits I have seen are from practice rounds. At least that's what Anissa said. "They're not the real deal. That's on a different level altogether."

"Bella."

There's a warning in his voice. I ignore it. "I want to see it. All of it. Including you in the ring."

"I don't think that's a good idea."

I press my hand flat against his chest, feel the rapid beat of his heart. "Please."

"Dammit, you don't know what you're asking." His voice has gone rough. "Watching me fight—it's not like watching a boxing match on TV. It's brutal. Bloody. I become something else in that ring."

"The Beast."

"Yes." The word sounds like a confession. "And not like you've seen. I don't want you to see me like that."

"Why not?"

He starts pacing the room. His back is to me, shoulders taut. "Because you might not look at me the same way after. Because there's a difference between knowing what I am and actually watching me tear someone apart with my bare hands."

I follow him, stopping just behind him but not touching. "After everything we've been through, do you really think watching you fight is going to be the thing that drives me away?"

"I don't know." The rawness in his voice makes my chest ache. "That's the problem. I don't know what's going to be too much. What's finally going to make you realize that the man you loved is gone and all that's left is—"

"Don't." I close the distance between us, then fist the front of his shirt. "Don't you dare finish that sentence. The man I love is standing right in front of me. Changed, yes. Scarred. But still here. Still fighting to come back to himself." I rise up on my toes, brush my lips against his. "I need to see all of you. We need this. Both of us."

He's quiet for so long, I think he's going to refuse. Then his forehead drops to mine, and he exhales, long and shaky.

"I'm terrified," he whispers.

Two words. That's all. But coming from a man who's spent five years armoring himself against any hint of vulnerability, they feel like a revelation.

"I know," I say. "That's okay. We'll be terrified together."

His laugh is more breath than sound. "That's not exactly comforting."

"It's the best I've got." I pull back so I can see his eyes. "Soon? Will you take me back there soon?"

He studies my face for a long moment, searching for something—doubt, maybe, or the first cracks of fear. Whatever he's looking for, he doesn't seem to find it.

"Okay," he finally agrees. "But not today."

"No?"

"No." He pulls me closer, his hands settling on my hips. The tension in his body shifts, transforming into something warmer. "Today I just want you."

The heat in his voice sends a shiver down my spine. But I make myself hold back, make myself ask the question that's been circling in my mind all morning.

"I want that, too. But could you…just right now, I mean…can you be gentle with me?"

He goes still.

I watch emotions flicker across his face—surprise, uncertainty, something that looks almost like fear. "What?"

"Last night was intense. Necessary, sure. But pretty damn awesome, too." I trace patterns on his chest, feeling the raised ridges of scars through his thin t-shirt. "But I don't want intense right now. I just want...you. Simple. Tender." I look up at him. "Is that something you can give me?"

The silence stretches between us, heavy with everything he's not saying.

"I don't know," he finally admits. His voice is barely above a whisper. "You know how I've been living for years. I'm not sure I remember how to be gentle."

The confession breaks my heart a little. This man who used to paint me like I was made of starlight, who used to trace every inch of my skin like he was memorizing a sacred text—and now he's not sure he remembers tenderness.

They did this to him. Those bastards in Aspen. They tried to burn his heart out of him.

But I refuse to believe it's gone completely.

"Then let's find out together," I say. "And for the record, raw and wild and deliciously kinky are definitely on the menu. But right now, I want slow and sweet. And I think we can do that."

I don't give him a chance to protest. I take his hand and lead him toward the bedroom. When we reach the bed, I turn to face him. Slowly, I pull my shirt over my head. He watches, his eyes, dark and hungry, but he doesn't reach for me.

"Bella—"

"Shh." I step closer, work the hem of his t-shirt free from his sweatpants. "No thinking. Just feeling."

I push the shirt up and over his head, revealing the map of scars that covers his torso. In the light from the high windows, they look almost silver—burn marks and cuts and that puckered bullet wound just below his ribs. Evidence of everything he survived.

I lean in and press my lips to the scar nearest his heart.

He shudders.

"That's it," I murmur against his skin. "Just feel."

I kiss my way across his chest, tracing the topography of his suffering with my lips. Every mark, every ridge, every place where they tried to destroy him. And with each kiss, I feel something in him start to unravel.

"Bella." My name comes out broken, barely a breath.

"I'm here." I look up at him, hold his gaze as I ease his sweatpants down over his hips. "I'm not going anywhere."

He's hard already, straining toward me, and I want nothing more than to touch him, taste him, make him lose control.

But that's not what this is about.

I strip, then ease back onto the bed and pull him down with me. He hovers over me, weight braced on his arms, and I can see the war playing out behind his eyes. The beast wanting to take, to claim, to dominate. And the man—the man I fell in love with all those years ago—fighting to stay present.

"Kiss me," I beg.

He lowers his head. His lips brush against mine, tentative and questioning. Like he's forgotten how this works. Like he's learning the shape of my mouth all over again.

I thread my fingers through his hair and pull him closer, deepening the kiss but keeping it soft. No desperation. Just the slow, sweet slide of mouths learning each other again.

When he finally pulls back, his eyes are glassy. Overwhelmed.

"I want to be inside you," he whispers. "But I don't know if I can do this without—"

"Without the beast taking over?"

He nods, jaw tight.

"Then we'll go slow. And if you need to stop, we stop." I cup his face in my hands. "No matter what, I'll still be right here."

Something in his expression cracks open. "Day by day," he whispers. "And minute by minute."

He enters me slowly. So slowly it feels like an act of worship as warmth spreads through my body like honey. His eyes stay locked on mine the whole time, as if he fears he'll look away, and I'll freak out.

"Okay?" he asks, barely breathing.

"More than okay." I roll my hips, drawing him deeper, and watch his eyes flutter closed on a groan. "Gabriel. Look at me."

He does. And in his gaze I see everything—the love he thought was dead, the tenderness he thought was burned away, the man he's been fighting so hard to bury.

He's still there. Scarred and changed, but still there.

We find a rhythm that's nothing like the desperate coupling in the gallery or the intensity of last night. This is something else entirely. Something new and softer. Something that feels terrifyingly like hope.

The pleasure builds gradually. I feel it in my belly, in my thighs, in the curl of my toes. And I watch Gabriel's face as he fights to stay present, to keep the beast at bay.

To give me exactly what I asked for. Gentle. Tender. Himself.

"I love you," I whisper as the wave crests. "I love you, Gabriel. All of you."

He shudders, and I feel him let go—not to the beast, but to the feeling. To the overwhelming vulnerability of being truly loved.

We come together, his face buried in my neck, my arms wrapped tight around him. And when the aftershocks finally fade, and he lifts his head to look at me, I see something in his eyes I haven't seen since before Aspen.

Peace.

"I told you so," I say, and he actually laughs, then rolls to his side, pulling me with him. We lie tangled together, his hand tracing lazy patterns on my back, and for the first time in longer than I can remember, everything feels quiet. Still.

"I have a meeting this afternoon," I murmur eventually. "Supplier negotiations. I should probably..."

"No." Gabriel's arms tighten around me. "Stay."

"Gabriel."

"Five more minutes. Then you can go save the casino." He presses a kiss to my hair. "Let me have this. Just a little longer."

I shouldn't. There are things I need to do, a business to run. But when I look at his face—relaxed, almost peaceful, so different from the haunted mask he's worn for days—I can't bring myself to move.

"Five minutes," I agree.

Twenty minutes later, I'm still in bed, and we've somehow ended up having sex again—even slower this time, lazier, both of us half-asleep and moving on instinct. It's the kind of morning I used to dream about during the five years he was dead. The kind of morning I'd given up on ever having again.

By the time I finally drag myself to the shower, there's no way I'll get to the meeting on time. Thankfully, that's what subordinates are for, and I call my Assistant Manager from the bathroom, apologize profusely, and pass off the task to him.

I end the call and realize with a start how good I feel. Not about passing off a meeting, but about my life with Gabriel. I've been carrying a weight in my gut for what feels like an eternity. But I feel lighter now. Like the world is settling back on its axis and turning the right way again.

I get dressed again in my dark slacks and silk shirt—the kind of outfit that says *boss* without trying too hard—and find Gabriel in the kitchen, making an afternoon pot of coffee. He's wearing sweatpants and nothing else, and the sight of him barefoot and domestic makes me smile.

"Meeting handled?" he asks.

"I dumped it all on Greg." I accept the cup he hands me. "What about you? Any fires to put out in your criminal empire?"

His mouth twitches. "Nothing that can't wait. I've got some emails to deal with, but I can do that from here."

"So you'll be here when I get back?"

"I'll be here." He pulls me close, coffee cups pressed between us. "Always."

The word settles into my bones, warm and certain. *Always*. We might actually get there. We might actually build something real out of all this wreckage.

I'm halfway to the Monarch when my phone rings. It's one of the food and beverage managers panicking about a liquor delivery that got sent to the wrong loading dock. I handle it, then get pulled into an impromptu meeting about a staffing issue in housekeeping, then spend an hour reviewing the quarterly numbers with the CFO. So much for pawning off my first meeting and having a less stressful day.

It's afternoon by the time I finally make my way back to Gabe's apartment. My feet ache from walking the casino floor, and I'm starving. But mostly I just want to see him. To confirm again that we've really turned some kind of corner.

When I step inside, his back is to me, staring at his phone. Every line of his body is rigid, tension radiating off him in waves.

"Gabriel? What's wrong?"

He turns, and my heart stops.

The peace from this morning is gone. In its place is something cold. Something dangerous. The mask he wore when he first came back—the one I thought we'd finally shattered—is firmly in place.

"You're scaring me. What happened?"

He holds out his phone. "Listen."

I take it with trembling hands and press play on the voicemail.

The voice is AI-generated, but it's the words that make my stomach turn.

"Death comes for everyone eventually. Some deaths are quick. Merciful. Others...well." A pause. "I'm told some victims would consider three days of torment in a cabin a mercy compared to what's possible. And it seems to me that you'd hurt more knowing someone you love is waiting for that slow death. And believe me, wanting you to hurt more is very much on my agenda.

The message ends.

I lower the phone slowly, ice spreading through my veins. Three days. A cabin. And a clear message—*I did that. I can do worse. I can hurt someone you love.*

"When did you get this?" My voice sounds strange. Distant.

"An hour ago. Maybe two." Gabriel's jaw is tight enough to

shatter. "Anonymous email, AI voice, routed through a dozen different servers. Untraceable."

"My father sent this." The words make me shiver, but I know they're true. He paid Dekker and Webb, after all. He tried to murder the man I love.

"Sterling Hart, that fucker." The words are harsh, but his hands are shaking. I've never seen his hands shake.

"He's not even hiding anymore," Gabe says.

I meet his eyes, and all I see is rage. Pure, burning fury, the kind that could level cities.

"He's trying to scare you," I say. "To make you back off."

"Then he's a fucking idiot." Gabriel takes the phone from my hand and sets it aside with deliberate care. The control in his movements is more terrifying than any explosion would be. "All he's done is remind me exactly why I spent five years building an empire designed to destroy him."

"Don't you dare do anything stupid," I say, fresh terror rising inside me. "The evidence is coming together. Leo found the money trail. We have Dekker's confession. And surely we'll have Webb in custody soon, too. The FBI—"

"The FBI." He laughs, but there's no humor in it. "Your father has cops in his pocket, judges on his payroll, politicians who owe him favors. You think the FBI scares him? You think *justice* scares him?"

"It should. The walls are closing in. That's why he sent this— he's desperate. Please, Gabriel. Please don't be rash. I can't lose you. Not again. Not when I've just gotten you back." I taste salt and realize I'm crying.

"Do you really think I'll sit around and wait? I got away from him, and that pisses him off. He wants to hurt me, and he knows how—by hurting you. And since he's up and disappeared, we don't even know where to look for him."

"Then we get the police involved."

But he's not thinking about cops or the FBI or even justice. He's thinking about blood.

"Gabriel, please." You go out chasing vengeance, and I'll lose you again. Even if they don't arrest you, I'll lose *you*. The man inside. The man I love. Please, please. We have to do this the right way."

"The right way." He says it like the words taste bitter. "The right way is watching your father walk free because he can afford better lawyers than God. The right way is waiting for a system that's been rigged in his favor since before either of us was born."

"Bullshit. The right way is not becoming what he made you."

The words land like a slap. Gabriel goes still, something flickering behind his eyes—pain, maybe, or recognition.

"I'm already what he made me," he says quietly.

"Dammit, Gabriel, no."

"He had me tortured, Bella. For three days. Left me to burn alive in that cabin. And now he's promising to do worse—to you."

"He's threatening. But he won't hurt me. I'm his daughter."

Gabriel turns, and the look on his face makes my blood run cold. "You think that matters to him? You think blood means anything to a man like Sterling Hart?" He crosses back to me, grips my shoulders. "He's already proven what he's willing to do to protect himself. You're not a daughter to him—you're a liability. An asset that's outlived its usefulness."

I want to argue. Want to tell him he's wrong, that whatever my father is, he wouldn't actually hurt me. But the words stick in my throat because they're a lie. I've watched my father operate for years, and I know exactly what he's capable of.

"Then let the FBI handle it," I say instead. "Let them build their case. Let justice—"

"Justice." He spits the word like it's poison. "There is no justice for what he did to me. There's only ending him before he ends us."

"And if ending him ends you too?" My voice cracks. "If you go down this path—if you become the weapon he forged—you won't survive it, Gabriel. Even if you win, you lose. The beast will take over completely, and I lose you anyway."

He goes very still.

"Is that what you think?" His voice is low. Dark.

Dangerous.

"You really think I'm one bad decision away from losing myself completely?"

I force myself to hold his gaze. "I think you're standing on the edge of something you can't come back from. And I think my father knows exactly how to push you over." I step closer, then take his face in my hands so he has no choice but to look at me. "This is what he wants, Gabriel. He wants you to come after him. He wants you to give him an excuse to put you down for good. Don't give him that. Don't let him win."

For a long moment, Gabriel just stares at me, the beast prowling behind his eyes, hungry and restless.

Then something shifts. Not surrender—nothing that simple. But a crack in the armor. A moment of doubt.

"Day by day," I whisper. "That's what we said. Day by day."

His jaw tightens. "Day by day doesn't feel like enough right now."

"I know. But it's what we've got." I press my forehead to his. "Stay with me. Please. Whatever we do next, we do it together. Not from rage. Not from fear. Together."

The silence stretches between us, heavy with everything he's not saying.

"Together," he finally agrees.

But the beast is still there, watching and waiting. And I don't know how long *together* will be enough to keep it at bay.

CHAPTER
THIRTY-THREE

Two days pass.

Two days of Gabriel pacing like a caged animal, of terse phone calls with Leo, of silence that feels like a held breath.

He hasn't touched me since he got my father's threat. Hasn't painted. Hasn't done anything but pace and plan and stare at his phone like he's waiting for permission to unleash hell.

When I walk in after hours of chasing fires at the Monarch—and finding no evidence of my father or Mina on site at the Casino—I find Gabe shirtless and sweating, beating the shit out of the heavy bag in the corner of his studio, his fists wrapped, his breathing rough, his jaw tight with determination.

He must have been at this for hours, and it looks like he could keep going for hours more. Like an Olympian. Or a machine.

No. Like a weapon honed by five years of fury. Every muscle carved, every movement precise. Shoulders that could carry the weight of the world—and have.

A body I know so well, now coiled with well-honed rage.

I push my worry deep into my gut and try to sound casual when I say, "You promised to take me to The Beast."

He doesn't stop punishing the bag. In fact, the blows come faster.

"Not now, Bella." His breathing is hard. Ragged.

"You said we'd go soon. That was days ago. We're way past *soon*."

I move closer, facing him from the other side of the bag. "You promised to show me all of it. All of you." I reach out and hold the bag still. "It's time."

"Fuck." The curse sounds ripped out of him, and he steps back. His eyes are so bloodshot they're practically solid red. "You don't know what you're asking."

"Not really the point." I move around the bag to his side and draw a breath, softening a little. "Gabe, it's time."

Finally, he looks at me and nods, like all along, it was as simple as that. "Fine," he says, with an edge to his voice. "Let's go."

He pulls on a black tee that clings to his chest and torso, then takes my hand. I've never wandered all the corridors that lead into the belly of The Beast. My corner of this world is a small, plain studio apartment.

This is something else entirely.

Gabriel leads me through a steel door and down a corridor lit by caged bulbs, the concrete walls are painted black, and gurgling pipes run overhead as our footsteps echo behind us, the only sound we're making because Gabriel hasn't said a single word since we left the studio.

I pushed him into this, and now I'm getting the silent treatment. Fine. I can handle pissed. Pissed is better than the alternative.

Maybe I'm a little pissed, too.

The air seems to change as we go deeper—warmer and more humid, and carrying the faint copper tang of old blood and fresh sweat.

We pass doors marked with numbers, but no other labels. A muffled thud reverberates out from somewhere. Then another. And another.

Training rooms. Fighters preparing for what comes next.

The corridor turns, then turns again. A labyrinth. I'd never find my way back alone, and I think that's the point. This place wasn't built to be found. It was built to be hidden.

We move down yet another long corridor, but this one opens up at the end. And when it does, I swear I stop breathing.

A massive space stretches before us—part arena, part underground cathedral. Exposed pipes and industrial lighting, but also velvet ropes and gleaming bars.

Money and violence, dressed up pretty. The crowd hits me like a wave—bodies pressing, voices layered into a roar, the bass of music I can feel in my teeth. The energy is electric, primal, hungry. We're in the heart of The Beast, and it's like walking into a twisted Oz.

I turn to Gabriel. "Holy shit."

For the first time in two days, something like a smile tugs at the corner of his mouth. "Welcome to my world."

"Gabe...I, I mean, *wow*."

He almost laughs. "From you, that means a lot."

Since there's a ring in front of us, I'm about to ask him when the fight will start, but I'm silenced by the incongruous sound of my name echoing off the walls.

I turn, looking for the source, and find Anissa, waving and calling out, "Bella!"

I wave back and gesture for her to come over. She trots up, then sidles against Gabe and gives him an easy hug. I know there's nothing but friendship between them, but little green-eyed monsters start a protest march in my belly anyway.

Which means I guess I owe Gabe a slice of apology for being pissy about David.

"Dad didn't say you were coming." She grimaces at a look from Gabe, then rolls her eyes. "Sorry, *Travis* didn't say. Referring to him as my father isn't professional."

"No, it's not," Gabe says, but there's affection in his voice.

I shoot a sidelong glance at Gabe as I speak to Anissa. "I kinda had to twist his arm."

"I'm surprised he let you. I mean, your first time and it's

tonight?" She glances toward Gabe with a disbelieving shake of her head. I look at him, too. My expression hopefully demanding an explanation.

"Take her to the Owner's Box," Gabe says to Anissa. " I need to go warm up."

I look between them. "Warm up?"

Anissa's eyes go wide. "You didn't know? He's on the card tonight."

I've never heard the term before, but I'm pretty sure he's going to be in that ring soon. "What? Seriously?" I cross my arms and aim a mock glare at him. "You'd been planning on bringing me here tonight all along."

He chuckles, kisses my forehead. "Busted," he says, then slides through the crowd, pausing only to say a few words, sign a few cards, and shake a few hands.

"This really is Oz," I mutter as Anissa takes my arm. "Come on. Best seats in the house."

She leads me through the crowd—already rowdy enough that a private box sounds just peachy—then up a set of stairs to a raised platform overlooking everything. There's a leather couch, comfy chairs right at the edge for prime viewing, a video feed, presumably for playback, a small bar, and freedom from the jostle and shove below.

Pretty damn cool, actually. "So," Anissa says, settling onto the couch beside me. The crystals around her neck catch the light— amethyst, quartz, and a few others I don't recognize. "You're really going to watch him fight?"

"As of about forty-seven seconds ago, yes."

"Good." She stretches her legs out, utterly at ease in this place. Of course, she is. She's been part of Gabriel's world for five years. Longer than me, in some ways. The thought stings more than it should.

"You were there," I say. "In Colorado. After."

She nods, then pulls her feet up onto the seat and hugs her knees, as if the memory is one she doesn't want to get too close to.

"Dad found him in the woods. Half-dead, burned, out of his mind with fever." Her voice is low, and she's looking at her toes, not me.

"You didn't call the police?"

She shakes her head. "Dad didn't want to. Told me he'd heard some chatter." She shrugs. I don't know how. Just that he got wind that there was a hit out on someone in the area. He figured it was for the guy who owned this ramshackle old cabin through the woods from our place."

She shrugs again. "Somehow, Dad learned that the owner was one of the Grimm brothers. I found out later that one of his 'hunting mornings,'"—she makes quote marks with her fingers— "was really a jaunt to meet him and warn him. Except he was too late."

My heart is racing. "Does your dad know who tried to kill Gabe?"

She shakes her head. "He tried to meet up with his informant guy later to ask that. But the guy was dead." She shudders. "Honestly, I don't even know how he survived Dad dragging him home," she adds. "But he did, and we nursed him back. Took months. He'd wake up screaming your name, and I'd sit with him until he stopped shaking."

Jealousy flares through me, hot and irrational. She was there when I wasn't. She saw him broken, held him together.

Comforted him.

Anissa must see something in my face, because she puts her hand on mine. "Whatever you're thinking, don't. I love Gabriel like a brother. That's it. And trust me, even if I'd wanted more— which I didn't—it never would have happened. There was always someone else. Someone he couldn't let go of, no matter how hard he tried."

She looks pointedly at me.

I brush away tears. "He thought I shot him. He actually believed I could do that."

"Yeah, well, if you'd seen him then, you'd know what a mess

he was. He could barely breathe, much less think straight." She grins. "And now he knows better."

I manage a half-smile.

"For what it's worth, I never believed it."

My brows rise. "Why?"

"I don't know. Hopeless romantic, I guess. The way he talked about you—it was clear he thought you hung the moon. So of course I had to believe you thought the same, too, and it was all a big clusterfuck. Like Shakespeare or something."

I actually laugh. "Professors all over the world are cringing at the thought of works like *Romeo and Juliet* being categorized as a clusterfuck."

"Maybe," she says with a shrug. "But I'm right."

And, yeah. Maybe she is.

"I'm glad I was right," she says quietly. "I'm glad you found each other again. He's been half a person for years. Walking around with a hole in his chest where you used to be. And now..." She gestures vaguely at me. "Now he's got a chance to be whole."

Below us, the crowd is getting louder. The fight before Gabriel's is brutal—two massive men trading blows that would kill an ordinary person. One of them goes down after what feels like hours, blood streaming from a cut above his eye, and the crowd roars its approval as he's dragged from the arena.

I've never been so grateful for violence in my life. It gives me somewhere to look that isn't Anissa's too-kind face. Something to focus on besides the tears burning behind my eyes.

Anissa's fingers twine with mine.

Then the announcer's voice booms through the speakers:

"Ladies and gentlemen...the main event. You know him. You fear him. The owner, the champion, the man himself...THE BEAST."

The crowd loses its mind.

Gabriel steps shirtless into the pit, and I don't recognize him.

Gone is the man who held me two days ago, who agreed to do this together, who whispered "day by day" against my hair.

In his place is something else entirely. Something cold and controlled and utterly terrifying.

The Beast.

His opponent is bigger. Taller, broader, with arms like tree trunks and a neck thick as my thigh. He looks like he could snap Gabriel in half without breaking a sweat.

Gabriel doesn't seem concerned.

They circle each other, testing, feinting. The crowd is screaming, but I can't hear them anymore. All I can see is Gabriel—the fluid grace of his movements, the predator's focus in his eyes, the coiled power waiting to be unleashed.

The big man lunges first.

Gabriel sidesteps, drives an elbow into his opponent's kidney, spins away before the counterpunch can land. It's beautiful. Brutal. Like watching a dance choreographed in hell.

"Breathe," Anissa murmurs beside me. I realize I've been holding my breath.

The fight lasts longer than I expected. The big man is skilled, and lands several blows that make me wince, including one that opens a cut on Gabriel's lip that sends blood streaming down his chin. But Gabriel keeps coming. Keeps pressing. Keeps finding openings where there shouldn't be any.

And then, suddenly, it's over.

One moment they're trading blows, evenly matched, both breathing hard. The next, Gabriel's behind him, arm locked around his throat, squeezing with a cold efficiency that makes my stomach turn.

The big man taps out. Goes limp.

Gabriel releases him, steps back, and looks up at me.

His face is bloody. His eyes are wild. The beast is fully awake, fully present, and it's staring at me with an intensity that should terrify me.

It doesn't.

I stare back. Hold his gaze. Let him see that I'm still here. Still watching. Still not running.

Something in his expression shifts. Softens, just slightly.

Then he turns and disappears through a door at the edge of the pit.

I'm on my feet before I realize I've moved.

"Back corridor," Anissa calls. "Third door on the left."

I push through the crowd, relieved when I reach the relative quiet of the corridor. I follow the sound of running water until I find an open door—third on the left, just like she said.

Gabriel is inside, washing blood from his hands in a sink. His back is to me, muscles still taut with unspent adrenaline. Water runs pink down the drain.

I shut the door behind me and lock it.

"You should have stayed in the box," he says without turning around.

"Since when do I do what I should?"

A sound escapes him—not quite a laugh. He braces his hands on the edge of the sink, head bowed, water still running.

"Now you know," he says quietly. "What I am. What I have to do to stay human. To keep the demons at bay."

I cross the room. Press myself against his back, wrap my arms around his waist. Feel the tremors running through him—aftershocks of violence, the beast slowly retreating into its cage.

"Now I know," I repeat, then press a kiss to his shoulder blade. "And I'm still here."

He stills for a moment, then turns in my arms. His face is a wreck—bloody lip, bruise forming along his jaw, that wild light still flickering in his eyes. He looks feral. Dangerous. Beautiful.

"I don't deserve you," he says.

"Yes, but who would, really?"

As I'd hoped, he laughs, and I take advantage of the moment to pull his head down and kiss him hard.

His control snaps.

One second I'm standing in front of him, the next I'm pressed against the wall, his body pinning mine, his mouth devouring me with a hunger that borders on violence. But it's not the beast—not entirely. There's desperation in it. Need. The raw, ragged edge of a man who—I hope—finally realizes that he's not alone.

"Bella." My name is a growl against his throat. "Tell me to stop."

"No."

"Tell me you don't want this."

"I want this." I arch into him, feel his cock pressing against me. "I want you. All of you. Man. Beast. Everything."

There's a cot in the room, and he throws me down onto it. I gasp, reaching for him, wanting him right there with me.

And then he is, his mouth on mine as his hands make quick work of my top and my slacks until I'm naked beneath him, and his shorts have disappeared as well.

I squirm until he lets me up, then I straddle him, his cock hard against my ass as I let my hands roam over his torso. Every scar, every ridge of muscle, every place that makes him gasp when I press my mouth to it after my hand maps the way. Not tender, but wild with teeth and hunger and need. To have him. And—oh, dear god, yes—to be had.

This isn't tender. This isn't controlled.

This is something else entirely.

He takes me completely apart. Every touch is electric, every kiss feels like a bruise. And when he finally thrusts inside me, I feel the last wall between us crumbling to dust.

We move together like we're trying to crawl inside each other's skin. Like if we get close enough, nothing can tear us apart again. His hands are everywhere—my hips, my breasts, my throat. Claiming. Possessing. And I give him everything, holding nothing back, meeting his intensity with my own.

When I shatter, his name tears out of me like a violent prayer. He follows moments later, his whole body shuddering, his face buried in my neck.

For a long time, neither of us moves. We just breathe together, tangled on the narrow cot, his weight pressing me into the thin mattress. I don't mind. I want to feel him everywhere.

Eventually, he rolls to his side, pulling me with him so we're facing each other. The wild light has faded from his eyes, replaced by something softer. Something almost peaceful.

"I love you," he says quietly. "I loved you when I thought I hated you. And I'll love you until there's nothing left of me."

"Then don't let there be nothing left." I trace my fingers along his jaw, feeling the bruise forming there. "Don't let the beast consume you. Don't let my father win."

Something shifts in his expression. Sharpens.

"Is that what you're afraid of? That I'll kill him?"

"I'm afraid you'll destroy yourself trying." I press my forehead to his. "I just got you back, Gabriel. I can't lose you again. Not to death. Not to prison. Not to the darkness."

He's quiet for a moment, his hand stroking slow circles on my back.

"I do want him dead," he finally says. "Every time I think about what he did, what he would have done to you—"

"I know." I kiss him softly. "I know. But want and action aren't the same thing. You can want him dead and still choose to let the courts handle it. You can be the beast and still decide what the beast does."

He stares at me for a long moment. Then something in his face breaks open—not grief this time, but something else. Something that looks almost like hope. He pulls me closer, tucks my head under his chin, and I feel his chest rise and fall beneath my cheek. For this one moment, the beast is quiet. The darkness is at bay.

This is what we're fighting for.

Us. A life we can build together.

I just have to hope he's brave enough to choose it.

CHAPTER
THIRTY-FOUR

The next few days settle into something almost like normal.

Gabriel paints. I run the Monarch. We meet in the middle—breakfast together, dinner together, and deliciously slow, sweet nights that make me more and more confident that this fragile thing we're rebuilding might actually survive.

"You're thinking too loud," Gabriel murmurs against my shoulder as we cuddle in bed, the morning light sneaking into the closet he calls a bedroom through the cracked door.

"Sorry. Occupational hazard."

He pulls me closer, presses a kiss to the curve of my neck. "And what occupation is that exactly?"

I laugh. "Hanging out lazily with you. I happen to have a PhD. Highest honors.

"I'm impressed. And what does your doctoral brain say you should do?"

"It's debating whether I should get up and be a responsible adult or stay here and let you do that thing with your tongue again."

His laugh is low and warm. "I vote for the tongue thing."

"You would."

I'm about to roll over and take him up on that offer when his phone buzzes on the tiny nightstand. He ignores it, his hand sliding down my hip, but then it buzzes again. And again.

"Someone really wants to talk to you," I say.

Gabriel sighs and reaches for the phone. I watch his face as he reads whatever's on the screen—watch the softness drain away, replaced by something cold and hard and terrifyingly familiar.

"What is it?"

He doesn't answer right away. Just stares at the phone, jaw tight, a muscle ticking in his cheek.

"Gabriel. What?"

"Leo." His voice is flat. Controlled in a way that makes my stomach clench. "Your father made a move last night. Tried to have one of Leo's informants killed."

"An informant who was working for my father, you mean?"

He draws a breath, then nods. "The guy survived, but barely. Sterling Hart doesn't take betrayal well." His eyes are locked on mine as he says the words, and I have to force the bile back down my throat. Because haven't I betrayed him more than anyone?

I push that lovely thought down as I sit up, pulling the sheet around me.

"The real kick in the gut is that this informant was helping us build the case against your dad." Gabriel's eyes meet mine, and there's nothing soft in them now. Nothing of the man who was kissing my neck just moments ago. "He's cleaning house. Eliminating anyone who can connect him to what happened in Aspen."

The words hit me hard.

I've known for ages that my father is an all-out prick capable of terrible things. But knowing it abstractly and watching the fallout in real time are two very different things.

"We need to go to the FBI," I say. "Now. Before he can do anything else."

"The hell with that. That fucker needs to die."

The words hang in the air between us, cold and final.

He's not joking. He's not venting. He's stating a fact.

He's making a plan.

"Gabriel..." My voice is laced with a very sharp edge.

"Don't." He's out of bed now, moving out of the tiny bedroom and into the hallway where he can pace. I slide into my robe, then stand in the doorway and watch him, naked and furious, every muscle coiled tight.

"Don't what? Don't involve the authorities? That's nuts."

His eyes flash to mine. "Don't tell me to let the system handle it."

"Why not? That's the point. It's why we have a system in the first place."

"Bullshit. Did the system keep Leo's informant from almost dying?"

He stops pacing and faces me. "Sterling already tried to kill me. Now he's eliminating witnesses. How long before he decides you're too dangerous to leave alive?"

"So your solution is to what? Emulate him and kill, too?"

"My solution is to end a fucking threat against me and the woman I love."

He stalks toward me, and I have to fight the urge to shrink back. "He sent that message, Bella. The AI voice. You think that was an idle threat?"

I step toward him, my hands clenched at my sides. "I think going after him is exactly what he wants you to do. "He's baiting you. Pushing you. Hoping you'll do something stupid so he can—"

"So he can what? Have me arrested? Kill me?" Gabriel laughs, but there's no humor in it. "He's already tried to kill me once. And he'll try again. The only question is whether I get to him first."

"Listen to yourself." My voice is shaking now. "You sound exactly like him. Eliminating threats. Ending problems. That's his language. That's how he thinks."

Something flickers in his eyes. Pain, maybe. Or recognition.

"If you do this, you really will become a monster. Just like he is. Please, Gabe. Please do the right thing."

"Goddammit, Bella," he says, his voice barely a whisper. "They tortured me. They left me for dead. Your father was walking around like a modern-day prince while I had Death holding me by the scruff of the neck. How the fuck can letting that prick of a man live be the right thing?"

"But it is," I say, gently taking his hands. "You already know that." I move my hands to his cheeks and force him to look at me. "If you kill him now, he becomes a martyr. A victim. But if we do this the right way—with police and courts and news reports and evidence—he'll lose everything. His reputation. His freedom. His legacy. Everything he's spent his whole life building." And for a man like my father, that's a fate worse than death.

Gabriel is quiet. I can see him struggling, the beast and the man at war behind his eyes. His hands have come up to cover mine where they rest on his face, and for a moment, I think I've reached him.

"He'll find a way out," he finally says. "Men like him always do. Money. Lawyers. Connections. He'll slither free, and then he'll come for us. For you—not just because you sided with me, but because you're how he can hurt me."

"Maybe he will," I concede. "But at least you won't have blood on your hands." I soften my voice, stroke my thumb across his cheekbone. "I just got you back. I can't lose you again. Not to death. Not to prison. And definitely not back to the darkness."

For a moment—just a moment—I see the real him. The man who painted me sleeping, who whispered "day by day" against my hair, who's trying so hard to claw his way back to the man he used to be.

Then his expression shutters. Goes cold. His hands drop back to his sides.

"You're asking me to let him live."

"I'm asking you to let justice happen."

"There is no justice for what he did to me."

The silence stretches between us, thick and suffocating.

"I can't do this," I say quietly. "I can't stand here and listen to you plan a murder. If you do this—if you kill him—the beast wins. And I won't watch you disappear into it."

"Bella."

"No." I'm gathering my clothes now, pulling on whatever I can find. Shirt inside out, doesn't matter. Slacks wrinkled from where they landed on the floor last night. I can feel his eyes on me, but I can't look at him. If I look at him, I'll stay. And staying means watching him destroy himself.

"Don't go back to the Monarch," he says, his voice barely a whisper. "Your father will have people there. You're not safe."

I draw in a breath. About that, at least, we agree. "I'll stay with David at the Mercer Casino."

"No. Don't draw him into this. I'll tell Leo you need to crash at Grimm Tower. Harper's staying there, too, I think."

I nod. "Great. Perfect." I sling my purse over my shoulder, then head for the door, wondering if the man I love is still in there, or if the beast has finally won.

I'm at the door when his voice stops me.

"I'm doing this for you." The words are raw. Ragged. "To keep you safe from him."

I turn. Look at him standing there in the wreckage of our morning, beautiful and broken and so lost it makes my heart crack open. Still naked. Still furious. Still the man I love, even when I want to shake him until his teeth rattle.

"So far, yeah, maybe. But don't you dare say that vengeance and murder are for me. That's not a gift, and it's not love. And I wouldn't want it if it was."

I look him up and down. "If it's really all for me, then prove it. Choose me over vengeance. Choose us over blood. Because I won't build a life wondering when the darkness is going to swallow you whole."

I wait, giving him one last chance to say the words I need to hear.

He doesn't—and I walk out the door, navigating this underground maze until I climb a set of stairs and slip out through one of the basement exits, happy to avoid going through the hotel.

I stand there for a moment, blinking in the brightness, letting my eyes adjust. Atlantic City spreads out before me—the boardwalk in the distance, the ocean beyond, seagulls wheeling overhead. Normal life. Regular people going about their regular days, completely oblivious to the underground empire beneath their feet.

I take a breath. Then another.

And then I start walking toward Grimm Tower, leaving the beast and its master behind.

CHAPTER
THIRTY-FIVE

Gabriel Grimm had ridden in this elevator to the Grimm Tower penthouse a million times and was certain it had never once moved this slowly.

He gave the polished interior a hard kick as he stared at the climbing numbers and tried to figure out what the hell he was going to say. He'd never been good at apologies. Never had to be.

He was a Grimm, after all. And the Grimm men didn't apologize—they maneuvered, strategized, outplayed their opponents until they were the ones saying sorry.

Gabriel knew that well. He'd been his father's favorite. The bright and shiny heir. The one that had the family's friends trembling—and their enemies pissing themselves.

And none of that mattered.

Isabella wasn't an opponent he could out-maneuver. And it damn sure wasn't a game he could win with strategy.

The number climbed. Forty-two. Forty-three.

He'd called Leo on the way over, just to confirm she'd arrived safely. She had, and Leo left her alone to chase a lead on Sterling's location. He and Mina had been away from the Monarch for days now, and the lead was hot. Hopefully, it would go somewhere, but Sterling was slippery enough that Gabe doubted they'd get that lucky so soon.

Harper was also crashing at the penthouse, but Leo said she'd be gone until morning. Some sort of work crisis had sent her off to Manhattan.

All of which meant Isabella was alone there. She was safe—Grimm security around the residence was top-notch—but that didn't mean she was settled. She was probably stewing in the same toxic cocktail of anger and hurt that had been churning through Gabriel's gut since she'd walked out.

Forty-seven. Forty-eight.

He watched the floors go by, wondering what he was going to say? That he was sorry? That he'd been wrong? That the thought of letting Sterling Hart breathe another day made him want to claw his way out of his own skin, but the thought of losing her was worse?

All of it was true. None of it felt like enough.

Fifty. Fifty-one.

He'd spent three hours at The Beast after she left. Not fighting. Just standing at ringside, watching other men trade blows because he couldn't make himself get in there to burn it off. Couldn't find the will to get in that ring and picture each and every one of his opponents as Sterling Fucking Hart.

He'd tried, dammit. But he couldn't find the right headspace. Instead, he just found her, over and over, telling him that he was on the verge of becoming what he despised. A monster. Just like Sterling Hart.

She was right. He hated that she was right.

Fifty-four.

Finally.

The doors slid open, and Gabriel stepped out into the foyer. The penthouse was quiet, lights dimmed, the massive windows showcasing Atlantic City's glittering sprawl. He could see her silhouette on the balcony, wrapped in what looked like one of Leo's hoodies, staring out at nothing.

His chest ached just looking at her.

He crossed the living room slowly, giving her time to hear his footsteps, to decide if she wanted to flee before he reached her. She didn't move at all. Just stood there, her back to him, arms wrapped around herself, shoulders tight with tension.

Finally, she said, "Leo told you that I'm alone here tonight, didn't he?"

"Don't blame him. I'm older and can take him in a fight."

She didn't turn, but the way her shoulders moved suggested he'd won a smile.

That was something.

"He also said you probably don't want to see me, but I'm an asshole and came anyway."

This time, her shoulders didn't move.

"Can I come out there with you?"

She was quiet for a long moment. Then, "I don't know. Can you do it without telling me how my father needs to die?"

He still believed it. Probably always would. But that wasn't why he was here.

"I can try."

Another pause. Then she shifted slightly, making room at the railing. Not an invitation, exactly. But not a rejection either.

The wind was cold this high up, but he barely felt it. All he could feel as he moved to the rail was her—the distance between them, the wall she'd built since this morning, the fear radiating off her in waves.

Fear of him. *No.* Fear *for* him. Fear of what he might become.

And that hurt worse than anything Sterling Hart had ever done to him.

"I'm sorry," he said.

She didn't respond. Didn't move away. Didn't shrug. Didn't look at him.

He cleared his throat. "This morning, I was wrong. The way I talked about your father, the things I said—I made you feel like your opinion didn't matter. Like I'd already made up my mind and you just had to live with it." He gripped the railing, knuckles white. "That's not okay. That's not the man I want to be. Not with you."

"And what man do you want to be?" She finally turned to look at him, and the pain in her eyes nearly broke him. "Because the one I saw this morning scared me, Gabriel. Really scared me."

"I know."

"Do you?" She stepped closer, and he could see the tracks of dried tears on her cheeks. "Because here's what I keep coming back to. You believed the worst about me for five years. Five years of hating me, planning to destroy me. But then, when it really mattered, you chose to believe in me without proof. You took a leap of faith."

"I remember."

"So why can't you do that now?" Her voice cracked. "Why can't you have faith that the system will work? That my father will face real consequences? Why does it have to be blood?"

The question cut deep. Deeper than she knew.

"Because systems don't work for men like him." The words came out raw. "Sterling Hart has been committing crimes for decades. Money laundering, bribery, attempted murder—and he's never spent a single night in jail. And right now, he's out there eliminating witnesses while we wait for warrants to get signed."

Bella said nothing, her expression unreadable.

"I know what you're asking me to do," he continued. "I know the courts are the right answer. I know killing him makes me a monster. I know all of that." He turned to face her fully. "But every time I close my eyes, I see that cabin. I feel the ropes. I hear them whispering your name." He stopped. Breathed. "And then I think about him walking free. Again. Like he always does. And the beast wants blood."

She wrapped her arms around herself, not in defense of the cold, he thought, but in defense against him.

"So you're going to give it to him? Blood?" Her voice was

barely a whisper. "That's the plan? Kill him and damn the consequences?"

"The plan is to protect you the only way I know how."

"By becoming someone I can't love?"

The words hit like a physical blow, and he swallowed. Hard.

"No," he said softly, then took her hand, and when she didn't pull away, something loosened in his chest. "I can't lose you over this. Over him."

He dragged the fingers of his free hand through his hair. "This morning, you asked me to choose, and I couldn't give you an answer. But I have one now."

"And?"

"I choose you." He lifted her hand to his lips, pressed a kiss to her knuckles. "I choose us. I choose being the kind of man who lets the courts handle it, even when every cell in my body wants blood."

Her smile bloomed as he continued.

"I choose day by day, one step at a time, figuring out how to be someone worthy of you."

Bella looked at him, her eyes searching his face as if for cracks. For any sign that this was just another pretty speech.

He let her look. He had nothing left to hide.

"I want to believe you," she finally said.

"But?"

"But I've heard a lot of promises from a lot of men that weren't worth a dime. My father. David. Even you—you promised to come back from Aspen, and then you were gone for five years. You were right here. Right under my nose, and I never had a clue."

She pulled her hand gently from his. "I need more than words, Gabe. I need time."

"Time." The word tasted sour and felt like a slamming door.

"Time to think. Time to figure out if loving each other is enough." She wrapped her arms around herself again, pulling away. "I hear what you're saying. And I believe you want to mean it. But wanting and doing are different things."

"Bella."

"Please." Her voice was barely a whisper. "Please just let me sleep on it. Let me figure out what I need."

Every instinct screamed at him to stay. To argue. To hold her until she believed him, until the wall between them crumbled and they were back in bed, tangled together like this morning had never happened.

But that wasn't what she was asking for. And if he was really going to be different—really going to choose her better angels over his demons—then this was where it started.

"Okay," he said.

She blinked. "Okay? Really? Okay?"

"You need time. I'll give you time." He stepped back, putting distance between them even though each inch made his heart ache more.

"Oh."

He heard the surprise in her voice and almost laughed.

"Gabe. Thank you."

"I love you." He said it simply, without expectation. "I'll love you tomorrow, and the day after, and every day until you tell me to stop. And I'll keep loving you then, too, because stopping's impossible. But I'll be quieter about it."

She smiled, and the sight of it squeezed his heart. "Seriously. Take whatever time you need. I'll be here when you're ready."

He made himself turn. Made himself walk back through the penthouse, past the expensive furniture and the stunning views and all the trappings of the Grimm empire that suddenly meant nothing.

At the elevator, he paused and looked back.

She was still on the balcony, silhouetted against the city lights, small and alone.

He wanted to go back to her. Wanted it more than he'd ever wanted anything.

Instead, he pressed the button and stepped into the elevator.

The doors closed, and Gabriel Grimm did the hardest thing he'd ever done in his life.

He let her go.

CHAPTER
THIRTY-SIX

I don't sleep.

After Gabriel leaves, I stand on the balcony for a long time, watching the city lights blur through tears I refuse to let fall. The wind is cold up here—fifty-four floors of cold—but I barely feel it. All I can feel is the hollow ache in my chest where Gabe used to live.

He said all the right things. Made all the right promises. And I believe he meant them. In that moment, standing in front of me, he meant every word.

But moments pass and promises fade. And I've spent my whole life learning that the people who love you are the same people who hurt you most.

My father loved me. In his own twisted way, I think he really did. Maybe still does. And look what that love cost Gabriel. Cost us.

So, yes. Gabriel loves me. I don't doubt that anymore. But love isn't always enough. Sometimes love is the dark thing that destroys you.

I close my eyes, blocking the view when I'm trying to block my thoughts. Trying to simply *be*.

Turns out, just existing is harder than it sounds.

Eventually, I go back inside, and I wander through the rooms, too restless to sit, too exhausted to stand. The kitchen is stocked with things I don't want to eat. The bar is stocked with things I probably shouldn't drink. The massive flat-screen TV offers a zillion channels of nothing I want to watch.

I try anyway.

I curl up on the leather sofa, wrapped in a cashmere throw as I flip mindlessly through channels without seeing any of them. News—too depressing. Reality TV—too vapid. A romantic comedy that makes me want to throw the remote because the couple on screen is fighting about a forgotten anniversary instead of, oh, I don't know, whether one of them is going to murder the other's father.

I turn it off.

Silence is better. Much better.

Except it's not. I'm completely at loose ends. The penthouse feels too big. Too empty. And the silence is pressing in from all sides like something physical.

On top of all that, I keep glancing at my phone, waiting for what? Gabriel to text? To call? To tell me he's changed his mind, or I should change mine, or that somehow in the last hour he's figured out the magic words that will make all of this okay?

There are no magic words. I know that. But I keep hoping anyway.

I think about calling Harper and pouring out everything to her —the fight, the apology, the impossible choice Gabriel is asking me to make. She'd listen. She'd probably even have something wise to say, or at least something sarcastic enough to make me laugh.

But it's late, and she's probably still in New York, dealing with her own crisis, and I don't want to be the friend who interrupts someone else's crisis to whine about her own.

So I sit. And I stare at the ceiling. And I sip whiskey and consider a bubble bath and try to figure out what the hell I'm supposed to do now.

Do I believe him?

The question circles through my mind like a shark, restless and hungry. He said he'd choose me. Choose us. Choose the courts over blood. But I've heard promises before. My father promised to protect me while he was plotting to kill the man I loved. David promised our engagement was just business while he was falling in love with me.

Even Gabriel. For those first two years he gets a pass. But once he was fully entrenched at The Beast? Once I'd moved from Connecticut to the Monarch so I could learn the business inside and out? Once he was literally just a few blocks away?

And still he stayed silent?

Honestly, it makes my heart hurt.

Of course, if my father hadn't tried to kill him—hadn't made him believe I was in on it—well, of course, he'd have come back.

Is that what's making me so pissy? That he lost faith in me?

I shake my head. *I just don't know anymore.*

Except I do. At first, yes. That stung. His hatred. His fury. And all directed against a woman that wasn't really me.

That about killed me, that lack of trust.

But we got through it.

That was the hard one. Now? Well, I'm okay with him believing my dad deserves to die. God knows, I believe that myself. But thinking he *should* die is a lot different than playing executioner.

And so long as Gabe means what he says—so long as he doesn't take off like a vigilante to take out my father before the law can handle it—well, then I think we're good.

I hope so.

On the whole, I don't ask the world for much. But I'm asking now. I want him back. I want him to work through the trauma that's eating him alive. To push past all those hurts he never should have had to bear and didn't deserve.

I think he can. I hope he can.

But that's the thing about trauma. It doesn't care about fault. It just...is. And Gabriel's trauma has teeth. Has claws. Has a beast living inside it that wants blood.

Can he really keep that beast leashed? Could anyone?

I don't know. And not knowing is the worst part.

At some point, I must have dozed off. Now my neck aches from sleeping at an awkward angle, and my mouth tastes dry and bitter.

My phone chimes with a text, and I snatch it up. *Harper.*

You there?

I tap out a reply—*Here. You still in NYC?*

Her reply comes fast.

Can you come down to the parking garage? Stuff to carry. Save me from multiple trips?

Not my idea of a fun morning activity, but I'm hardly going to say no. Besides, I need to move. I'm all stiff from falling asleep on the sofa.

I drag myself off the couch, still wearing yesterday's clothes. I don't bother changing. Don't bother checking my reflection. What's the point? It's just Harper.

I grab my phone and keys, pausing briefly to look at my reflection in the entryway mirror. My own exhaustion stares back at me. Dark circles under my eyes, hair tangled, skin dull and pale.

Gabriel would tell me I'm beautiful anyway. The thought makes my chest ache.

The ride down takes forever. Fifty-four floors of piped in music is cruel and unusual punishment. For what condos in this building cost, there should be a live orchestra right there in the corner.

The elevator opens onto the parking garage, and I step out into concrete and fluorescent lights and the smell of exhaust and damp asphalt.

"Harper?"

My voice bounces off the walls. No answer.

I walk deeper into the garage, past rows of expensive cars that belong to the building's other residents. BMWs and Mercedes and a Tesla or three. Nobody else is around. Too early for anyone to be leaving for work, too late for anyone to be coming home from a night out.

"Harper, dammit where are you?"

Still nothing.

I pull out my phone and send a quick text—*I'm going back up. Meet me there, and we'll ride back down together.*

I know there's a guard at the gate, and I consider asking him to check all his cameras and tell me where she is, but it's a long, circular walk. And even though I'm sure it's only paranoia, I'm getting a little creeped out.

That's when I see him.

A tall man, stepping out from behind a concrete pillar. I take a step back. Then another.

"Ms. Hart." His voice is almost polite. "Your father would like a word."

My blood goes cold. "I'm not going anywhere with you."

"I'm afraid that's not optional." He gestures toward a black SUV idling near the exit, its windows tinted dark. "We can do this quietly, or we can do it loud. Your choice. But you're coming either way."

I think about screaming. About running. About the self-defense moves Gabriel tried to teach me, back when the most dangerous thing in my life was a handsy investor at a gallery opening.

But this guy's a professional, and even if I screamed, who would hear me? It's not yet five in the morning in an empty parking garage. By the time anyone responded, I'd already be gone. I need to buy time to make a plan.

"My father sent you?" I ask, stalling. "Sterling Hart?"

"Please come with us."

It's the *us*, that catches my attention, and that's when I feel something hard press against my lower back.

There's a second man. And he has the barrel of a gun pressed right against my spine.

"Like I said." The tall man's smile doesn't reach his eyes. "Not optional."

The gunman guides me toward the SUV, one hand on my elbow, the gun still pressed to my back. My mind races—looking for options, looking for escape routes, looking for anything that might give me an advantage.

There's nothing.

The SUV door slides open. Gun Guy pushes me inside. The other one zip-ties my wrists before I can even think about fighting back. As if I would. *Gun.*

"Hand over your phone," Gun Guy says.

I consider saying I left it upstairs. But they'll search me anyway, and the punishment for lying will be worse than the punishment for compliance. "Back pocket."

He roughly pushes me forward, pulls it out, then drops it on the garage floor. Then he stomps on it. Hard. After that, he shuts the door, circles around to the driver's seat, and starts the car.

The engine roars to life, and I fight the urge to vomit.

But as we pull out of the garage into the gray morning light, I hold tight to one absolute certainty—Gabriel Grimm is going to burn the world down looking for me.

I just have to stay alive long enough for him to find me.

CHAPTER
THIRTY-SEVEN

The call came at 6:47 AM.

Gabriel was in the ring at The Beast, sparring with one of his trainers, trying to burn off the restless energy that had been crawling under his skin since he'd left Bella at the penthouse. He hadn't slept. Hadn't even tried. Just paced his apartment until the walls started closing in, then came down here to hit something.

It wasn't working. Every punch he threw, he saw her face. Every combination, he heard her voice. *I need time to think. Time to decide if loving each other is enough.*

He should have stayed at the tower. Should have fought harder. Should have found the words to make her understand that he'd already chosen—had chosen her the moment he decided to believe in her innocence, had been choosing her every day since, even when he didn't know how to show it.

His phone buzzed against the bench where he'd left it. He ignored it. Threw another combination. Ducked a counter punch.

It buzzed again. And again. And again.

"Boss." His trainer stepped back, dropping his hands. "Might be important."

Gabriel caught his breath. Looked at the screen.

Harper. Four missed calls in three minutes. And as he stood there, a text from her. *911.*

Something cold slithered through his gut. He snatched up the phone and pounded the button to call her back.

"Oh, thank god." Harper's voice was wrong. Tight. Scared. As if she was trying very hard to hold herself together. "Bella's gone. I think someone took her."

The world stopped.

"What are you talking about?"

"I got back to the penthouse, and she wasn't here. Her purse, her keys, everything's still here. Just not her. So I used that location service thing, and her last location was the parking garage."

Harper's breath hitched. "I went down to check. Oh, god, Gabe, her phone is on the floor. Smashed. Like someone stomped on it."

Fear and fury poured through him. And the beast woke up.

He made it to Grimm Tower in seven minutes. It would have been faster if he hadn't hit every red light on the way, if his hands hadn't been shaking so badly that he'd nearly sideswiped a delivery truck.

The parking garage was dim and cold, fluorescent lights buzzed overhead like insects. Harper was already there, standing near the elevator bank, her face pale and drawn.

"Where?" Gabriel demanded.

She didn't answer. Just turned and led him deeper into the garage, past rows of luxury cars, past the reserved spaces with their brass nameplates, to a spot near the exit ramp.

And there, on the concrete floor, was Bella's phone.

"I didn't think I should touch it," Harper said as he bent to pick it up, using a tissue just in case there were prints.

"You did good." He managed to keep the words level, despite the rage roiling through him. Not aimed at Harper. No, this rage was aimed at Sterling Hart and the flunkies who'd taken her. At the bastards he was going to kill.

"Security cameras." His voice came out steady. Controlled. He had to hold onto that control if he was going to get her back. "This building has security cameras."

"I called," Harper said. "They're pulling the footage now. He said to come to the security office when you got here."

He nodded, then held out his hand, then pulled her close and wrapped her in a hug. "Tell me she's going to be okay," he said.

"She will," Harper whispered. "Of course, she will. Have I ever lied to you?"

"Not and gotten away with it."

She laughed, then rose up to kiss his cheek before cupping his face in her hands. "No tears," she said.

"I was an ass," he said, his voice so low he was amazed she heard it. "I was an ass, and so she went to the penthouse instead of staying with me. If something happens to her…"

He trailed off with a shudder, holding Harper tight, and hoping for all he was worth that he'd soon be holding Izzy."

"Come on," Harper said. "The sooner we find her, the sooner you can bloody whoever took her."

He didn't laugh, but his lips twitched.

And she damn sure wasn't wrong.

She held his hand as they walked to the security office, a cramped room on the ground floor filled with monitors and blinking lights and a building manager named Patterson who kept wiping his palms on his slacks.

"Here," Patterson said, pointing at one of the screens. "I'm sorry to say, this is the only angle we have of that section of the garage. But at least it's something."

Gabriel scowled as he watched the footage play. A grainy, low-resolution image with a starting timestamp of 5:20:27 AM.

At 5:24:10, Bella walked into frame. Even in the poor-quality video, Gabriel could see the exhaustion in her posture, like she was carrying a weight too heavy for her shoulders.

His fault. He'd put that weight there.

She stopped. Looked around. Called out something. Harper, probably, based on the shape of her mouth.

And then they appeared.

Two men. Big. Professional. They'd positioned themselves carefully—faces angled away from the cameras, baseball caps pulled low, nothing that could be used for identification. They knew exactly where the blind spots were. Knew exactly how to move through the space without giving the cameras anything useful.

Sterling had sent pros. Not surprising.

He watched as Bella tried to back away, then as one of the men circled behind her to press something—a gun, it had to be a gun—against her back.

That's when he saw the change. When all the fight went out of her.

They guided her toward a black SUV idling near the exit. She didn't fight. What choice did she have?

The SUV door opened. Hands pushed her inside. The door slammed shut.

And then she was gone.

"I got back to the penthouse about twenty minutes before I called you," Harper said. "I thought about crashing in New York, but I figured Bella needed me. And then I realized she wasn't there when I stuck my head into the bedrooms to see if she was awake. If I'd just skipped the damn coffee and left earlier—"

"No." Gabriel took her hand. Squeezed it. "None of this is on you. You did exactly the right thing." He turned to Patterson. "And that's it?" His voice was deadly quiet. "That's all you have?"

Patterson nodded jerkily. "I'm sorry, Mr. Grimm. The cameras in that section... They're older. Lower resolution. We've been meaning to upgrade, but the board keeps pushing back on the budget."

"Get out."

"I'm sorry?"

"Get. Out."

Patterson fled. Smart man.

Gabriel stood there staring at the frozen image on the screen. The last frame before she disappeared. Bella, being pushed into that SUV, her face turned just slightly toward the camera.

She looked scared. She looked brave. She looked like a woman who knew she was in trouble and was already planning how to survive it.

God, he loved her.

"I'm going to kill them. Those men. Sterling. They're going to pay for this."

The words came out flat. Matter-of-fact. Not a threat—a promise.

"Dammit, Gabe, think." Harper crossed her arms as she stood in the doorway. "For one thing, where? You haven't got a clue where he took her. You planning to burn down the Monarch? Because that won't work.

"Guess we'll find out. At the very least, I can take that away from him. But, no. I'm only going to his penthouse. I promise you, he's there. And he knows where she is."

He stood up, and she moved in front of him. "You're playing into that asshole's hands. You go in there guns blazing, you'll either end up dead or in prison, and then who's going to save Bella?"

"Get out of my way, Harper."

"No." She moved to the security room's doorway and spread her arms. "I know you're scared. I know you're angry. I'm scared and angry too—she's my best friend. But Bella needs you thinking clearly, not running off to do something stupid."

"He has her." The words tore out of him, ragged and raw. "Sterling Hart is a goddamn monster, and he has her, and every second I stand here is another second that she could be—*No.*

He couldn't go there. Couldn't let himself imagine what Sterling might be doing to her. What those men might be doing.

"Leo's already got people checking Sterling's properties," Harper said. "His known associates, anywhere she might be. The

FBI has a warrant for his arrest—they're looking for him, too. We will find her."

"I'm going to the Monarch."

"Gabriel—"

"He might be there. He'd probably take her there. Where she and David pulled one over on him. Where she and I have the Gallery. It's the place she'll inherit when she marries. And it's the place where she finally started standing up to him."

His eyes met Harper's, hard and sure. "He'll take her there. And I'm fucking terrified that he'll kill her there, too."

CHAPTER
THIRTY-EIGHT

The drive to the Monarch took seven minutes. Gabriel didn't remember most of it—just the blur of streetlights, the white-knuckle grip on the steering wheel, rage howling in his chest.

He left the car running in the valet zone and stormed through the front doors.

The lobby was quiet at this hour. A few early-bird gamblers at the slots, a couple checking out at the front desk, staff going about their morning routines with the glazed efficiency of people who'd been awake too long.

They all stopped when they saw him.

Gabriel knew what he must look like. Sweat-soaked from sparring, still in his workout clothes, his face a mask of barely contained violence. The guests shrank back. The staff froze.

He stalked to the front desk.

"Where is he?" Gabriel's voice echoed off the marble floors. "Where is Sterling Hart?"

A manager appeared—young, nervous, probably fresh out of a hospitality program. His name tag identified him as Jesse.

Sir," Jesse said, "Mr. Hart isn't on the premises today. He called in sick two days ago, and we haven't—"

"Don't lie to me."

"I'm not lying, sir. I swear. He's not here. Perhaps I could help you?" He didn't sound happy about the possibility.

Gabriel grabbed the man by the collar, lifted him half off his feet. "Help? Hell yes, you can help. You can tell me where the fuck Sterling is."

"I don't know!" Jesse's voice cracked with fear. "I don't know, I swear, please, sir. "

"Gabriel." Harper's voice, behind him. She'd followed him. Of course, she had. "Gabriel, let him go. He doesn't know anything."

Everything hard and furious inside him wanted to squeeze. Wanted to shake this pathetic man until answers fell out of him. Wanted to burn this whole fucking building to the ground and sift through the ashes until he found what he was looking for.

But Jesse didn't have what he needed. Didn't know where Sterling was hiding. Didn't know where Bella was.

Gabriel released him. The man stumbled backward, gasping.

Gabe turned away, Jesse forgotten as he looked out over the Monarch's lobby. This keystone of the empire that Sterling Hart had built.

He looked—and he felt something crack inside him.

She was gone. Bella was gone, and he didn't know where, and every minute that passed was a minute she might be hurt, was definitely scared.

He wouldn't let him think that she might be dead. Think that, and he'd crumble.

"Gabriel." Harper's hand rested on his arm. Gentle. Grounding. "Come on. Not here. Not like this."

He let her guide him toward the doors. His legs felt like they belonged to someone else. The fury was still there, still burning, but underneath it was something worse.

Fear. Pure, paralyzing fear.

He'd lost her once, but he'd been given a second chance he didn't deserve.

He couldn't lose her again. He wouldn't survive it.

"The gallery," he heard himself say. "I need to go to the gallery."

———

La Galerie LaBete was quiet at this hour, of course. But Chris was there, hunched over his laptop at the front desk, fingers flying across the keyboard, a croissant on a plate beside him.

He looked up when the door opened, and Gabe watched as his face cycled through surprise, confusion, concern.

He said nothing, though. Smart man. And Gabriel strode past him without even a nod of acknowledgment. Through the main gallery, past the newer acquisitions, past the pieces by other artists —talented people whose work meant nothing to him right now. All the way to the back showroom where Caged was again mounted and on display.

He stopped in front of it.

The painting he'd created when they were still planning this gallery. When he thought they had forever. The image of Isabella behind bars of her own making, her arms reaching through toward light she couldn't quite touch, her face a study in longing and beautiful despair.

He'd painted it as a promise—that he would be the one to set her free from her father's control. From the gilded cage of the Hart empire. From whatever shadows held her back from the light.

He'd failed that promise. For five years, he'd let her stay trapped. Worse—he'd tried to lock her in a cage of his own making.

But she'd refused to stay there.

She'd stood on a balcony and asked him to choose her over vengeance. She'd tied him to a bed and forced him to feel something other than rage. She'd looked at the beast inside him and loved it anyway.

Now, she was counting on him to find her.

"I'm coming for you," he said quietly. The words felt like a vow. Like a prayer. "Do you hear me, Bella? I'm coming for you. And God help anyone who gets in my way."

The painting didn't answer. But something in Gabriel's chest settled. Solidified.

He'd spent five years as a monster. Five years feeding the darkness, nursing the hatred, letting the beast consume everything soft and good inside him.

But Bella had found him anyway. Had seen past the armor to the broken man beneath. Had given him something to live for beyond revenge.

She'd saved him.

Now it was his turn to save her.

His phone buzzed. Leo.

"Tell me you have something."

"Maybe." Leo's voice was tight with urgency. "One of Sterling's shell companies owns a property in Margate. Old warehouse, supposedly abandoned for years. But we've got movement—vehicles coming and going in the last few hours."

"Send me the address."

"You should wait for backup. I can have a team there in—"

"Send me the address, Leo."

A pause. Gabriel could practically hear Leo weighing the options, calculating the risks, trying to figure out if there was any point in arguing.

"It's in your texts," Leo finally said. "But Gabriel—be smart. Cornered men do desperate things."

"So do I."

"I know. But—hang on."

He heard Leo's sharp intake of breath, and the moment nearly destroyed him.

"What?" Gabriel demanded. "What happened?"

"Mina," Leo said. "I just got a text. Found dead at an abandoned car wash. A single bullet to the brain."

Bile rose in Gabriel's throat. "Sterling," he said through a throat clogged with fear. "If he killed the woman he supposedly loved, he damn sure won't have mercy for the daughter causing him trouble."

"We'll find her," Leo said, but Gabriel was already hanging up. He turned, letting fury rage through him. Gathering its strength. It's power.

When he turned, he found Harper standing in the doorway, watching him with worried eyes. Chris hovered behind her, still silent, his face pale.

"I'm going," Gabriel said. "Don't try to stop me."

"I wasn't going to." Harper crossed the room, pulled him into a fierce hug. "Bring her home."

"I will."

He looked at Caged one more time. At the woman behind the bars. At the reaching hands, the desperate eyes, the face he'd painted when he still believed he could save her.

Never again, he promised silently. *Never again will you be caged. Never again will you be afraid. I will burn down the world before I let anyone hurt you.*

He walked out of the gallery. Got in his car. And drove the short distance toward Margate.

Toward Bella.

And toward blood.

CHAPTER
THIRTY-NINE

The drive takes forever. Or maybe it takes no time at all. It's hard to tell when you're zip-tied in the back of an SUV with a hood over your head, your mouth taped shut, and terror clawing at your throat.

My heart won't stop racing. Every beat feels too fast, too hard, like my body knows something terrible is coming and is trying to outrun it. My wrists hurt where the ties dig into my skin, and my mouth is dry.

The air is stale under this hood, and I can barely breathe—each inhale pulls in the smell of my own sweat and the filthy scent of the material, like decay. Like someone died wearing this hood.

Like I might.

Please, no. Please, God, no.

I try to track our movements—left turn, right turn, the bump of a pothole, the hiss of tires on wet pavement. But I lose the thread. Atlantic City's streets blur together even when you can see them. Blind and bound, I have no chance. And how would I get a message out, anyway?

The men in the SUV don't speak. Not to me, not to each other. They're professionals.

Not surprising. My father always did hire the best.

When the SUV finally stops, hands grab me roughly and haul me out. I stumble on uneven ground—gravel, maybe, or broken asphalt—and nearly fall. Someone yanks me upright by the arm hard enough to wrench my shoulder. I bite back a cry. I won't give them the satisfaction.

There's a new smell now. Something chemical I can't identify. An industrial plant? I know there are a lot on the outskirts of the city. Some busy. Some abandoned.

The kind of places where people disappear, and no one ever finds them.

Gabe. Please, Gabe. Please find me.

They march me forward. A door creaks open, the hinges screaming with rust.

The acoustics change—we're inside now, our footsteps echoing off hard floors and high ceilings.

The hood's ripped off.

I blink in the sudden light. It takes a moment for my eyes to adjust, and when they do, I almost wish for the darkness back.

We're in an industrial warehouse. Old and abandoned. Water stains streak the concrete walls. Pigeons nest in the exposed rafters, their cooing eerily soft against the cavernous silence. The windows are so grimy they barely let in the gray morning light.

And there, standing in the center of the space like he owns it—which he probably does—is my father.

But not the Sterling Hart I know. Not the master of the universe. This man looks fragile. Like one strong kick would break him.

He's aged ten years in the few days since I've seen him. The silver hair that always seemed distinguished now just looks gray. The tailored suit hangs wrong on his frame. And his eyes—those cold, calculating eyes—are rimmed with red, like he hasn't slept in days.

"I wish it hadn't come to this," he says. Almost casual. As if I'm still sixteen and he's imposing a curfew.

"Then let me go."

He sighs. Actually sighs, like I'm being unreasonable. Like I'm the one who had him kidnapped at gunpoint.

"I can't do that."

"You can. You just won't." I yank against the zip-ties behind my back, even though I know it's useless. The plastic bites deeper into my wrists. "I'm your daughter. Your only child. Whatever you have planned—don't do this."

"You need to understand—"

"Understand what?" The words explode out of me. "That you're a murderer? That you tried to kill the man I love? That you've been lying to me my entire life?"

"I've been protecting you your entire life." His voice sharpens, and for a moment I see the father I grew up with—the one who controlled every room, who made grown men cry in boardrooms. "Everything I've done has been for you."

"Bullshit."

"You don't understand how the world works, Isabella. You never have."

"Then explain it to me." I keep my voice steady, even though my heart is hammering. "Explain how torturing Gabriel was protecting me. Explain how shooting him and leaving him for dead was for my benefit."

Something flickers across his face. "That was never supposed to happen. I wanted him convinced that staying away from you was in his best interest. The men I hired went too far."

"And you just let them."

"By the time I found out, it was too late."

"You could have stopped it. You could have saved him." My voice cracks. "You could have done the right thing for once."

"The right thing." He laughs—hollow, exhausted. "Gabriel Grimm was going to destroy everything I'd built. And you were going to hand him the keys."

"I love him."

"Love is a weakness." He says it like he's reciting a fact. Like it's something he learned long ago and never questioned. "I thought I taught you better."

I stare at him—and for the first time, I see him with perfect clarity.

"You taught me nothing," I say quietly. "Nothing except how to pretend everything's fine when it's not."

His jaw tightens. "I didn't bring you here to argue."

"Then why did you bring me here?"

Silence. The warehouse creaks around us. Pigeons coo in the rafters.

"The FBI has a warrant," he finally says. "My accounts are frozen. My allies have abandoned me." He meets my eyes, and I see something I've never seen in him before. *Fear.* "Forty years, Isabella. Forty years of building an empire. And it's all crashing down."

"Good."

He flinches. Actually flinches, like I've slapped him.

"I'm your father."

"You're a monster." But even as I say it, something twists in my chest. Not grief for him, grief for the father he could have been. The one who might have come to my school plays. Taught me to ride a bike. Told me he was proud of me without expecting anything in return.

That father never existed. Maybe he was never even possible.

I let the grief wash through me. Let it hurt.

Then I let it go.

"Gabriel is going to find me," I say. "And when he does, I hope you're ready. Because the man I love has spent five years wanting you dead. And I'm not sure I want to stop him anymore."

Something hardens in his expression. The fear crystallizes into calculation. The look of a cornered animal deciding its next move.

"Then I suppose we'd better make sure he doesn't find you."

He nods to the men flanking me. Before I can react, hands grab my arms and drag me toward a door at the back of the warehouse.

"Father—"

But he's already walking away.

The last thing I see is his back. Straight. Rigid. The back of a man who's already decided I'm expendable.

Then the hood's back on, and I close my eyes in the dark and pray for Gabe to find me.

———

THEY PUT ME IN A ROOM. A cell, really—concrete walls, no windows, a single bare bulb hanging from the ceiling that flickers every few seconds like it might die at any moment. There's a chair bolted to the floor and a bucket in the corner that I refuse to think about.

The men cut my zip-ties, at least. Small mercies. I rub my wrists, wincing at the raw skin, the sticky smear of blood. Then they leave, and the door locks behind them with a heavy metallic clunk that echoes in my chest like a death knell.

I stand in the middle of the room, trying to think. Trying to breathe. Trying not to fall apart.

Gabriel will come. I know he will. Harper will realize I'm gone. She'll call Gabe. And then nothing on earth will stop him from finding me.

The question is whether I'll still be alive when he does.

My father's parting words echo in my mind. *I suppose we'd better make sure he doesn't find you.*

Is he planning to kill me? Use me as a bargaining chip? Disappear to some country without an extradition treaty and drag me along as insurance?

I don't know. And not knowing is almost worse than any of those options.

The silence is oppressive. Thick. The kind of silence that makes you hear your own heartbeat, your own breathing, the blood rushing through your own veins.

I strain to hear something—anything—from beyond the door. Voices. Footsteps. Some sign that the world still exists outside these four concrete walls.

Nothing.

I sink down against the wall and pull my knees to my chest. The concrete is cold through my clothes. The air tastes stale and damp, like something died in here a long time ago and no one ever bothered to remove the corpse.

Maybe that's what I'll become. A corpse no one bothers to remove.

Stop it.

I close my eyes and think about Gabriel.

He'll come. I know he will.

I think about our first date, back when we were young and stupid and didn't know how dark the world could get. He took me to a little Italian place in SoHo, and we talked for hours about art and family and dreams. He drove me home afterward, and when he kissed me goodnight, I felt like I was standing on the edge of something enormous. Something life-changing.

I was right. And even after everything, I still love him, and he still loves me.

Even after five years of believing I'd betrayed him. Even after the rage and the hatred and the beast that tried to consume him from the inside out.

He loves me.

And he's coming for me.

I'm certain of it.

I just have to survive long enough to see it.

I wrap my arms around my knees, put my head down, and let myself cry. "Please," I whisper into the darkness. "Please find me. Please."

The flickering light doesn't answer. The silence doesn't break.

But somewhere in my chest, in the place where fear and faith live side by side, I feel something warm. Something steady.

Gabriel is coming.

I just have to hold on.

CHAPTER
FORTY

Gabriel killed the engine a half a block away and studied the broken-down building. Two vehicles in the lot—a black SUV that matched the description from the security footage, and a silver Mercedes that probably belonged to Sterling. No visible guards outside, but that didn't mean anything. Men like Sterling didn't leave their perimeters unprotected.

Gabriel checked his phone. Leo's team was fifteen minutes out. The FBI was twenty, maybe more—they were mobilizing a tactical unit, which meant paperwork and protocols and all the bureaucratic bullshit that got people killed while lawyers covered their asses.

Fifteen minutes was too long. Twenty was an eternity.

Bella was in there. Every second he waited was a second something could go wrong.

He got out of the car.

The gun was a comfortable weight at his back—a Glock 19, the same model he'd trained with for years.

He moved carefully to the side entrance, gun in hand, as he checked the door. Unlocked.

Either Hart's men were sloppy or they were setting a trap.

Gabriel didn't care either way.

He slipped inside, moving silently through the shadows. The warehouse was cavernous—high ceilings, rusted equipment, the smell of mold and pigeon shit to give it that extra homey feel. And something chemical underneath it all.

Light filtered through grimy windows, casting everything in shades of gray.

He heard voices ahead and pressed his back against a wall, the gun held ready if they came his direction. The voices were low. Male. At least two, maybe three.

He held his breath and listened.

"We need to move."

"Move where?"

Sterling. That was Sterling Hart's voice.

"The feds have eyes on every port, every airport," Sterling continued. "We try to run, we're done."

"But they're out there." The speaker had a slight accent. The Bronx, maybe. "You're saying we just sit here and wait for them to kick down the door?"

"We have leverage," Sterling said. "As long as we have the girl, we have options."

Gabriel's hands curled into fists, and the beast stirred within, hungry and eager.

Carefully—silently—he slid away from the door, then moved deeper into the warehouse, skirting pools of light, keeping to the shadows. The voices faded behind him as he worked his way toward the back of the building, where a row of doors lined the wall. Storage rooms, maybe. And wouldn't those make handy cells?

The first two were empty. The third was locked.

Gabriel tried the handle. Solid. Industrial. The kind of lock you couldn't kick through, not without making enough noise to bring every guard in the building running.

He pulled out his lockpick set—another skill he'd learned in the years after Aspen, when he'd had nothing to do but plan and prepare and teach himself all the ways a man could destroy another man's world.

Thirty seconds. The lock clicked open.

He pushed the door inward, gun raised, ready for anything.

Bella was huddled against the far wall, knees pulled to her chest, face streaked with tears. When she saw him, her eyes went wide—shock, then recognition, then something that looked like a prayer answered.

"Gabe!"

His name was barely a whisper, but the love and relief behind it filled him to the brim.

He pressed a finger to his lips, then crossed the room in three strides and dropped to his knees even as he pulled her into his arms. She was shaking. Trembling. But alive. Whole. *His.*

"I've got you," he breathed against her hair. "You're safe now."

"I knew you'd come." Her voice cracked. "I knew it."

"Always." He pulled back just enough to look at her—checking for injuries, for damage, for any sign that they'd hurt her beyond the raw skin at her wrists where they must have bound her. "Can you walk?"

She nodded.

"Then we need to move. Leo's team is on the way."

At a sound from the doorway, Gabriel spun, shoving Bella behind him, raising his gun in one fluid motion.

Sterling Hart stood in the threshold.

He looked worse than Gabriel remembered. Older. Grayer. The polished facade cracked and crumbling. He had a gun of his own —a sleek silver pistol pointed directly at Gabriel's chest.

"Mr. Grimm." Sterling's voice was calm. Almost pleasant. "I had a feeling you'd show up eventually."

"Let us walk out of here." Gabriel kept his voice steady. The beast was howling for blood, but he forced it down. For Bella. For the promise he'd made. "Do that, and maybe you live long enough to see a courtroom."

Sterling's laugh was dry. Hollow. "And endure years of trials? My name dragged through the mud? Everything I built dismantled?" He shook his head. "I don't think so."

"You don't have a choice."

"Everyone has choices." Sterling's eyes flicked to Bella, then back. "I could let you walk out. Or I could end this on my own terms."

Behind him, Bella's hand found his back, gripped the fabric of his jacket.

"You'd kill your own daughter?"

Something flickered in Sterling's eyes. Pain. Regret. Then it vanished.

"She stopped being my daughter when she chose you."

"Father, please." Bella's voice was barely a whisper.

Sterling's gun hand trembled. "Don't."

Gabriel felt the beast strain against its leash. Every instinct screamed at him to attack—to close the distance, to rip that gun from Sterling's hand. But Sterling's finger was on the trigger. And Bella was directly behind him. Any sudden move, and the bullet meant for him could find her instead.

So he waited. Watched.

The distant wail of sirens grew closer. Leo's team. Or the FBI. Cavalry coming, but not fast enough.

"Put down the gun," Gabriel said. "It's over."

For a moment—just a moment—something in Sterling's expression shifted. Softened. The gun wavered.

Then his eyes went cold.

"You're right," he said. "It is over."

Everything happened at once.

Sterling's finger twitched, and Gabriel whipped around, shoving Bella to the ground with one hand as he used the other to fire his own weapon in time with Sterling's shot. The gunfire exploded through the warehouse—deafening, disorienting—and for one horrible second Gabriel didn't know who had fired or who had been hit.

Sterling staggered.

The silver pistol clattered from his hand. He stood there for a moment, swaying, a look of surprise on his face. Then he looked down at the red bloom spreading across his chest.

"Well," he said quietly. "I suppose that's that."

He collapsed.

Gabriel stood frozen, gun still raised, smoke curling from the barrel. Behind him, Bella was scrambling to her feet, her eyes fixed on her father's body.

"Gabriel." Her voice sounded far away. "Is he dead?"

He forced himself to move. To lower the gun. To check for a pulse, even though he already knew what he'd find.

"He's dead."

Gabriel stared at the body—at the man who'd stolen five years of his life, who'd tried to kill him, who'd threatened everything he loved. He waited for the satisfaction. The triumph. The vindication of finally, finally seeing his enemy destroyed.

It didn't come.

All he felt was tired. And sad. And desperately, achingly grateful that Bella was still alive.

He turned away from the corpse. Bella was standing now, arms wrapped around herself, staring at her father's body with an expression he couldn't read.

"Bella?"

Slowly, her eyes lifted to his. They were dry. Shocked. But not grieving. Whatever complicated feelings she had about Sterling Hart, she'd worked through them before Gabriel ever walked through that door.

"Is it over?" she whispered.

Gabriel crossed to her, pulled her into his arms. Held her tight against his chest, feeling her heart beat against his, proof that she was alive, that they were both alive, that this nightmare was finally, finally finished.

"Yeah," he said. "It's over."

The sirens were closer now. Louder. Blue and red lights flickering through the grimy windows as vehicles pulled into the lot outside.

Gabriel held Bella and waited.

He'd made his choice. He'd chosen justice. Chosen the courts. Chosen to let Sterling live if Sterling would let him.

Sterling hadn't let him.

And Gabriel couldn't bring himself to regret it.

Later—after the FBI had swarmed the building, after statements had been given and evidence had been catalogued, after Leo had arrived and wrapped Bella in a blanket and pressed a cup of terrible coffee into her hands—Gabriel found himself standing outside the warehouse, staring at the gray morning sky.

Bella appeared beside him. Silent. Warm. Alive.

"You killed him," she said. Not an accusation. Just a fact.

"He was going to shoot you."

"I know. If I'd had the gun I would have shot him myself." She slipped her hand into his. "I'm numb."

"That's normal after something like this."

"Is it?" She laughed—a small, broken sound. "I don't think anything about our lives is normal."

He couldn't argue with that.

They stood together in silence, watching the agents move in and out of the warehouse. Watching the coroner's van pull up.

Watching the end of Sterling Hart's empire play out in real time.

"What happens now?"

Gabriel squeezed her hand. "Now we go home. We sleep for about a week. And then we go on."

"Together?"

He turned to her. Cupped her face in his hands. Looked into those dual-colored eyes that had haunted his dreams for five long years—first with hatred, then with longing, now with love so fierce it burned.

"Together, Izzy," he said. "Always."

She rose on her toes and kissed him, soft and sweet. Like a promise. "Day by day," she whispered against his mouth.

"Day by day."

The sun broke through the clouds, spilling golden light across the wreckage of everything they'd survived.

It wasn't a happy ending. Not really. But it was a beginning.

And it was theirs.

EPILOGUE

THREE MONTHS LATER

The gallery opening is in full swing, and I still can't believe it's real.

La Galerie LaBete has a new home now—a sleek space carved out of the lower level of The Beast, all clean lines and dramatic lighting and Gabriel's paintings glowing on the walls. The art world lost its collective mind when the mysterious LaBete was revealed to be Gabriel Grimm, back from the dead. Critics call it the story of the decade. Collectors call it a goldmine.

I call it a miracle.

Gabriel stands across the room, deep in conversation with a collector from Manhattan. He's cleaned up for the occasion—charcoal suit, open collar, his dark hair actually combed. But that isn't what makes my breath catch.

It's the ease in his posture. The genuine smile. The way he gestures while he talks, animated and engaged, like he's finally remembered what it feels like to be part of the world.

The beast is still there. Will always be there. But it's quiet now. Content. Happy, even.

Harper appears at my elbow with two glasses of champagne. "You're staring."

"I'm allowed to stare. He's mine."

"That he is." She hands me a glass and clinks hers against it. "You did good, Bella. Both of you."

I look at the centerpiece of the exhibition—Caged and Free, hanging side by side. The woman trapped behind bars, and the woman standing in an open doorway, sunlight streaming around her, one hand extended toward the viewer.

The whole story, right there on the wall.

Later, after the guests have gone, after Travis and Anissa have spilled their congratulations all over us, and after Harper has made us promise brunch on Sunday—Gabriel leads me upstairs to the apartment he now uses only as a studio.

I expect him to tumble me onto the sofa. Instead, he takes me to the bathroom, where a straight razor, a brush, and a bowl of shaving cream sit waiting.

I look at him, confused. "Okay?"

"The beard was part of the armor." He picks up the razor, turns it over in his hands. "Part of the disguise. I don't need armor anymore." He holds it out. "I want you to be the one who takes it off."

My hands tremble as I take the blade. Not from fear, but from the weight of what he's offering.

He sits on the edge of the tub. I work up a lather and begin. Stroke by stroke, the beard falls away, revealing the jaw I remember. The face I fell in love with all those years ago. And the scar that had been partially hidden from me for months, now there for me to see, like all the wounds he's shared with me.

When I'm done, I wipe away the last of the shaving cream and cup his bare face in my hands.

"There you are," I whisper.

He pulls me onto his lap and kisses me. Not desperate. Not tentative. Something new. Something that tastes like the future.

"I love you, Izzy," he murmurs against my mouth.

I smile, relishing the sound of the nickname, so casual on his lips. Like we're back to normal now.

Like we've come home.

ABOUT THE AUTHOR

J. Kenner (aka Julie Kenner) is the *New York Times, USA Today, Publishers Weekly, Wall Street Journal* and #1 International best-selling author of over one hundred novels, novellas and short stories in a variety of genres.

JK has been praised by *Publishers Weekly* as an author with a "flair for dialogue and eccentric characterizations" and by *RT Bookclub* for having "cornered the market on sinfully attractive, dominant antiheroes and the women who swoon for them." A five-time finalist for Romance Writers of America's prestigious RITA award, JK took home the first RITA trophy awarded in the category of erotic romance in 2014 for her novel, *Claim Me* (book 2 of her Stark Trilogy) and the RITA trophy for *Wicked Dirty* in the same category in 2017.

In her previous career as an attorney, JK worked as a lawyer in Southern California and Texas. She currently lives in Central Texas, with her husband, two daughters, and two rather spastic cats.

Stay in touch! Text JKenner to 21000 to subscribe to JK's text alerts.

www.jkenner.com

www.ingramcontent.com/pod-product-compliance
Lightning Source LLC
Chambersburg PA
CBHW021020310726
48969CB00006B/1468